GENESIS

GOD'S CHAIN

Book one
in
GOD'S CHAIN

Nikolaus Baker

Published by Mikey Books [2016]
Jacketed case laminate published [23.03.20]
First Edition, 2010
Second Edition, 2016
[R1 15.10.16, R2 03.02.20]

ISBN: 978-1-9162589-2-1

Dedicated to my wife Aileen.

THE PROPHECY

They will come first and smite.
All will shake in terror.
Cold is the land.
Nowhere to hide.

The cursed will come and bite.
All will run in terror.
Pained is the land.
Nowhere to hide.

Devil's will come and spite.
All will fall in terror.
Dead is the land.
Nowhere to hide.

Darkness will come and blight.
All will bow in terror.
Black is the land.
Nowhere to hide.
Souless and suffering in the land of nowhere.
Nowhere to hide.

Index

PROLOUGE

CHAPTER I   The Prophet Monument

CHAPTER II   Genesis

CHAPTER III   Palazzo del Governmantorato

CHAPTER IV   Root of the GODS!

CHAPTER V   The Vatican Dungeons

CHAPTER VI   The Freemasons

CHAPTER VII   A warning from the grave

CHAPTER VIII   Death in dark places

CHAPTER IX   Secrets behind the Vatican Walls

CHAPTER X   The Visitors

CHAPTER XI   Operation Aequinoxium

PROLOGUE

⌐⌐ ⌐⌐ ⌐⌐⌐

It was on the morning of the sixth of
May in the reign of King Charles II and James
VII, 1685. One could almost see the translucent,
silvery green dew changing to a misty grey
vapour. Dancing droplets of water warmed
with watery energy and dissipated throughout
the green meadows. The sun's rays rose kindly,
chasing the early morning moisture over the
peaceful countryside and forming a distilled
mist around the brown trunks of a grove of
Scots Pines. The loose ground mist cleared in
sections that wisped around the bases of
enormous boulders that squatted on the top of
the hill. Fresh water condensed rapidly,
beading on the rough surfaces and, like the
many rivulets of sweat, ran down from the
rocks' stony faces.

Pilgrim was troubled. He stared
anxiously out from the tall shield of the great
stones that towered over him. Barely breathing
while peering from his hiding place long and

hard, he looked into the golden grey mist. He knew they were coming....

A black mood came on him because suddenly there they were! Numerous shadowy dark figures, cloaked in mist flitted in and out of his blurred vision as a group of obscure small figures, all hooded slowly ascended the hill from the village. Pilgrim had company. The Abaddon Clerics. Things from another place, another time and another world, *The Clerics – The Unliving* would not stop hunting him.

The sun's intensity increased as the orb began to rise up from the east and lift itself over and above the massive stone boulders, silhouetting them as powerful dark shadows. Stealthily, the supernatural beings crawled up to the hill top. Sparrows whistled tunefully as they flew from tree branch to bush and then fled suddenly in panic, soaring away from the hazy mists.

Inside the mist of dark grey shades and shadows of boulders, he knelt in prayer for the salvation of the men down in the village, hovering over an ancient stone slab imbedded in the earth. Pilgrim held high in his clenched fist the object—an object he would give his very life to protect. In his final worship, Pilgrim looked up high in wonder towards the Supreme Architect.

On the day before this fateful morning, a new regiment of royalist dragoons had arrived in the village and were billeted at the castle. They had come in support of the local garrison and were loyal to the crown. As five men were marched brutally in chains to the nearby Inn, the royal dragoons walked alongside to quell any thoughts of rebellion. It was Judgement day!

The covenanters in chains wore dirty clothes, ragged and threadbare. Their arms and legs were skinned and bloodied from the weeks-long forced march over the countryside. These men were ordinary men, with ordinary lives, ordinary families. And each had been pushed too far, as had many of their kinsmen. With tousled and matted long hair, they looked more like beggars than the farmers they were. Their beards were shaggy and unkempt, faces matted in hair, all except for one young boy who stood there in line with the others, staring out in terror.

After being held prisoner in the castle for several days, all were roughly assembled together by the soldiers this morning at bayonet point and musket barrel. Their wrists were bound and ankles shackled by iron as they stood proudly, resolute to mumble and muffle defiant sounds of insurgence before the Royal Jury.

Keeping his back to the haggard men who stood worn in a line behind him, the judge looked firmly forward, towards the assembled Jury. A few local villagers witnessed the trial but were greatly outnumbered by the royalists at arms.

The judge smiled, his lips extenuated by his thin moustache. His thick, long wig was tightly curled and well kept. He proudly stood in full uniform, his red sash and long grey coat perfectly stitched and tailored. Although now dressed as pretty as a peacock, Lieutenant-General William Drummond was a warrior who had seen a great deal of active service and campaigning.

He had surmised in deliberation that he would give them a last chance to repent if they gave him what he wanted and, in addition,

'All of you stand together accused of stashing weapons, conspiring against and attacking the King's Tower not far away in the village of Newmilns. How do you plea?' he shouted. 'I said, how do you plea?' striking his solid fist off the dock in pure rage.

Laughter again came from the court as the judge paced arrogantly back and forth, for he had done this justice many times before. There was a quill pen and paper on the dock.

'Place your mark here — it is your last act against the Reformation of Covenance.' The accused stood silently shaking their heads, every one of them uttering not a single word. They still were men and proud to be covenanters; they would not agree to this Inlet of Popery.

'One last thing,' the man secretively lowered his eyes to look at the ink pot and death warrants.

Here it comes, thought the young boy.

'Who knows of the whereabouts of the holy bond, it is said to be... *the Link of God?* It was rumoured to be in the hands of the Covenant. Is that so true?' snarling nastily, '*I have been told of this.*' he seethed more. Then changed and seemed almost friendly, too friendly. 'Speak and I will pardon that man. I will spare his life for knowledge of this kingly treasure.' Articulating his authority, the Lieutenant-General's red eyes of malice did not rise to meet the accused in case his black soul could be seen by theirs, and as he spoke his soft words of clemency, his lenient words of deceit. All worthless, all untrue, words of kindness and persuasion caressing their mortal fears. *Will they buckle…* he wondered coldly watching for a sign, a weakness. They said nothing leaving a heavy silence, his answer.

It was much more than a kingly treasure and much more than a priceless artefact. A relic dating so far back that no one could remember its origin and elusive as the Holy Grail. The darkness has many allies and as rumour would have it, this thing could exhibit strange and awesome powers. God's link, as it was called, was veiled in secrecy; if it had been found it remained masked somewhere in the kingdom.

The boy, Bruning, had been tortured and forced to expose his uncle's part in a rescue attempt at Newmilns and spoke much under duress to his captor, Bloody Claverhouse. He'd witnessed his uncle, John Brown, be shot six times in the head on his doorstep!

But he didn't tell Claverhouse that, days before the dragoons arrived, a visitor had come to his uncle's abode, a holy man who had visited for shelter and for prayers. That the visitor be known simply by name, 'Pilgrim', was a bearer of a great and holy gift! The young boy knew that he was doing wrong when he looked — he was starving and had peeked inside the man's satchel for food and saw the great charm. The holy man had discovered the boy's indiscretion and forgave his sin. How could he not? The boy's word of silence was enough. The boy had the wit not to speak of this thing but the fearful insight it gave him when he touched it, had told him of his future. It would be his bond until death.

The Lieutenant-General began closely scrutinising each one so accused, hatefully, his malice overwhelming and complete. The accused felt his chill breath on their eyes and said nothing.

'Where is it hidden?' he roared. No one would speak. Rebellion! Still, he had nothing

more than a rumour to go on. It was no use —
these men knew nothing!

The accused silently waited for his
judgement, their mouths gagged tight.

Such was their defence.

'Men of the Jury?' the Lieutenant-
General prompted.

They were his own men, his troops, the
men of the Jury. All stood up as if commanded
to do so. 'These men will not repent,' the
Lieutenant-General continued. 'They remain
defiant and are traitors to the King and unto
God! I have pleaded with them and offered
them pardon if they would speak. Such is my
clemency; they will not agree.' His tone
lowered. 'How do you find them — guilty or not
guilty?' he paused, for effect. 'Guilty or not
guilty?' he thundered.

'Guilty, Sir!' the men of the Jury
chorused, laughing loudly. The prisoners
moved with fearful excitement, trying to break
their bonds in defiance and moaning at the
injustice, voicing their disobedience aloud.
There could only have been one verdict. The
soldiers raised their bayonets, quickly
suppressing the men's attempted revolt.

CHAPTER I

THE PROPHET MONUMENT

Over three hundred years later, life in the village of Mauchline had become quite tiring and slow paced unlike the olden days of Reformation, things had settled. Most excitement occurred on Sundays, when the usual latecomers were running to church. It was late afternoon and the last warm embers of autumn rays streamed down their dying light, dousing the countryside with yellow-golden shades of sunshine. Scott took a deep breath of fresh air and sighed for a long moment, drifting his eyes lazily over the view from his bedroom window. Today, there was a great deal of activity. The boy listened to the sound of a waning, monotonous whine, and then saw Farmer Drew Kirkland's red tractor about half a mile away, making slow progress up the hill at the end of town. It was the last trim of the year — Drew Kirkland was cutting away the yellow-browning hedgerows of hawthorn and beech that divided the once green meadows from the quiet back road that led out of the village.

The autumn grass had become so long that it swished back and forth in a fast-flowing breeze. The boy listened sleepily as the wind swept across the high sloped meadows and rustled over the tree-lined hilltop.

The cows still pastured in the nearby fields outside his home would soon be herded into their byres for the winter. A sudden cold gust drifted through the cracked-open window frame and struck his young face. Scott narrowed his eyes and tightened his lips. It was a neat wind that touched his skin, warning him that the definite shift was on its way.

Scott still had not settled in after two years in the village and found life to be less than dull, especially compared to the busy seaside town of Ayr, which used to be his home. *Why did dad have to go away?* The boy thought forlornly of his father. God had not listened to any of his prayers...*why not?*

He continued to stare out towards that steep country road that divided the autumn pastures. Trying not to dwell too much on his past, Scott's watery eyes fixed onto those lonely far-off green mixtures of Scots pine and other blue-green Norwegian firs. The noble trees moving slowly in the breeze and stood banded tightly together on the hillside, forming a natural wind break to the winter harsh gales. This tall timber held the ridge above the village. The boy had never grown used to those creepy old woods on the hill.

Ancient standing stones could also be seen from the boy's window, small and delicate-seeming on the remote hill top northeast of the village. These seven solid bastions were rooted deep and firm in the rock beneath the thin hill soil, standing there in a natural formation at the highest height of the ridge. The tallest of the boulders far exceeded the rest; it dominated the hill. They all stood silently, rough and dry, ancient and true, sentinels.

The principal primeval rock was encircled by other sizable boulders, and all seemed to challenge on-comers, or so Scott imagined. The young man thought it odd that he imagined their presence, their ever-readiness to burst to life and crush anyone that might wander their way. How old and long they had been standing there, centuries maybe, millennia likely.... No one knew, no known written words told when these old stones had first come to be. The ancient monoliths had always been there....

In the twilight of October, the days were coming short. The light already began to fade, casting a yellow-orange tinge over the once rich-green pastures. The treetops swayed to and fro, gathering momentum, preparing themselves for another stormy evening. Near and far the branches of trees could be heard in the distance, creaking in unison, protesting the wind. Occasionally one heard the mighty groan as a branch was pressed too far...and then snapped. Scott shivered.

Scott's home was one of the village's original cottages, constructed by master stonemason's centuries ago and built to last. Those old stones would hold any storm at bay.

The boy turned his head and looked up at his bedroom wall, towards a mounted, framed photograph that hung there. It was a photograph of his older brother Christopher. Scott's mind began to drift to a much happier time, when he and his brother played together in the streets of Ayr.

Christopher had flown the nest at the beginning of this year and had not been in contact with his family for several months. The last they'd heard, he was gallivanting around in South America performing work for some multinational research company, exploring the rainforest for new species of insects....

Mmmm, what was it called again? A funny name...oh I can't remember. Something to do with bugs, anyway, thought Scott, quite perplexed with himself. *It was a stupid name,* he thought, trying hard to remember. The more he tried, the more the memory became like water in cupped hands—dribbling away. Scott was still infuriated that his brother had gone abroad again. *Mum still needed him to be here! Didn't he realise it?*

Scott missed his older brother, a lot. They used to have such great times, wrestling like the pros! *Why did we have to grow up?*

The photograph pinned up on the wall was one of Christopher wearing camouflaged trousers and similar styled vest top. *What a poser!* Scott smiled to himself, wishing that he could be more like his brother. Christopher had always been photogenic — his angular features gave him a kind of rough, model appearance and his somewhat long, marine-styled black haircut, fashioned with thin tramlines, displayed openly a degree of vanity very unlike the papal cloth that he so worshipped. His tall brother held a large spear in one hand and a wide-brimmed green camouflaged hat in the other. Proudly he grinned from ear to ear! A natural pioneer, Chris was truly in his element in the Amazon.

His photograph was set against a background of dense greenery with lines of large, fat tree trunks. Long sweeping vines and thick creepers covered everything! Lush greens and brown foliage was so ubiquitous that it almost grew out in the picture in a cascade of coloured flowers. The picture felt somehow alive!

Scott's bedroom walls were painted light blue and plastered with posters of his favourite football team interspersed between posters of wrestling heroes and computer games. There was a small television and an old game console sitting in one corner and a bookshelf with his magazines and several advanced school books on engineering science in the other. The rest of the room was a complete mess—clothes lay on the floor, abandoned after weeks of wear, causing no end of anguish for his mother.

"Scott!" shouted his mother. 'Dinner!'

Yes! His mind leapt into action. Dinner was going to be a favourite of his—cheese burgers and chips! Scott ran down the stairs, almost drooling with hunger.

'What were you up to, son?' asked his mother.

'Nothing much, Mum,' replied the boy.

'When are you going to get a haircut, my lad?' Laughing, she ruffled his thick, dark-curled mop.

'Dinner?' Scott smiled a little to himself, knowing that he had no intention of anything like getting a haircut.

'You can ask Cammy over to the house tomorrow night provided you tidy your room,' she granted.

'Aye sure,' Scott confirmed coolly, still with no intention of tidying his hair or his room. Mum was a complete pushover. Scott attended to his food. His smiling face wiped away, transformed from delight to disappointment, losing all signs of coolness from his youthful composure. He stared at his plate in miscomprehension—boiled potatoes, silverside, and broccoli steamed up at him. 'Aw, yuck mum!' he cried. Tonight's dinner was his worst nightmare on a plate!

'Cheeseburgers tomorrow,' she promised.

Later that evening, Scott toyed with a computer aided design project for school. He had already worked up part of a new wind-turbine system, attempting to increase the Betz limit and so reduce the overall costs of manufacture. A young rebel he was; engineering science was one of his true interests, if not his passion, along with computer games, although he had painted some outlandish graphic graffiti on the outer-structure sketch of the turbine, just to annoy his tutor.

Afterwards, tucked up warm in his bed, Scott listened carefully as the wind outside began to rise, blowing through the deciduous trees over at the manse, scattering single leaves from near-bare branches and flying them through the air until they slammed against his bedroom window. The trees would soon be all nude. Pulling the covers up over his head, Scott drifted into a disturbed sleep.

****

As Scott walked to school the next morning the wind was still quite strong and breezy. Black crows flew through the air haphazardly, pitching loftily above and then quite unpredictably diving down in steep swoops, squawking as they flew past his ears. The hand held school bell swung up and down, clanking metallically and waning in the gale as Scott walked aimlessly through the open iron-barred gates of the school, unperturbed by the mentors who waved with great urgency to all the stragglers.

The school had been a primary school for many years but, due to the declining population of the village and subsequent decrease in school roles, most of the younger kids received their schooling from a much larger school in a nearby town. Scott's school had been converted into a very successful grammar school for some of the area's most talented young students. Located remotely in this secluded village, far enough from the media mainstream, seats here were very limited and only for a few exceptional or privileged students. This suited some well-to-do parents, who pulled strings to include their children, while other youths, like Scott, were simply of exceptional ability, and of course the educational body was obligated to provide a certain number of places for students who lived in the local community. They would all have to pay, of course. Scott was blissfully unaware of the personal sacrifices his mother made to keep him at the school.

Like most other buildings in the area, the school was built with red sedimentary sandstone, mined from nearby quarries centuries ago. Stone masonry was evident throughout the village, although the masons' fine skills and trade secrets were no longer in use. The majesty and intricacy of these projects have never been surpassed by today's modern mode of construction. The main school building and outer stone structures bore enigmatic messages with detailed inscriptions describing the hidden story of their intricate and esoteric works.

The long main building stretched the length of the sizable school grounds, and contains about twenty or more large classrooms for learning languages and mathematics, there were science and engineering labs and music wings, a gymnasium, a dinner hall, a few large teaching huts, an administrative office and a staff room. The school was filled with over a hundred very gifted students from all parts of the United Kingdom.

For all its antique exterior and sixteenth century features, the school was an equal balance of old and new, well furnished with modern fittings and fixings, it also integrated various state-of-the-art communications equipment, including satellite-dishes discretely hidden by well-cultivated foliage at the rear of the school grounds.

Encircling the school was a high stone wall about a metre tall providing privacy and seclusion for the students. The only exception was at the front of the school, which housed a short, red sandstone dyke which was only a few feet high and topped with tall green-painted iron bars. The students would chat while sitting and standing on the edges of the sandstone wall, holding onto the iron bars that separated them from the rest of the world. Within the walls were lovely and well-tended gardens, maintained by the old school janitor, who was affectionately known by some as "Creepy".

On the facing front wall of the main building there was a large carving of a stone shield up at the apex of the roof. The shield bore the stonemason mark and the year of construction. Scott looked up with interest at the square and compass marking carved inside the stone shield as he approached the front door. It said the year it was completed... sixteen hundred and something...? It was difficult to make out from ground level.

'Hi Scott.' Scott's friend Cameron walked down the sloped grounds to meet him, appearing from behind another group of kids who jogged towards the building. The school ground was a busy place.

'Hi Cammy. Want to come over for dinner?' Scott smiled engagingly.

'Sure! I'll bring Zombie Killers, too.'

'The one with one head shot kills?' Scott said excitedly. 'The demo looks so cool!'

'Brilliant!' Cameron agreed.

'Mmmph, quite sick really,' came another young voice from behind. It was their science teacher, Miss Davies. 'Scott and Cameron, can't you boys think of anything better to talk about, something more constructive to do in your spare time? What about some extra science homework? Would that do?'

Embarrassed, the boys ducked their heads beneath their shoulders and scurried into the school.

Later that day, in the science laboratory, Miss Davies waxed poetic on her special subject — Chemistry. Although she was only twenty-four years old and no taller than most of her students, Miss Davies's enthusiasm for chemical equations made her seem quite old to the students. The laboratory also seemed old, although it was filled with modern equipment. The windows were tall and wide with painted wooden frames, topped with long poles with brass hooked end catches that could be used to open the windows by a metal loop or latch at the top. The room was hot, despite the brisk fall weather, and all the windows were wide open as the Bunsen burners burned blue at full blast.

Charity Fludd, a young girl who sat in the front of the class, wearily studied the young teacher in her long white laboratory coat as she paced around the lab.   Charity felt bored — very, very bored.

Her clear blue eyes glazed over as she yawned dramatically and began to braid her slick, black pony tail. Charity was a girl with a brilliant mind and a knack for disguising her true nature; she had always been a little mischievous and now, at seventeen years of age, anybody was fair game to her.   She looked impishly across the science lab towards Scott, the boy with the strange second name.

'What's your stupid second name again, Scott?' Charity taunted him in the middle of the lecture, longing to be the centre of attention again. Scott looked over at her, seeming slightly embarrassed — colour pulsed into his cheeks. *She's a pain!*

up in embarrassment. 'Could I have a private word with you later in my office, Miss Davies?'

The students gasped, wondering what sort of punishment a teacher would have.

'Of course, headmaster,' Miss Davies responded, her voice low and humble. The headmaster left with his cloak swishing, closing the cloak in the door on his way out. After a few tugs freed Mr Collins from the door, Miss Davies turned to the class.

'Well, that lesson went off with a bang...did it not, children?' The science teacher looked over with a smile at the astounded kids, and the children burst out again into fits of laughter.

****

When the old janitor shook vigorously his heavy, hand-held bell that afternoon, there was a short mad rush out the main wooden door as students ran through the front gates and past the tall sandstone column obelisk, shouting jubilantly their freedom. The old iron bars surrounded the column's square base; its four surfaces were covered with a patchwork of light green algae and partially eroded engraved writing. The thin obelisk stood gravely within the school gardens, positioned on the edge of a line of trees and shrubs outside the school gates. It was a testimony and a pinnacle to the Covenanters who were hanged in the village centuries ago, whose only crime was in reading God's words for themselves.

There was still a strong breeze pushing thick, dark clouds across the afternoon sky when Scott and Cameron at last appeared at the school gates and began their usual meandering. With no sense of purpose, the boys took the minor path that led away from the school in the opposite direction to home. The janitor locked up the large double iron gates of the school behind them.

'What's the plan for tonight?' Cameron asked.

'Probably play with my old games console?' came Scott's reply as they walked on.

The back path was fenced on their right, separating them from nearby farmlands and a nervous flock of sheep. Wild, overgrown bushes sprouted on the opposite side of the path, creating a natural border over fifteen feet tall in some places, making the narrow pathway seem private and secure, if a little claustrophobic. Thick shrubbery rustled madly in the rising wind seeming to speak to the boys at times about the coming storm.

Walking aimlessly along and talking with enthusiasm about their computer games, Scott and Cameron suddenly heard a loud cracking noise. The boys stopped. The noise had come from somewhere inside the thick bushes. They peered at the branches but could see nothing in the dark shadows. Both boys stared warily into each other's eyes for what seemed like too long a moment...

'Let's get out of here!' Cameron shouted, and they both bolted along to the end of the pathway, both nervously laughing as they jumped onto the main street.

Straight ahead of them was "the cross", which was a cross roads that split the antiquated village centre and led to all the different parts of the shire. Here at the cross were all the usual amenities — a small supermarket, student hostel, estate agents and bank, paper shop, Italian restaurant, family butchers and several taverns.

Meanwhile, Charity laughed in amusement at her own prank as she dropped a broken branch to the ground. She had been watching the boys pass by her hiding place as she stood out of sight in the centre of the tall bushes, where the branches were thicker and there was some free space. How odd her laughter seemed to sound, muffled by the dense branches — no one could have guessed she was waiting inside.

Charity then, for no particular reason, began to feel somewhat uneasy. She realized that she was all alone, that everyone had left school... but the mood was more than just that. She was overcome with a strange sensation, a sort of unexplained dread and an awareness of being watched....

Alarm bells rang in her head and the girl suddenly jumped out of the bushes and onto the path. Running quickly after the boys, she never looked behind her.

If she had, she might have seen the dark shadow that stood where she had been only a moment before — a figure that bent slightly and picked up her snapped branch. Silently standing there for a moment, the shadow moved away, deeper into the darkness and back under cover....

Standing next to a public hostelry, Scott and Cameron looked to a small café that was attached to Mauchine's new Italian restaurant. Both the restaurant and the tavern were built on Hilltop Road, and both establishments adjoined the cross. Violin music drifted through the air as did the delicious aroma of Italian cuisine. Everyone who passed by smiled to the irate chef arguing with his prep staff about the herb sauce for this evening's menu.

The church dominated the village centre, constructed in large red sandstone blocks and perfectly positioned. With a green-slated roof covered with a light moss, the church had a venerable sort of run-down appearance. A gothic tower soared upwards from the centre, featuring a short spire at each its four corners. This godly structure could be seen for many miles around.

A large clock face was set in each side of the tower and above the large-arched, vented belfry, which was made of wood. The fine mechanics of the church clock had never broken down or stopped or slowed—the gears kept perfect time, thanks to the village's elderly watchmaker, chiming the hours with noisy church bells on Sunday mornings and holidays. Underneath the clocks and belfry levels were beautiful stained glass windows, each set into the church's stone walls. The road split around the church; to the right and downward through an alley behind the old church squatted the dilapidated Freemasonic lodge and castle ruin. There hadn't been any masons living in the village for many years.

Standing at the cross and looking east, the road went out of the village and up towards the hilltop, past Crows Wood, through Kirkland's farm, and then further onwards to the lowland hills about five or six miles away. Beyond the hills, the route led out of the shire and further into the countryside.

'I don't want to go home yet,' Scott announced, standing at the village cross.

Cameron nodded. 'I know what! Let's go up to the Prophet Monument,' he suggested, pointing the way up to the main road.

Scott was a little scared of the monument, but he felt a rush of excitement run through him. 'It's supposed to be haunted,' he reminded his friend.

'Yeah! It'll kill some time,' Cameron urged. 'Don't be a pratt. Come on!' he ordered with a mischievous smile. 'We can go right to the top of the tower and look through the telescopes!'

'Yeah, ok...it might be a bit of a laugh!' Scott nodded slowly, excitement building inside him. *It's Mauchline!* he reminded himself. *Nothing ever happens here, anyway. It's time to take a few risks!*

Laughing and joking on their way up the long road, Scott and Cameron gave each other courage to follow through on their dare. It was late afternoon and the daylight was dimming quickly with each minute that passed. Scott noticed a policeman's tall shadow silhouetted against the inside of the station window; the constable was nodding and speaking to someone. It was old Drew Kirkland—his red tractor was parked outside.

The Prophet's Monument was not the tallest built, although it had the highest vantage point. It dominated the top ridge to the north; like a citadel it watched over the village.

Beyond the monument, the roads ran away west and north to the hamlet of Crookedholm and the larger town of Irvine on the coast and the busy commercial city of Glasgow to the north.

The boys stood outside the tall sandstone building, which was protected by a low triangular sandstone dyke. The Prophet Monument was built in traditional Masonic fashion, made with the red sandstone quarried locally. Even from the outside the structure oozed with ancient history and folklore — old scripts were carved and cut all around the base of its walls by the masons, rumoured to verse cryptic warnings although no one knew what it really said....

Scott stood for a long moment at the entranceway to the enclosed grounds, wondering if it might not be such a good idea to enter.

'Having second thoughts?' Cameron teased.

'No way!' Scott grinned, although his face became somewhat sober as he looked up at the ominous long windows that stretched before them.

happened in this place, that much was obvious to the boys. It was dead....

A thick, stale odour in the calm air stung their nostrils and caught just the tip of Scott's nose, making his eyes water a little and causing him to sneeze. The boys tilted their heads to hear the monotonous noises of clocks, ticking...upstairs?

'Two tickets, is it then, lads?' the caretaker nodded jovially to them from behind his dark oak counter. 'That'll be two pounds.' Giving Cameron his change from the old fashioned cash till, the man's thin, white-gloved hands shook minutely. The boys saw that his hands were extraordinarily large – almost as big as shovels!

A slim man with short, grey cropped hair, the caretaker stood much taller than the teenage boys. Although the whites of his green eyes were filled with unsightly veins that resembled little red rivulets, his gaze was keen and alert. He wore a dark casual suit, shirt and tie, and his evident care for personal appearance surprised them. Considering the remoteness and unpopularity of the place, it seemed unlikely that he would have many visitors. Even at the best of times, most people would be almost too scared to enter.

Chuckling the man strode a little to the front entrance and turned the sign on the door behind them to 'closed' and then said,

'No electricity, either, lads — it is a plain, old fashioned till. Well, up you go and I hope you find the place interesting. Don't be too long now, it is getting late.'

The boys darted quickly towards the corner of the room and climbed the steep spiral of stairs. They were excited about what lay ahead. Forgetting the caretaker for the moment, they ran up, around and around, as quickly as they could, holding onto the thick banister for assistance as they leapt two steps at a time. Laughing and giggling with excitement, they went right past an open doorway on the first level and continued straight up to the second. It was all a wonderful game! Out of breath, they stopped on the second landing for a minute before entering the large room that opened off of it. What a strange place this was!

The room was dimly lit and very noisy. There were several large bookshelves overflowing with clocks of all types, as well as one way and then another. It was a despairing and awesome sight!

All combatants were locked in a military mêlée to the death against some unnamed and unholy dark host of heavily armoured devils with evil black eyes and sharp, pointed teeth. The demons had sharp and dangerous spikes on top of their black helmets and gripped bloody battle-axes in their fists! The boys could almost hear the battle cries and blood curdling screams of the people depicted in these oil pictures, who seemed to struggle in some long forgotten land — a land of mountainous sand dunes, a dry place extending over many, many leagues now wet with blood. Grains and grains of the desert were covered over with wet, slick scarlet blood. A weird crimson sun doused over the macabre red sands. End was inevitable.

'Mmmm. Spooky.' Cameron looked at Scott, who did not reply.

The atmosphere somehow felt heavier after they'd seen the dessert battle, and the boys walked on to another wall, which also held a large mural. The painting seemed to be of an impression of the universe. A mighty explosion of wondrous colours expressed a cataclysmic energy into the room and introduced a myriad of stars that appeared to twinkle madly. Thousands of stars!

'It must be an optical illusion,' Scott spoke uncertainly. It looked so real, though...the boys could almost feel the attraction of this great void drawing them inside.

In the centre of the wall hung a drawing of some monstrous looking nebula shaped like a deformed, masked visage made up of purple and blue gases and a spiralling-out-of-control Milky Way. An image of a great comet exploded out from the left side of the wall, streaking towards many different worlds. Devastation of all the planets in the twisted system seemed certain — the painting appeared to be a grim depiction of Armageddon.

The last mural, if you could call it such, was somehow both stronger than and in complete contrast to the other oil paintings. It was a plain white wall, with no features at all...except, with closer investigation, Scott discovered various clusters of finely dotted brushed black marks, which looked almost like a light dust or mist forming on different areas of the enigmatic white surface.

'What a load of old rubbish,' stated Cameron, as Scott stared at the wall more closely.

The boys turned around, ready to escape this peculiar room, when suddenly their hearts jumped. It was the caretaker! He had quietly entered without warning and was standing silently right behind them.

'I thought you lads were going to the top?' spoke the man in a soft voice.

'Where di...did you come from?' Cameron said, startled.

'I have been here only a moment,' replied the man, staring at the scenes. 'Amazing, are they not? I have always been fascinated with this room,' he paused. 'It's sad and yet, so wonderful.'

'What are they about? Who painted them?' Scott probed as the caretaker continued to look thoughtfully around the room. Suddenly, the caretaker's face seemed to open up with surprise and he startled, as though he did not recognize the boys.

'Wh...?' he breathed.

Then his gaze seemed to achieve its former composure.

'Come now, come out of here and go up to the top and onto the tower and have a good look outside, before it gets too dark to see anything. You'll find it much more fun up there. Hurry up—I will be closing up soon!' The thin man ushered them out of the pentagonal room and quickly locked the door behind.

At the top of the staircase, the boys jumped out of a small turret and onto the flat rooftop. The stair door flew open as Scott turned to close it and smashed against the turret wall. A gale was blowing over the exposed, red sandstone roof, but a stonewall barrier surrounded the roof like a safety fence, rising to about chest height and making the boys feel comfortable about being up high in such a wind.

The whipping wind was so much better than what the boys could have ever imagined! They were instantly blown and buffeted about to the far wall as the wind cycled around them on the tower top. Their hair waved around insanely above their heads and both lads were taken completely by surprise as the wind pushed them about from one walled barrier to the next, almost blowing them off their feet! It was great fun. Scott and Cameron half-ran from one wall to the next, laughing wildly as they looked over the edges and lifted themselves a little onto the stone barriers, exhilarated by the simple boyish fun and daft bravado! They could hardly hear their own shouting for joy and the wind of it! It had been all worthwhile. Scott and Cameron were ecstatic with energy!

Daylight had nearly gone when the floodlights suddenly switched on. The lights shone upwards towards the boys from the ground below, dousing each red sandstone wall with an amber splash. Looking over the edge, Cameron began to feel a bit dizzy as it was a very steep drop!

The gargoyle replicas crouched on the walled perimeters and quietly watched the boys with imagined stony intent. These small, carved caricatures cast queer silhouettes over the stone turret; the boys had almost entirely forgotten their legendary menace.   Suddenly, the air pressure increased. The atmosphere seemed to become heavier.

'Do you feel it, Scott? My ears are hurting!' Cameron shouted in pain, holding both sides of his head with his palms.

'Yes! What is happening?' screamed Scott as the increasing atmospheric pressure intensified sharply and he was overwhelmed with the feeling of being on an airplane in steep ascent.

'Hold your nose and blow into it!' Cameron shouted again, his face screwed up in complete discomfort as he attempted to equalise the pressure inside his head.

Scott plugged his nose and blew. Pop! It worked! Just as he began to grin with relief, Scott heard a deep and low rumble that shuddered through the ground and reverberated also in the clammy air. A colossal and incredible BANG! floored him as a wild explosion shook the monument!

The sky flashed brightly with white sheet lighting. The tormented countryside was instantly illuminated for a split second, dazzling Scott's eyes. The blank and startled faces of the villagers in the streets were suddenly revealed, highlighted along with the macabre and ill-omened stone devils.

The villagers waited with bated breath to see what would happen next. Their questions were answered with another low rumble as the earth began to slowly wobble and then undulate in long waves, which flowed like a sheet flapping in the wind. Scott collapsed as the building buckled beneath him, riding up and down with the trembling landscape. Without any warning, the ground suddenly stopped heaving and was completely still. A deathly silence instantly ensued, washing over the frozen shire — the atmosphere eased and the air pressure returned to normal. Birds began to squawk and whistle, flying from tree to tree in a mixture of alarm and relief; dogs barked and yelped to each other in the distance. The winds calmed to no more than a cool breeze. The tremor was over in less than half a minute....

'What happened?' Cameron held his still-churning stomach with both hands.

'It was an earthquake, I think,' Scott replied in disbelief, bewildered as an eerie hush fell over the shaken village. A fire engine siren and a flashing blue light passed quickly below them, charging down the road and into the village, mingling with the distant, distressed shouts of village folk.

'Let's use the telescopes' shouted Scott, wanting to see more of what had happened in the village. The telescopes were positioned at each corner of the tower and the boys took turns at each vantage point to observe as best as they could where the fire engine was going. Scott watched as the truck disappeared in the narrow village streets and then headed up the steep hilltop road.

Scott ran over to the other telescope at the west viewpoint, trying to spot what damage had been done. His eye was distracted by a darkish mist that seemed to shift slowly over the moor near the disused sandstone quarry.

What is that? he wondered. The low-lying mist appeared to be hugging close to the crags of the deep red-sandstone quarry...or was the deeper dark grey actually coming from within the quarry? In the low light, Scott was unsure. Perhaps the earthquake had fractured something deep inside the quarry, and gas was now escaping....

'I think you should go now,' came a stern voice from behind them. It was the caretaker, who stood over at the tower door, his face pale and serious. 'I will take you home — we must go quickly!' the man insisted.

'What is happening?' Cameron asked anxiously. The man did not answer and instead guided them down the spiral staircase, his former friendliness disappearing into a frosty sternness that seemed almost more horrible than the earthquake. After he slipped into his heavy coat, they all started walking fast down the road. A few automobiles swerved wildly around the sharp corners of the rural roads, and people walked quickly toward the village, all talking excitedly and sharing worried glances.

The old man tapped the front door of Scott's home and his mother appeared within seconds. Her face lit up the moment she saw Scott. She was so glad that her son was safe she gave him a big hug, to his complete embarrassment.

'Where have you been, young man?' she spoke sternly. 'You should have come home straight from school! And you too, Cameron! You, my lad, are in big trouble — your mother has been phoning here ever since it happened. We had no idea where you boys were!' Scott's mother finally seemed to notice the caretaker, and she seemed to shake off her panic. 'I hope these boys haven't caused you any trouble, er, Mr...Mr...I'm sorry, I don't know your name.' the woman said hesitantly.

'No, they were fine,' the caretaker intoned. 'Good evening to you.'

Scott's mother seemed to shiver slightly. 'Come in boys, let's get you something hot in you,' she said kindly, glancing up only once in puzzlement as the man disappeared down the dim street.

Luckily, little or no damage had occurred in the village to any of the houses and buildings. Only a few loose slates, damaged chimney pots and burst water mains were reported. The Masons had built their works strong.

****

Drew Kirkland happily put another whisky away as he sat on his tall wooden chair at the village pub. Drew was middle-aged and in his prime; his well-worn and somewhat soiled breeches, tattered tweed jacket, and dirty deer-stalker hat lent him a somewhat older air than he could actually claim, and a distinctly unpleasant odour. Dirty and unshaven, the man rubbed his dark-stubble face. He precariously balanced himself for another evening at the bar and another malt whisky chaser.

'Mmm that's a fine dram, Mr McCourt,' Drew spoke with a passion in his rough country accent, smiling contentedly as he savoured the distinct taste. The man's weather torn and kipper hardened face cracked a little more as he finished off his fifth. Only a handful of patrons were inside the bar at this moment, but the place seemed lively and friendly banter bounced from every corner.

"Another, please," Drew slurred as Tom Milligan, another regular, entered from the freezing cold night, rubbing his chilled hands.

'It's a cold one, Drew,' he said, referring to the bitter turn in the weather.

'Aye, that it is Tom. That it is. Cold for the time of year,' Drew replied in a broad Ayrshire dialect as he tossed off the drink set before him. 'I'll be away to milk my herd.' His voice had a pleasant lilt to it, oscillating up and down tunefully as it did.

'One for the road, then?' Tom queried, nodding to the barman.

'Aye why not Tom? A whisky,' Drew replied, only too glad for the excuse to stay inside. The men settled in their seats, grumbling a little and grunting appreciatively as their drinks were set before them.

'What do you think that was then, you know, last night?' asked Tom, finally.

'Do you mean all that shaking and shoogling? No idea, Tom. It woke me up — the bedstead was bagging off my head!' shouted Drew in distressed remembrance. 'Woke me up good and proper. I could not get back to sleep after that — not a wink all night.'

'Aw, too bad, it is a bit worrying, you know. The papers don't know what to print!' came a voice from by fireplace across from the bar. The man was an estate worker named James, who was a distant relation of Baron Murray Argyll Thom — he worked the estate on the outskirts of the village over and past the Hilltop, to the east of Ayrshire. James kept rubbing his hands over the heat of the small fire for comfort.

'I'm sure that it'll be no good for my beasts—it'll be sour milk tomorrow,' added Tom.

'It's to do with all that "Global Warming," so they say—they're always talking about it in the television,' added James with a nod.

'Maybe... the paper is full of it,' Tom agreed. 'What do you think, Mr McCourt?'

The owner had a reddish complexion and curved moustache. He just smiled and nodded his agreement, focusing mostly on polishing the silver tankards that hung above the bar. He took them off from their hooks one by one, seeming lost in thought. Mr McCourt was the superstitious sort—he looked a little panicky and did not reply.

'Aye, strange happenings, indeed Tom,' Drew cackled strangely. The two men smiled smugly at each other.

The tavern stood cosily warming, in stark contrast to the Italian restaurant that glittered from shadows directly across the road. The restaurant had been established only a few years ago, and was called Giovanni's Bar Napoli. Unlike the bar, Giovanni's was frequented by strangers, often rather unsavoury types—unknowns in the smallish village, which was unusual and nerve-wracking. Mr McCourt had thought the restaurant would never take off, but unfortunately it had proved very popular with incomers from neighbouring larger towns and some well-to-do families.

****

The earthquake story never even reached the national papers, and the story only ran in a few local newspapers in front page headlines that screamed:

"EARTHQUAKE STRIKES VILLAGE as INSURANCE HITS ROOFTOPS!"
and
"TREMOUR in TOWN — OLD FOLK SCARE!"
then
"THE EARTHQUAKE that NEVER WAS!"
and then
"COUNCIL BLAMED for QUAKE FEARS!"

The closest university, thirty miles away in the city of Glasgow, had advised the *The Village Chronicle* that there had been very little abnormal seismic activity in that area, although acknowledging that there was a well-known natural fault line that ran through this part of the country side. The university professionals claimed that the quake was an overreaction of villagers unused to shaking earth and *The Chronicle* followed their lead, to the consternation and outrage of locals who had seen and felt the massive disturbance.

There were a few rumours of a national cover-up and claims that the council was in denial run in local pamphlets, but these did not strike the attention of the community and eventually the whole matter was forgotten or ignored. One thing that could not be denied, however, was the change. The whole county experienced a sharp drop in temperature, felt even in the dusty city of academics. Somehow, after that fateful day, the world had changed.

The only people who put two and two together were the villagers, in whose minds the earthquake and the temperature drop were inextricably linked. But for the rest of the world, which did not acknowledge that the quake had ever happened, this possibility went entirely unnoticed.

****

CHAPTER II

Genesis

⅂□•□V⌐V

Thus the heavens and the earth were finished,
and all the host of them.
— Genesis 2:1

Don Luzio Ilario was not a particularly light humoured gentleman. He was ruthless, in fact, or so he seemed to anyone who really knew him. A more accurate description might be lethal although most people were unwilling to say so aloud. But everyone knew that unless you wished to casually end up swinging over the side of a bridge with your neck stretched, he was a man who commanded respect. Of course, Don Luzio had a variety of faces to fit his numerous business interests — his shifting personality could be both persuasive and witty when required, and he had a light-hearted, diplomatic charm that belied the gravity of his purposes.

Don Luzio owned many casinos and other businesses in Italy. Most of his companies were honest businesses, built up over generations by his father and grandfather. Unlike his forefathers, Don Luzio built other businesses upon his solid family foundations, diversifying into the utilities and manufacturing sectors. He now supplied many services to the government, and billions of pounds flowed through his fast growing empire. His lifestyle had made him a little fat, almost jovial to look at; the man would not walk anywhere far, and he did not need to. With a still-young look and smart, short-brown hair, an outsider would consider him nothing more than a brilliant young entrepreneur.

Today marked the bidding of another lucrative contract, and his organisation was busy preparing the many tender documents for perusal. Although everything was nearly ready, the team would wait until about ten minutes before the deadline before they made the final document transfers. It was a tried and tested procedure that had won them many e-government tender contracts. Their competitors never knew that the real reasons their bids were unsuccessful — even if discussions with candidates or tenderers took place afterwards, even if someone filed a debrief or complaint, no other offers would succeed if the Ilario Holdings expressed an interest. To win contract after contract with the central government would eventually force other companies out of business, and then Don Luzio's competitors would be ripe for the picking. Ilario planned to eventually own all the utility suppliers in Europe — be they cleaning services, road repairs, parks and recreation, security or the supply and manufacture of gas equipment. The Don was already a prominent and very powerful figure in Italy, and well on his way to expanding his organisation.

Most governments he considered for his growing empire used a formal mechanism for assessing pre-qualification of contracts through tendering exercises. European governments required assurance that potential suppliers of services and products were suitable to tender for public contract opportunities in terms of their legal, financial, and technical capacity, as well as their honest integrity and credibility.

His subsidiary companies always passed these credibility quality checks with flying colours!

Ilario's companies used and owned an online supplier information database service available to all supplier companies or competitive organizations. Many suppliers accessed the databases via the internet and the information service was truly global, crossing all natural borders worldwide.

Likewise, government buyers would interrogate this common database using the same system or suite of internet applications. These applications would then ask certain supplier companies to "Express an Interest" in various buyer contracts, depending on what kind of tenders were on the offering. The buyer and suppliers were presented with their own dedicated portal interfaces, although the underlying database was the same.

Ilario Holdings was the parent company of a small software company called Ventisei Software Solutions Ltd, which specialized in electronic tendering, known glibly as "e-tendering". The Managing Director of Ventisei, a tough business woman named Nina Ventisei, had for her sole purpose the development and

company acted as a middleman by providing essential electronic tendering software tools in order to exchange confidential documents. He'd already fulfilled contracts for the warship R & D Support to Modify a Northrop Grumman AN/APN-241 radar system to develop an Anti Ship Missile (ASM) simulator and the IRL-Dublin apparatus for measuring radiation. The title attributed to the contract by the contracting authority was: Upgrade of Italian National Radioactivity in Air Monitoring Network.

This contract Ilario decided he wanted and would keep a lucrative eye on the Stingray Intensive Munitions Programme Ltd Insertion, which was a single-source contract for the manufacture of 112 Insensitive Munitions Warhead Systems and the integration of these systems into the Sting Ray Strategic Defence Department. Codenamed A400M, the project aimed to provide tactical and strategic mobility to all three services. The Ministry of Defence required that the contractor be able to: operate from airfields and semi-prepared rough landing areas in extreme climates and all weather conditions by day and night; carry a variety of equipment, including vehicles and troops over extended ranges; air drop Para-troopers and equipment; and unload with a minimum of ground handling equipment.

The Strategic Defence Review confirmed that the A400M would meet these requirements. It would replace the remaining Hercules C-130K fleet. A400M is a collaborative programme involving eight European nations (Germany, France, Turkey, Spain, Belgium, Luxembourg, UK and Italy) and a total of 180 aircraft. The program was, all in all, considered "chicken feed" — because the UK Ministry of Defence fielded thirty billions of pounds sterling to be awarded in contracts alone.

Don Luzio wanted this award badly and would see it achieved! Procured through a contract with Airbus Military Italian, also owned by Ilario Holdings, the deadline was this Friday and worth billions of pounds. A large share of the contract money would be transferred to a few the Don's individual Swiss bank accounts, of course.

Ventisei Software Solutions (VSS) had just provisioned the UAE Armed Forces General Headquarters' (GHQ) new electronic tendering portal, enhancing the efficiency, speed and transparency of the GHQ's procurement process and bringing the system on par with international standards. A joint press conference was attended by the Armed Forces and UAE's leading IT solutions provider, ITQAN, who implemented the project in association with international partner Ventisei Software Solutions Ltd of Italy. ITQAN and its strategic partner, VSS, were entrusted by the UAU Armed Forces to provide a state-of-the-art IT solution to automate GHQ's procurement process. The press conference was held on the sidelines of the International Defense Exhibition (IDEX) in Abu Dhabi. The portal's capabilities would also be enhanced in the future for use by other directorates of the Armed Forces.

Power, wealth and ambition were Ilario's middle names, although far from the world he'd known as a child, raised as he was in the Sicilian village of Petralia Soprana, located in the Madonie Mountains about 1500 metres above sea level. The village was always a step or two behind the modern world. As a young man, Don Luzio had firmly gripped the modern age of technology with both hands and used it easily to his full advantage — technology was like the tree of knowledge of good and evil to him; it raised him up above others, and yet....

The Don he hoped his father would have been proud of him and all his work.

****

Now the serpent was more subtil than any beast of the field which the Lord God had made. And he said unto the woman, yea, hath God said, Ye shall not eat of every tree of the garden?
— Genesis 3:1

The love of money, it is said, is the root of all evil. And yet some roots grow much deeper than that...

The Cardinal lived just outside Rome in the village of Acilia. He owned a fine villa with peaked central turret and a generous main building on two levels; it dominated the hill upon which it sat. A sandy coloured building with different shades of light pastel yellows and dull oranges, its windows were large and arched and from this vantage point the house looked out and downwards through a gorgeous system of valleys and creeks far below. The landscape was characterized by its natural warm colours—fertile soil and the rich clearness of water streams produced lush vegetation and a forest of oaks.

Lying comfortably on his basket lounger in the shaded veranda as the sun rose early this October morning, Cardinal Giovanni Dalla Gassa contemplating in deep solitude as he looked over the world....

The mission is almost complete, he thought. *Benedict has not sat in his holy chair for long — he is unfamiliar of the immediate office issues within the Vatican and, like Pope John Paul, he may not be in office for the normal term....*

With a silent prayer to God, the Cardinal viewed the successful transfer of another $300,000,000 into the Vatican purse. The day was beginning well.   Sipping a tall glass of red wine, harvested from his own vineyards, the man felt warm and satisfied. Placing the slim wineglass on the side table, the man began typing again—playing the keys with the confidence of a skilled organist.

The Cardinal tended to the dollars like a shepherd to sheep, gathering the flock into its pen while making sure that no wolves were sneaking around. Pleased with his success, the Cardinal surveyed the latest figures in the financial spread-sheets.

The weak-coloured tiled floor was cold to the touch of his toes as he readjusted his sitting position. The day began to heat up slowly as he studied the electronic marketplace. *Where...where is it?* the Cardinal wondered. *Si, there!* It was not the largest company he had acquired but one that was very healthy. Biotechnology! That was always a sound financial investment. The Cardinal had earned early recognition by the Vatican when he'd demonstrated his skill in the acquisition of all types of companies. He was certainly destined for greatness.

Under divine instruction, the Cardinal was able to buy stocks and shares to fund projects that helped to build the Catholic faith throughout the world and especially in those darkest, uncivilized places. Indeed, the

Cardinal's was a true and holy mission! If the church had a solid financial base, then the faith of the masses would follow. Governments would bend their knees for the short and immediate financial reprieve the Vatican could offer and would in exchange allow God's missions in their countries.

Giovanni Dalla Gassa had been in the service of the Lord all his life and, by the grace of God; he was fifty eight years old and had known several Holy Sees. Like many entrepreneurs, the man had lowly beginnings — he'd worked up through his community church from a simple choir boy to a priest, ascended the steps to the Holy Order and then became a Cardinal. The rest of the story was well known. He'd learned his financial wizardry on his consecrated ascension to the Vatican City as he worked through all the hours God blessed him with. Cardinal Giovanni Dalla Gassa was now the "Secretary of State" to the Pope. Not only was he much respected and trusted at the highest levels, his reputation of generosity made him much beloved by the greater Italian community. Many paid him homage and pleaded if not prayed for his sacrament, his sanctifying financial grace....

After checking the morning financials, His Grace drove himself into the Vatican City in his dark green Mercedes Benz cabriole. Today's mission was not in the civil administration building, where most of his corporate offices were located. This morning, he would conduct his religious duties inside the St Peter's Basilica.

All things in his grand office were unique and priceless — in stark disparity of the man who had previously occupied this holy office. There were many priceless works of art, including *Madonna in Glory, Tempera on Panel,* and *The Holy Trinity*, which had been acquired from the Galleries. Magnificent and breath-taking would not fittingly describe this man's shrine to the Holy Conclave! The rich colours of each painting jumped with life with flickers of the moody lamps that highlighted them. Sitting at his polished marble desk, the Cardinal scratched quickly a scripture with his long-quilled pen.

A portrait of his Holiness Alberto Luciani, Pope John Paul (I), adorned with red and gold robes and holding a golden, jewelled crucifix with his right hand, hung above the entrance doorway. The portrait was twenty-five feet tall and ten feet wide and topped with a shining silver crucifix — it dominated the majority of the Cardinal's dimly lit office. John Paul's eyes seemed patient, thoughtful and ever-watching from his elevated position.

Cardinal Giovanni Dalla Gassa dipped his quill in and out of holy ink whipping as the heavy bronze doors to his outer-office slowly opened. Multi-coloured tones of red, green, blue and golden yellow light shone through stained glass windows set just outside his office, in the main hall. Two men were silhouetted for a moment against the jewelled light before the door closed behind them with an echo that reverberated off the polished marble walls. The men quickly approached the Cardinal's office, each step echoing louder and louder as they passed beneath the five large golden chandeliers that hung from the high ceiling of the Cardinal's outer office. The holy lights did not provide much luminescence in the Cardinal's personal and private chamber within the Secretariat quarter inside the Basilica.

A rich and heavenly mural with gold rimmed carvings felt heavy on the men's heads; they felt as if it was pressing down on them from the lofty arched ceiling. Colourful frescos hung on the walls and noble sculptures stood and guarded the corners of this astonishing chamber. His great office was nothing short of breath-taking! They knocked quietly, and then entered through the heavy wooden doors.

The Cardinal's table was elevated a few inches above floor level on a raised, white-marble base. Behind him, a magnanimous gold-framed mirror, thirty feet wide by twenty feet long, hung atop a marble mantelpiece. The mirror was etched with detailed and holy patterns, while solid silver crucifixes sparkled on either end. The mirror was curved and angled by skilled craftsmen so that it reflected the Pope's image opposite from his real and eminent blessed portrait above the door, including the cross, which shone brilliantly above his head.

The image was quite remarkable and so genuine that the men felt their nerves frazzling.

door behind him, the Cardinal walked towards the less noble wooden desk.

Sitting down, he switched on his laptop and, a minute later, typed in his login name (ggassa) and his password (cometh). This combination always amused him, and his mouth curved into a wry smile. There was a pause while his computer appeared to think. Then a message appeared on the display and his smile became a frown.

God is at work against me again! Why now, damn it?

'Just when I wanted to get on!' he exclaimed out loud, picking up the phone nearby with a hidden vengeance.

This is nothing like the ECB system I used earlier this morning! Grumping, *what's my secretary's number again? There is going to be hell to pay and someone is going to be sorry they came into work today!*

The Cardinal swore loudly as the phone rang and rang without answer, his eyes bulging in wrath when he read the next message.

Sorry, System Unavailable
Please Contact Your System Administrator.

CHAPTER III

PALAZZO del GOVERNMANTORATO

It was a normal working day in the Palazzo del Governmantorato, which was located not far away from the magnificent St Peter's Basilica. Francesca DeRose was running fast and running late—anxiously she ascended the large granite steps towards the building entrance. All Information Technology services had since been moved to the refurbished administrative offices and were all now housed in the same secured building as the Papal Civil Service, Press Office, Prefecture for Economic Affairs, the Secretariat and other top Vatican Executives.

The Palazzo del Governmantorato was a considerable building of outstanding architecture in its own right, with sandy salmon-pink granite stonework constructed into two, four-level wings of similar height that flanked the main central structure. The central, front-facing elevation was inset back from the two protruding outer wings, but was built two levels taller than the wings.

The Holy See administration and bureaucratic machine was located in the right wing, and continued to keep the Catholic Church at the forefront of the civilised religious world by provisioning copious productions of religious papers, activities and doctrines in all languages. The left wing housed the Information Technology (I.T.) core services and other administrative sections. Inside the central construct was the finance department, the cardinals and other high executives. Mission-critical data transmission links were maintained internally for the Istituto per le Opere di Religione (IOR) services, also known as the Vatican Bank, securing much more than the numbers that were published in the public domain.

It was 9:20 A.M. on a Monday morning in the last week of October, and the trains had been running slow. 'Points failure-technical difficulties' is what the engineers had claimed this morning, but that was always what they said. In the past, the Italian rail network had been very efficient and timely. However, a year ago a new company began providing train service, and nothing had been the same since.

Wearing a pair of tight-fitting dark blue jeans and silk, navy-coloured blouse beneath her expensive brown leather bomber jacket, Francesca took the final staircase two steps at a time. A small golden crucifix with red rubies at top and bottom, and diamonds at left and right, glinted in the morning sunshine that beamed through the tall office windows; the cross hung around Francesca's slender neck.

Francesca was about five feet eight inches tall, and her long legs and womanly curves always raised an eyebrow as she navigated the office. The young lady wished she had taken her vintage automobile into work this morning, but was trying to keep it in the best condition possible — which meant no city driving.

She was aware of being watched as she strode down the aisle to the far end of the office. Used to these backward primordial glances, she smiled confidently, continuing to walk just out of their virtual reach. *Si,* it was a normal day, except...Michaelangelo was not at his desk. The phones were ringing!

Eager eyes watched her, moving in time with her body. Yet although the IT contractors looked more than lustfully at the girl, they also hoped that she would quickly sit down and sort out their immediate problems. *Such a boring bunch*, she thought, passing them to assume her rightful seat.

Looking ahead towards her division, which supported most of the Vatican Banking System, she tapped her login details into her computer with one hand while tying back her springy auburn hair with the other.

Only Gabriella? Where is Michaelangelo? Her co-worker was usually on duty well before she arrived.

Francesca finally swooped down picking up the phone terminating the constant synthetic jingle. "Hello?" She tried to sound pleasant. It was the database administrator, the Englishman. Jonathan.

'Hey! Francesca!' his loud and irritating English voice seemed condescending to her. The man spoke with a quick-firing rat-a-tat-tat set of questions.

'What going on? You've got a network problem! I can't login. It is poorly designed and a crap network, we all know it—it's been slow for years and now it's dead. *Where have you been?'* he baited her. 'What about Michaelangelo—where is he? You are going to be in *deep...* if you don't sort things out fast.'

The man knew also that time was passing as he spoke, exacerbating the problem. She flushed with infuriation and hung up the phone without a word.

Leering at her with a warped and delighted smile from the other side of the room, Jonathan observed her suppressed discomfort. *I'll get her to blow her top yet!* he thought. Her face blushed even more deeply as she scanned the messages in her e-mail....

The Englishman loved it when the network was not working. His team was fine—being paid by the hour to sit at their desks and wait for the system to become available again was right up their alley. Most of them were having coffee as the network team of T&O sweated desperately to fix the immediate problems of the day. *A perfect start to a Monday...* he smirked.

Jonathan was Project Leader and responsible for a small team of contract Programmers and Database Administrators (DBAs) that maintained the contract staff workforce's "database-working environment". They primarily provided disk space and logical schema designs on database servers, as well as performing many additional scripting and admin duties. The entire multi-lingual staff; people from a variety of backgrounds, and English was spoken as the universal language of business. He laughed a little with another developer and lowered his voice a little, although he knew Francesca would still be able to hear him just fine.

'They are just rubbish,' he said distinctly as another man laughed with him.

'Si, we've known this for a while,' the man agreed.

'That lot is crap and this login denial just proves it again,' Guieletta snidely added to the conversation. Guieletta was a Unix Systems Admin Contractor and Developer who sat next to Jonathan. She loved stirring up trouble for the other women in the office and revelled in trying to cause disharmony and division between the teams.   She had a good mentor in Jonathan, for sure!

Bitch! Francesca thought, and then ignored the rest of their ridiculing conversation. Technical & Operations were always an easy target for annoyance and finger pointing when the systems were unavailable. The more a contractor caused some kind of problem for the T&O staff, the better — for then their position seemed to become stronger in the eyes of the Vatican Executives and Holy Order. It guaranteed their continued employment at very, very lucrative rates.

Jonathan's arrogance was endless, but he was a smart arse, a very smart arse, and not to be argued with lightly as he knew his area of the business intimately and was articulate in debate. Although in truth, the contractors would be completely lost without Francesca and the team. Maybe that was the true reason why T&O was hated so ardently.

Ignoring his rudeness, Francesca finally turned a deaf ear to the group. She could never let them know how hurtful they had been or that they were denting her armour, getting to her. Her full red lips moved softly near the receiver.

'Hello, Francesca speaking,' she said, speaking with rising trepidation of who was on the other end of the line.... Francesca listened for only a brief moment to the Chief Executives Secretary, Silvia.

'I'm just checking the systems, Silvia, it's not a big issue and we'll get back online for you as soon as we can.' *She always phones me directly – never the helpdesk. What a pain in the ass.* Francesca looked over at the smiling Jonathan and his sarcastic grin...

He's a bitch, too, she thought as a headache began to remind her why she was happier at home than at work. *This is the last thing I wanted, to give him an opportunity to be right! Steady, keep cool girl....* Francesca thought of a calm lake, its tiny lapping waves smoothing her mind.

Some of the other analysts in the office were bewildered; they tapped furiously at their keyboards, seeming bemused, scratching foreheads with dismay and looking around in confusion. Some, panicking slightly, focused their attention towards Francesca with mixed looks of terror and pleading. With each minute that passed, the noise of the office became louder and louder. More people were arriving at the office to begin their daily workload and found that they were unable to perform. The phones rang and rang without cease.

Normally there would be four people on duty working as an I.T. support team to solve network and systems administration problems. Team-members included Francesca, Massimo, Michaelangelo and Paulina, who was the Unix T&O member of the team. *Where is he?* Francesca thought, feeling a little isolated. *Where is Michaelangelo?*

Gabriella Siciliano popped her head up from above her console screen and smiled sympathetically. Gabriella was in her early to mid-twenties with short, straight black hair. The young girl was the *Change Control Officer*, and it was her job to coordinate any configuration changes to the many systems and services within the Vatican Bank and Administration. She was a small and attractive girl, with warm brown eyes, although her good looks were not quite as spectacular as

Francesca's. She had a friendly but quiet personality.

'Morning Francesca, it looks like your morning is full already. I'll speak to you in a while,' she spoke in a somewhat gentler voice, 'once it is a bit quieter.' The girls had been friends for a few years now, and often found that they made good company for each other at parties, dancing or shopping. Francesca was always the more outgoing personality of the two, but Gabriella had a subtle wit that kept everyone on their toes.

Francesca groaned as she saw Ciriaco from the helpdesk striding up the aisle towards her, the young man looking worried from being hassled by constant and incensed client demands. His phone had been ringing red-hot for an hour! He would be with her in seconds...

Francesca's computer finally accepted her login and password and agreed to let her in. *Phew! No problem here,* she thought, relieved to leave behind her the world of angry co-workers and enter into her domain, her system.

The backdrop on her computer screen was that of a 1956 Austin-Healy 100-4 BN2,

British Racing Green in colour with grill front, spotlights, and perfect alloy wheels, the windscreen tilted back to form a wind reflector. *What a car!* She sighed.

At the same time, Francesca's mind was whirring around the problems experienced throughout the system.

The login stage one, authentication complete...now, where is the difficulty? Why can't the others login?

Sharply, her penetrating eyes staring wide across the screen, she ignored the endless ringing of her own phone. Instead, she studied her system alerts, the green square indicators that began filing down the left window of her computer screen, top to bottom it filled like water dropping from a tap.

Things looked ok... all on the green. So why can't people login? Let me just ping a few connections... servers seem ok, file system volumes all mounted fine; health checks all on the green, except login monitor which was on the red...?

Good replies, too.... That was to be expected. *The switches seem ok as well, so the problem can't be the network... let me check the monitor console.*

Francesca logged in remotely from the additional computer system she maintained on the desk to her left.

Shit... the logins have been disabled on the Directory Services Tree! But who could have done that? Who would want too? The systems administrator tried to analyse the extraordinary puzzle in her mind as she took quick steps to restore login capabilities for the rest of her co-workers.

The term "Tree" was a database network structure containing a list related computer objects representing different items inside the main Vatican Bank computer systems — it controlled Users, Printers to System Resources, access to files, services like e-mail and flowing access control to other systems resources like Unix Databases. It was a strategic system that put great responsibility on T&O, who were not highly paid individuals, as was always the case.

'What's the status, Francesca?' Ciriaco complained as he arrived. 'They need to know! We don't want our Holy Father's Bishop boys boot team, bible bashing us again?' he was trying to sound light-hearted but not really pulling it off. His half-awkward smile and unusually shaky voice revealed his nervousness.

He must have been getting a real hassle, Francesca realized, feeling sorrier than ever that she had been so late today. She typed at the console the command "Enable logins" and then looked up with her large brown eyes towards Ciriaco, smiling into his anxious green eyes with a reassuring nod.

'That's it Ciriaco, its fixed.' speaking calmly and quietly, totally confident that the problem was resolved. 'All the disciples are online, ready and on the green now. All systems and services working normally, kid.' She was not telling the whole truth, of course, but as far as he needed to know everything was just fine.

Ciriaco's expression changed as she gave him the news—his flushed face became much cooler and easier in tone, normal again. Just like the system. Francesca also began to relax as her tension melted into her imaginary lake.

Ciriaco Esposito was only about twenty, if that, but was a bit too highly strung to be a

good Helpdesk Operator. How he got the job
Francesca could never guess, but did not regret
the opportunity it had given her to meet him.
Ciriaco was handsome, with short, dark
designer-stubble on his strong chin and an
athletic, if compact, frame. He wore his short,
spiky hair gelled up in the "wet" look, like a
model. Francesca liked his starry green eyes,
although she would not dream of indicating her
attraction.

Mmm... she thought.

'*Grazie*! I'll get on the telephone pronto!'
He smiled with deep admiration for her skill
and cool head — or was it his affection for her?

He shifted his slim frame and slowly
headed back to the helpdesk area with renewed
confidence. Francesca watched him as he
walked back up the aisle to the glass door
entrance to the office about twenty metres from
her. Her heart raced a little more quickly than
usual.

Oooh, I'm sure he likes me... she pondered
after Ciriaco, her lake rippling a little. A new
alert suddenly turned on within to red alert, but
it was nothing to do with computing!

'Oh! Snap out of it, Francesca, he's too young for you. Baby snatcher!' Paulina Toscano teased clearly but not too loudly. 'You're no better than those contractor guys, perv.' she joked. 'That cutie is only eighteen or nineteen year old.' she paused smiling at the other girl with her mouth hanging a little to open. 'So what's been going on, then Francesca?' Paulina sat down at her seat and logged into the system, effortlessly as usual, unaware of the emergency that had happened in her absence.

With mixed thoughts, Francesca laughed a little in embarrassment as she brushed scattered wisps of hair out of her face. She turned to Paulina as her colleague spoke with excitement.

'Login issue, its resolved.' said Francesca.

'By the way,' Paulina's eyes lit up. 'Did you hear the latest? Last Friday night the commissionaire at the door — it was Mario who spoke briefly with Michaelangelo.' She paused, 'Michaelangelo handed him an envelope, said *buonanotte,* and seemingly left for the weekend. When Mario opened the envelope, it contained

Michaelangelo's ID card and the keys to the office, server and communications rooms! What do you think is up with him? I *do not* think he is coming back! He must be gone for good...strange, eh?' Paulina rattled on, oblivious to Francesca's reaction.

Francesca had been in such a rush this morning that she had not had time to speak with the Commissionaire. Again her mouth dropped slightly, this time with dismay, although she'd known that Michaelangelo had been very unhappy for a while now. He was a disgruntled by the way support staff members were treated by the glorious Holy style of management, crucifixion mandatory. She'd never expected him to do this and get up and leave...

'Not Michaelangelo!' she exclaimed. 'Conditions are bad here but not *that bad*. Why did he quit?'

Paulina shook her head mutely.

Unsettled and raw-nerved, the girls got on with their daily administration duties.

****

The Technical and Operations Manager, Anatolio di San Angelo, called a meeting, later that morning in his office. Francesca arrived with Paulina and Gabriella. Massimo Rossi was not at the meeting, as he was on holiday for the day. The room was located on the Executive level floor, right at the top of the building, room six.

The girls entered a large room that was furnished with Anatolio's large oak desk, on which his grey-coloured laptop sat opened and humming quietly. The smell of black coffee was strong in the air. A dark brown leather swivel chair, its back to them, moved in a pendulum-like motion — to the left a little, and then to right.

Peering out the large middle window towards the old city skyline, Anatolio could see the Ethiopian Seminary below and the Lourdes Gardens in the distance near the old city wall, to the left. The new Gardens were to the right. It was a dull and cold day — not the best time of year to view the magnificent blossoms that would bloom below in warmer seasons. The mood of the miserable day was cast into the room by the wide windows.

Swivelling around to face his Network Support team, Anatolio's leather chair creaked a little.

'*Buongiorno,* make yourselves comfortable, please. Coffee is in the pot, it is freshly made.' He smiled lightly and surveyed his depleted ground troops. Francesca crossed her legs comfortably, resting a small notepad on her lap. Paulina walked over to the percolator as it bubbled and hissed like a steam engine.

There was an eye catching picture of the *Night Watch,* 1642 from the Rijksmuseum, Amsterdam — a Rembrandt — on the left wall near the poorly placed coffee pot. It was misnamed *Night Watch* because of a very dark varnish that covered it until the 1940s. It should have been titled *The Company of Captain Frans Cocq.* It is a group portrait of a company of civil guards under the command of Cocq and his lieutenant, Willem van Ruytenburch. In this painting, Rembrandt solved the problem of the group portrait by introducing a dynamic scene; making it so few artists after him could skilfully sit or stand their subjects in a static line or grouping. *Night Watch* depicts a powerful scene of Cocq and his men in motion, their lances askew and muskets primed as they prepared for battle. On the opposite wall was a picture of St Peters Basilica at night, lit up to display figures on top, looking over the city.

An oil lamp sat on Anatolio's desk, casting shadows onto *Night Watch*. A large, flat-screened LCD monitor glowed light onto the man's left face, creating stark contrast to the heavy atmosphere of the dark room.

'Ok,' he began, looking stony faced at Francesca, 'I have had a few concerned calls from above.' He looked at the ceiling above his head although there was no floor above his office. 'The Cardinal and a few of the Holy Order have become a bit agitated with our lack of commitment in this section. This morning's system network issues have not gone unnoticed, and they are only the latest in a series of recent problems.' He paused, and then continued in a low voice. 'In our defence, I mentioned that we are understaffed and that there was no lack of enthusiasm from my team. We have the skills and the commitment with less than adequate resources. In fact, I believe

we are doing a very good job under very
difficult circumstances,' he concluded, praising
his team despite the massive discontent with
their work throughout the organisation.

The system administrators nodded in
appreciation of his solid support. Anatolio was
quite charming and had a persuasive manner —
everyone except Francesca who was puzzled.

Di San Angelo smiled again. 'With a hail
Mary I managed to convince them that events
such as what occurred this morning are few
and far between....' A short pause ensued as he
looked at each and every member of the team.
'But when we are not online, guys, we lose our
credibility. To the big bosses, losing credibility
has severe financial implications, and that is all
they care about.' paused 'We missed the boat
this morning, did we not?' frowning at
Francesca. Francesca cut in. before he said
anything else,

'That is completely unfair, Anatolio. I
was able to resolve the issue within minutes of
arriving.'

'Si...and I heard you arrived *late*,' he
stated, with a hint of annoyance evident in his
reply. His tone deepened and turned to iron as

he addressed the greater group. 'The Cardinals know nothing of the sudden departure of our Michaelangelo. I have to say that I am really shocked to say the least and cannot believe this has occurred. It is totally out of the blue and makes us all look bad.' Anatolio turned again towards Francesca. 'And do you know, Francesca, why our escapee made such a rude departure?' he asked with some degree of sarcasm. Silence fell in the darkening room.

'Anatolio, I am as surprised and confounded at his untimely departure as you,' Francesca replied composedly.

'What caused the problem this morning?' Anatolio tried to establish some kind of connection but, drawing no answers, a gaze of dissatisfaction came over his brown eyes, lending an aged look to his broad, tanned face.

'After a few system checks,' she answered, 'I quickly narrowed the issue to "Luke's" console. The effects were widespread, affecting all users, so preventing login on all systems, but it was easy enough to resolve. I issued the "enable logon" command and everything began to work as it was supposed to.'

'How did this happen, Francesca? Who would try to do this? Was it Michaelangelo or Luke?' Anatolio drilled her for quick answers, clearly trying to lay blame for the major inconvenience which had made him look a fool.

Francesca sipped her black coffee with a steady hand and sat back easily in her chair, taking her time before answering.

'I looked at all the "disciples", but it was on Luke—his logger screen, sir, where the disable command was issued—not Michaelangelo's.'

'Then who did it, my dear girl—who?' Anatolio betrayed signs of losing his patience as his tone raised an octave.

'My analysis is not complete, but the login name was that of "Apostol". The login is not one that I know, it hasn't been in our naming convention for system users... but, as I said, my analysis is not complete. The *tree* was disabled about 03:00 hours Monday morning. No one should be on the system at that time,' she concluded with a bewildered expression, trying to ignore Anatolio's rudeness.

'Why would Michaelangelo play such a trick, knowing the problems that this would cause?' his tone a verdict.

'It's not him. Did you not listen to Francesca?' Gabriella chimed in. 'It was not his login. It would never be him; anyway, he is far too professional!'

'So professional that he left with only a "arrivederci", eh?' Anatolio interrupted angrily. 'Well, it's up to you, Francesca. Complete your analysis and report back to me. I will contact the Human Resources section and see if they know anything about the user name Apostol. I want you to disable Michaelangelo's login with immediate effect. However, keep this Apostol login open and monitor it.' Francesca nodded in understanding of his direct orders, but not with agreement.

'I would also disable if not delete the "Apostol" account, Anatolio, just in case it causes any more damage,' Francesca allowed her concern to show on her face.

'No, Francesca — I know what I'm doing. I'll have one of our VIA guys observe the Apostol account. I want *you* to find out what you can and report directly to me and no one

else. Is that clear?' Anatolio commanded
sternly.

Francesca showed no emotion other than
looking at *Night Watch* with disinterest. The
last thing she needed was the heavy Vatican
hand snooping about and preaching its
bureaucratic doctrine on her turf....

*That's all I need, a few of those idiots from
VIA sticking their noses in where they are not
wanted and causing havoc with things they do not
understand. Just brilliant!*

Gabriella moved slowly to get another
cup of coffee, her pastel pink sleeveless
designer top and short, light-red skirt with
black leather belt off-setting the gleam of her
short black hair.

'He was having some problems with his
girlfriend, I saw them having a bit of a tiff, an
argument outside the office, just the other
week,' Gabriella said quietly, seeming pleased
to have knowledge that they did not. 'It was
something to do with his not coming home one
night. Not that I was listening too closely, mind
you, but anyone in the street could hear what
was going on. I think he had been out in the

city with a few mates and gone to an all-night party.'

Francesca was grateful for Gabriella's friendship, but now, as she often did, felt that the girl was a little too gossipy.

It'll be her undoing someday, thought Francesca.

Anatolio di San Angelo rolled his eyes a bit and then continued for another hour or so discussing the other systems issues and updates in a manner more typical of a network team meeting.

He was never easy going and always one for sending e-mails to back up everything he said in order to have a paper trail, which Francesca viewed as an indication of his own insecurity. More than once he'd used e-mails to prove to her an error she'd made, digging a remote e-mail from years ago in order to make an irrelevant point. Anatolio would send an e-mail to God, if the Lord had an account set up, in order to cover his holy ass.

****

Francesca, Gabriella and Paulina exited the lift on the ground floor foyer and passed the inside of the front entrance of the bank. The foyer had undergone a recent facelift that gave it a more modern interior while maintaining its unique classical, Italian architecture. Mario the Commissionaire stood smiling at the girls, but then what man wouldn't?

Two Swiss guards stood outside the entrance day and night, keeping a watchful eye on anybody who passed by and checking their identification with complimentary salute. The Administration building like most building inside the Vatican City walls was out of bounds to the thousands of general public standing in their infinite queues in and around St Peters Square and the exterior walls heading for the Museum.

Mario was a retired policeman and now a Commissionaire at the entrance to the palace. Standing behind his desk in pressed uniform and skipped commissioner hat each day, he was a little bit stout and always had a wide, friendly smile extended beneath his upward-curving moustache.

'*Ciao*, ladies, looking fantastic as usual,' he greeted them, smiling at their catwalk.

Paulina wore a set of silver-rimmed eyeglasses that suited her petite features and a pin-striped black trouser suit that showed her figure to her best advantage. She had let her short, wavy blonde hair to flow loosely glancing licentiously to her left, through the glass door towards the Swiss guards outside.

'Hi Mario, you still here?' asked Paulina in jest. 'Working too hard, eh?' as Mario chuckled a little, his stomach wobbling slightly.

'Still here and at your service, Paulina, as always.' He tapped the skip of his hat in salute. 'Have you been upstairs to heaven's gate, then?'

Paulina answered with a nod. 'Just collecting *your* marching papers, Mario.' She joked and laughed a little.

The girls walked past the friendly commissioner and headed towards their office. The integral crystal fountain of the foyer sprayed a geyser twenty feet tall towards the high ceiling; it fell downwards noisily, like heavy rain, into the large circular, glass pool below.

Coins had been tossed into the fountain at different times, and would be routinely and unknowingly collected and then added to the Papal funds to keep the waters clean. The sound of the waterfall was deafening when the girls came close to it — the noise echoed off the granite floor and walls, which were made of solid and ancient marble stone. There was a natural sparkle, a speckled crystal within the walls that glittered in the light, contributing to the sparkle of the water.

The network team swished their ID cards at the entrance to the office and the thick glass door clicked each time; Gabriella opened the door and the girls stepped into the action.

The clacking of tapping fingers sounded like machine-gun fire in the closed room. A few people raised their voices above the sound, competing with the words of the helpdesk team, who was still fielding calls from the Vatican.

All helpdesk team members were now in full flow since August, covering not only the local, Godley calls but also the new link to the European Central Bank, the ECB building in Frankfurt and the Vatican's banking service.

This part of the business was not going so well, and had become an 18 hour operation with only one person on call at any given time. It all boiled down to what the priorities were in the Vatican, and I.T. support was always last on its Christmas list.

A few loud laughs could be heard as the girls walked back to their desks; Paulina heard a few derisory comments at their expense. This behaviour was the norm coming from the contractors, who believed they were better than anyone else. *Not all contractors are like that,* Paulina reminded herself. Some even took up permanent employment at the Vatican.

****

Tuesday was uneventful, and consisted of the normal routine checks and admin duties of the T&O section. The database guys were busy, too, with another system upgrade that involved "change control".

Nothing else occurred with regard to the mysterious Apostol login, which was being monitored by Francesca. Meanwhile, the girl had tried to piece together everything that had happened, but could not make sense of Michaelangelo's disappearance. She couldn't help but think that he was in some kind of trouble....

Francesca phoned him at home, to make sure he was ok, and received no answer but a continuous ringing; his mobile went straight to voice mail after only one ring. The man lived in Albano Laziale, so going to visit was not an easy proposition, but she decided to drive to his flat that evening, anyway. In the meantime, Francesca looked through the computer logs to find a clue, but unfortunately she found nothing.

Francesca was puzzled by the whole thing, although she knew that there is no such thing as a completely secure system. Protecting the systems was a bit like sealing up as many holes as possible, making the proposition of attack less attractive to potential hackers. Security was tight physically and at the server and network levels, of course. Frequent security checks were made with various "penetration testing" provided by the pedantic VIA — Vatican Internal Auditors.

The money was no compensation for the kind of pressure placed upon Francesca, but the work excited her and the Apostol incident was an intriguing puzzle. She was like a bear drawn to a honey pot.... *Mysteries are fun,* Francesca thought, and smiled.

****

That evening, Francesca drove to the town of Albano Laziale in search of answers. Albano Laziale sits within the Rome province, about twenty-five km from Rome. 'All roads lead to Rome' thought Francesca as she glimpsed one of the old Roman roads running not far away. It was the Appian Way — its cracked and paved engineering surrounded on either side with tall cypress trees guarding the ancient ghosts that still trekked on to the Eternal City.

It was a lovely evening as Francesca drove into the quiet cul-de-sac off Via Cesare Colizza where Michaelangelo lived. The neighbourhood was good enough for Pompey, and so it was also good enough for Michaelangelo. Although the journey took about twenty minutes, Francesca decided that the view was worth it.

Michaelangelo's home was on the bottom floor flat of a three story building; whose light blue-grey stonework, tall, arched doorway and attractive wooden shutters indicated that the building was a superb place to live. It was not too far away to commute and yet outside the hustle and bustle of city life. The light, marine-sloped roof was almost flat. Francesca admired the large, paved courtyard which was surrounded by a tree and shrub garden as she approached.

A few cars were parked at the front, in the courtyard. Francesca stopped her automobile and looked at the building; it looked exactly like the last time she visited — clean and quiet. Getting out of her antiquated Mini Cooper, Francesca looked around for Michaelangelo's Puma. There were a few cars sitting there — a couple of Fiats, a Citroen and an Alpha, but Michaelangelo's Yellow 1978 Puma GTE Coupe was nowhere in sight.

Mmm..., this does not look too good — no car! All this way for nothing.... she wondered what the chances were of him being at home without his car, and decided there was nothing to do but to knock on his door. She entered the building's front entrance, shivering in the cool darkness of the entryway. Taking off her sunglasses, Francesca pressed his door buzzer and waited. There was no answer. She continued to press the buzzer a few more times and waited, but no one came to the door. Francesca knocked on the door and then turned the door knob gently. The door was unlocked.

'Michaelangelo! Ciao, ci sei, are you in?' she shouted apprehensively, feeling unsure about the unlocked door.

When she heard no response, Francesca opened the door wider and looked inside. His rooms seemed undisturbed, filled with bamboo furniture and comfortable, light-coloured mosaic cushions. Magazines with automobiles and racing cars were stacked here and there, and a few pictures of old cars adorned the brown- and red-toned walls. Green Swiss cheese plants stood in pots, as did ferns near his music system. Francesca noted the sharp smell of cigarettes that drifted about his flat, catching the tips of her nostrils.

He smoked, but it was cigars, she remembered, her sense of unease rising. A coffee cup sat on the small table. She touched it lightly as she walked past the living room and into his bedroom, popping her head around the doorframe slowly.

He was not in there either! His bed looked unused. A computer was set up near the bedroom window. She looked at it quizzically, moving quickly inside Francesca switched it on; it fired into action after about two minutes of warm up, and then gave a logon. Francesca was familiar with the screen and was able to enter Michaelangelo's personal profile, which was protected, but she gained entry by using the password she'd noticed him using recently at work, as he often logged in from his office desk remotely to his home personal computer.

Francesca decided that since she had already entered his house and logged on to his computer, she might as well look at his browser to see what web sites he'd visited recently. The following list caught her eye:

www.vintageautocars.com
www.sicily.com
www.vaticanbank.com
www.cashinhand.com

Nothing suspicious here, she decided, knowing his interests as she did. She closed down his computer and went to the bathroom and then the kitchen, touching her fingertips on top of the old kettle.

'Ouch!' she yelped in pain, surprised. The kettle was hot! *He must have been in here recently!*

Francesca opened the back door, which was also unlocked, and scanned the open country and hills beyond. *He has dashed for it, I think... It is so odd... what is he afraid of?*

Francesca returned to the living quarters and felt the coffee cup — it too was warm. She lifted a gaming magazine from the top of the coffee table and noticed something was circled with a pen: Dammusi Finances and Gambling.

He always liked gambling...maybe he is in financial difficulties? Something else was bothering her, in the back of her mind, however, agitating her. But she could not pinpoint what the problem was.

There did not seem to be evidence enough of foul play to call the police, but where was he? *I'll try phoning him on his cell-phone again,* she decided.

'Oh shit,' she muttered as she looked at her phone, realising that she had run out of power. 'What a bugger.' Francesca locked the back door of the flat and also locked the front door before she left, pulling the door firmly behind her. Then a deep voice echoed from the stairs behind her.

'*Buonasera*, good evening, *Signora.*' Startled she instantly turned to see a big man standing on the stair case, leaning carelessly against the rail with a cigarette wobbling out the side of his mouth.

'Oh!'

'*Come sta*? *Mi chiamo es Lucciano,*' he introduced himself charmingly. 'I live upstairs, above Michaelangelo, but he,' the man paused, and then corrected himself. 'I have not seen him since last week. Have you spoken to him lately?'

The man spoke through his nostrils slightly, giving his voice a congested sound. He was completely bald but had a little goatee on his chin. He wore a white open neck shirt and fawn trousers strapped with silver-buckled black belt. His muscles were like none she had ever seen before. He could easily have passed for some kind of a bouncer or weight lifter, a hard man and a rough one.

'*Come ti chiami?*' he asked.

Francesca instantly thought...

Michaelangelo never complained about loud music, Francesca mused. Looking at the man *neither would I.* She had never liked big men, especially anabolic ones!

'*Ciao!*' she responded finally. 'I have come for a visit, but it looks like Michaelangelo is out, unfortunately.' *He is a bit forward, this big bear of a man,* she decided, not wanting to give herself away, smiled back. 'I missed him again, I guess. Oh well, I'll probably come back tomorrow.' Looking upwards at the man's intimidating frame, Francesca warily stepped back a pace.

'Where are you from?' the man prompted with a smirk. 'I'll let him know that you came over to visit.' He looked at her slowly, his vulgar eyes stripping her from top to bottom.

'I am from the city, but thank you — no need to bother. I'll speak to him soon,' she replied. 'I have to dash off. Thanks for the offer, but I really must go now. *Arrivederci.''*

'*Buona fortuna*,' he called after her. 'See you again, *soon*', he said watching her speedily exit the corridor, going into the wide automobile courtyard.

I hope not, you cheeky ass, she thought, feeling a little awkward and wanting to leave as fast as she could. Then she remembered Michaelangelo.

Out of view, and not quite sure why, Francesca quickly turned and approached the building trying to peer through his front windows to make sure, he had not come back. Cupping her hands on the glass, she could see no sign of life. *Where is he?*

Suddenly, she noticed a movement inside Michaelangelo's flat, a shape like a man at the other end of his room. Had Michaelangelo, returned? The dark silhouette moved quickly, and her heart raced a little as it disappeared from her sight. Francesca strained her gaze inwards, trying magnetically to follow the figure's direction of travel with her face pressed against the window. Her jaw dropped.

Eyes instantly widened! A face appeared from the other side, looking right out at hers, right in front of her face; her eyeballs were only a centimetre from his!

Francesca did not recognise the face or even notice any of its features because of the darkness of the room on the other side of the window, but one thing she did know—it was not Michaelangelo!

A sudden panic swept over her and she turned quickly and ran to her car, heading back to Rome with a screech of burning rubber as her wheels spun on the hard cement. She drove swiftly, very much afraid for her friend.

Francesca did not notice the Silver Alpha Romero with dark-tinted windows that slipped out gently into the street behind her.

****

Wednesday was another busy day for the T&O team as they continued to field their skills from Estates to IT, from the Papal Office to Finance and the Vatican Banking people, from Arts to PR & Events — pulled first one way and then the other.

Massimo returned from the Communications and Server room and sat diagonally across from Francesca, looking a bit puzzled.

This twenty-six year old I.T. Technician was as surprised as anyone to hear of Michaelangelo's unexpected departure. Massimo, also called Mass, sat comfortably at his PC, typing with his long, piano key-like fingers. Mass was not a big man or the most attractive guy in the world — in fact, he was quite comfortably average, with a slim frame and unremarkable features. Wearing jeans and a white, short-sleeved collared shirt, he turned towards Francesca and updated her on systems states. Small laughter lines appeared around his eyes and cheeks as he spoke.

'Mark and John are stable, and Luke, too, Francesca. Mathew is beginning to degrade a little on his logical space. Do you think you might move the services onto Luke and reboot node four later for me?' he quizzed Francesca.

'*Si*, I will have time to do it later tonight, once those geeks have gone for the night and there is no more money on the table,' she replied with a hint of sarcasm.

Working late was a requirement of the job, and night was a time when many tasks could be performed without affecting most normal users on the Vatican Network Systems.

'*Grazie*, Francesca,' he grinned, happy to be let away early.

Later that evening, the office was deserted as Francesca settled down to maintain the disciples. The contract staff had all picked up their jackets on the dot and quick marched to the door bang on the five o' clock whistle.

Francesca checked the system logs and found nothing unusual or out of the ordinary, only a few logins left on the system – probably employees who forgot to log out earlier or remote logins. Francesca let these be, knowing that the intruder detection alert system would sort out these users later in the evening.

There seemed to be no obvious reason for the previous security breach, and yet something gnawed away at the back of her mind like a sensitive tooth, hurting her now and again...something did not ring true of everything she knew, but she could not figure out what.

Let's get on with this node problem, then, she reminded herself. The girl began to go through in her mind the step by step procedure of power down and start up for the server. Picking up her notepad she headed for the fifth floor, the one directly below the Executive floor.

On her way passing the front entrance on ground floor, Francesca saw the Swiss guards outside yawning until they noticed her through the glass doors. Smiling, the men prepared themselves for another long night on guard duty outside the security doors. The evenings were starting to get colder, and both men pulled up their collars, shivering slightly.

Mario had left for the night, and Francesca was surprised to find that no one was stationed at the helpdesk.

That's too bad – Ciriaco might have been about for me to talk to for a while. Feeling a little miffed, Francesca got out the lift at the fifth floor and entered the deserted corridor, which ran about fifty metres straight along past the offices used by the Estates and Office services.

All the office lights were out; the office was as quiet as the grave. Along the corridor, Francesca walked towards the server room which was hidden behind a secure door on her left, roughly about twenty metres ahead. The floor was carpeted with a dull-blue flat carpet, very uninspiring and corporate in its look. There was no natural light in the corridor and only poor, dimmed artificial light from sporadic fixtures above. Pictures to her left and right lined the walls, depicting bizarre, distorted images of absurd situations that seemed to have some meaningful significance, although Francesca hadn't a clue what that might be. *Yes, it's a bit spooky here,* she thought, feeling like she was rather out on a limb.

A door suddenly opened to her right with a loud noise!

Francesca's head turned quickly and her deep auburn hair swung round as she jumped a little, putting her hand to her chest and letting out a yell....

'Oh!' she felt as though her heart had missed a beat. Startled, Francesca turned right to the Events Office!

'I am very sorry, my dear,' Agata, the cleaning lady, said kindly as she entered into the corridor from the office opposite, staring regretfully at Francesca. 'I did not want to startle you. Just cleaning up—all done now. I'll be going down to the stairs now and then the next floor.' The woman's voice was rough and deep, as though she had been smoking for many, many years. Holding Francesca's arm in friendship, Agata's carved face showed deep wrinkles almost like crevasses; she'd had a hard life and been exposed to the erosion of years of toil. Despite her hard exterior, the woman was a friendly person and showed genuine sympathy.

'Thank God it is you, Agata. I almost jumped out of my skin just now!' Francesca replied to the small, concerned cleaning lady, trying to make light of the moment. She giggled, a little hesitantly, and then Agata joined her in a laugh.

'*Ciao*, see you tomorrow!' Agata nodded understandingly. She picked up her green cleaning bucket—Francesca wrinkled her nose at the sight of the dirty rags inside—and made her way to the stairs.

At the server room door, Francesca swished the security card and spoke her name into a voice recognition receiver. Her eyes glanced left, looking down the corridor as the little woman turned the corner and descended to the stairs on the right of the lifts.

Francesca listened to the buzzer alarm while she pushed the heavy metal door open and entered the main communications and server room. Francesca suddenly remembered scenting a brief wisp of alcohol from the cleaning lady's breath when she passed her a moment earlier. Then, electronic noises began to intrude and take over her thoughts.

The long room was well-equipped with a multitude of servers secured fast within metal communication cabinets. Servers were high precision pieces of computer hardware that provided the Vatican with all the IT services expected in the modern world, from e-mail and Web Servers to Finance Servers and Vatican Banking Systems, provisioning file and print and other large mission-critical operations.

The servers were organised and arranged one above the other and housed in metal racks or cabinets. The cabinets stood side by side at six feet tall, extending along the length of the room. Periodic gaps were spaced out to allow access to the other side of the light grey-coloured walls. These cabinets also contained and connected many of the super-fast fibre switches from these servers to other areas throughout the old Vatican City — from the Administration building to St Peter's Basilica — and fanned out from there to the rest of Vatican City. Cryptic instructions for the emergency shutdown procedure for servers now long-out-dated remained stuck on the walls.

There were also old network charts showing old cable runs, although where the old cable runs ended up, Francesca would never know. In fact, no one at T&O even cared. The cable runs were "old stuff", irrelevant and therefore uninteresting. Too many external telecommunication companies had been involved in pulling and running cables in every direction over the years, leaving old ones hanging all over the city, but surprisingly, it all still worked. A constant background noise of air conditioning, along with the fans of the communications and computer equipment, made the room a place in which Francesca did not want to stay for very long.

Francesca knew her way about the comms room and amongst the large mass of cable spaghetti. She could use her sense of touch on this mass of twisted cables to find their termination point, feeling inch by inch to the exact patch point and number that would trail to even his Holiness's Benedict's office. Occasionally she might read it wrong, which at worst would cause a little confusion for an end user. But such is life!

Whoosh! The air blowers from square grills in the ceiling above her blasted strong cool air down just before Francesca as she walked, her face narrowed a little at the bad timing. Her hair wafted about madly in the air.

Bloody hell! I'm here on my own up here with no one around. What a great start to a night's work! Those blowers are loud and a nuisance, but it's better than letting the servers go into a melt now, isn't it?

A sarcastic little voice crept into her mind. The room temperature was a little on the warm side, overall.

It looks like the air conditioning should be inspected by Estates, if not the health and safety division; I'll let Estates know about it tomorrow...

The room was windowless and the lighting artificial, as was the stale air which circulated through. In case of the remote chance of a fire in the rarely-visited room, the air conditioners would automatically switch off when the smoke detectors sensed any hint of smoke and, because the room had no water sprinkler system, there were large fixed green installation cylinders on the wall at each corner of the room. These hefty green extinguishers would rush Halon gas into the sealed room and thus smother any flames within a few minutes. The detectors also set off a siren in the corridor, and caused an alert to flash at the front office. These safeguards would ensure the equipment remained free from water in the case of an electrical fire, where contact with water could cause things to become worse. However, Francesca believed the gas had more to do with saving the equipment and money than anything else! This fire safety equipment was never popular with the team and most other organisations, excepting the military, refused to use it.

The system had never been fully tested, for one thing. One of the installations was straight across from the door entrance and near the "duct", almost blocking its metal access point. The duct was a small door leading into the internals of the building, where no doubt "management" in their esteemed wisdom had at one time stuck additional comms cabinets and switches, power and electronic gear. It could be a real nightmare trying to work in the dimmed light; these conditions were typical and always a bone of contention with anyone who found herself needing to work in those atrocious conditions.

Francesca passed rows of equipment with little flashing green, orange and red lights, displaying a myriad of activity that reminded her of a heavenly constellation representing the Old City. Rome was old and ancient in body, but behind its walls and tunnels, a complex network of communications technology hidden from view among the warren of ducts and small rooms scattered around the city buildings kept the Papal machine moving in the modern age.

The administrator approached the three disciples, which sat at the back of the large room twenty metres away from her at the far wall, feverishly working away. She approached them with confidence.

'Well, I hope you've all said your prayers, because one of you guys is about to get the boot!' she joked. 'Just whine away, eh? That's the spirit—no backchat!' Her loud voice gave her a sense of comfort in the room filled with electronics.

The disciples were responsible for the total organisation of files and documents for all people employed by the Vatican, as well as required access to printing and pathways to other systems, like Finance, and the databases that were Jonathan's areas of expertise.

Mark, John and Luke seemed outwardly quiet, but Francesca knew that Luke had been complaining and she would have to power cycle him, which required her to follow a complex set of steps to ensure that she switched the server off and on in a safe manner.

Francesca sat down at the console desk and logged in. She had checked the alert remotely before coming up. Focusing her mind on the task at hand, she made a last check before typing the command "Down server". This command began an unstoppable sequence of events that would result in a full system halt. She breathed easily as Luke revealed there had been no errors.

Casting her eye downwards to the rubbish bin near her legs, she realised that there was something really smelly next to her.

Massimo has been here earlier with a pizza, she thought, examining the bin while she waited on Luke to finish up. *And what's that yuck? More old food, remnants of his dinner, phew! He is a mucky pup. I wish he would not eat here... what's that, a can of Coke? Following procedures as usual, I see! A spillage in here and we will all be collecting our marching orders. I'll have to have a quiet word with him tomorrow,* she decided, feeling quite exasperated.

The fourth disciple, Mathew, was located down in lower ground basement area 2 (LGB2), below the Administration building, also known affectionately as the Dungeon!

Located in a separate physical area in case of disaster, Mathew was a backup node and server that could take over all Vatican services as a complete working system.

Francesca could logon to Mathew easily from here as if she was sitting in front of it. She hated going down to LGB2—it was a horrible place deep in the bowels of the old building, a cold and dark room with very poor lighting. But she could see the sense of having the redundancy at a distance and protected by thick walls.

She shivered a little. It seemed lonely up here, but this was nothing compared to the Dungeon. *Not tonight, though*, she reminded herself, directing her thoughts to Luke.

Luke was at this moment powering up. Francesca's trained eyes stared closely at the screen, looking for any errors as the data passed quickly down the monitor before her.

Modules were being loaded automatically, as planned. The nodes were beginning to speak again to one another and they exchanged data packets and protocols among themselves. Francesca understood the language, and so would be able to interpret any unusual events.

Let's make sure that they all have joined the cluster, she mused. *Yep, looking good boys! Now let's just see if that the logical space is ok.* A few taps at the keyboard gave Francesca a final check and she grinned, satisfied with the power up.

Things just don't ring true with Michaelangelo.... Francesca's mind drifted as she began to think about his quick exit again.

All the logons were disabled except mine! Whoever did it must have known I would be the first to find out who had done this. It can't be the malicious act of some disgruntled ex-employee... it's just not in Michaelangelo's nature. What about the ghost Apostol?

Si, he must have known I would find out. It must be some kind of a clue, but a clue to what? Where to look, what to look for? That is the secret. Once I figure it out, I will be a bit closer to finding out what is happening with Michaelangelo. Her mind jumped tracks as she pondered the situation. *Those guys from VIA have not shown up yet. Some help they are – the kind you don't want, of course! A hindrance rather than a help snooping around, arrogant with power.... It smells like some security breach, though. I thought my system was the securest. Let's start again this time on the Unix box.*

A thought at the back of her mind reminded her that this was not her system and therefore not her responsibility, but her curiosity pulled her into Paulina's system, Noah.

As she worked, the room became cold — icy cold. The heat of her breath vaporised in front of the screen and she shivered. Ignoring this discomfort, she worked her fingers furiously until they stiffened with cold. The temperature had been dropping rapidly all along, although she wasn't aware. Francesca concentrated purposefully. She stopped periodically to blow into her hands for warmth.

Let me search for the word 'Apostol'...but first I will install my own version of the sugrep OS utility...nothing too obvious, it is sure to be hidden.

Francesca spent the next twenty minutes scanning the directories for a clue, any clue to why everyone's login had been shut down, but still found nothing.

What if I just look for the word 'kit' in the Noah system... I better not tell Paulina.

waiting...waiting...Results

1 file
/usr/include/rpc/bible/KIT_OUT_POSTAI.TAR

Eureka! Francesca clapped her hands. *Found a Root kit, si! It's a hidden directory, alright...there seems to be a few a-type files 'ptyq' for kidding the netstat file.... We've been Trojaned, as well!*

A Trojan is a computer program that mimics real applications but does completely unpredictable things to systems when administrators are unaware that their security has been breached. Normal commands do not work as they should.

*I was lucky to find this out. Let's find out a bit more by sugrep on pty**

waiting...waiting...Results

4 files
/usr/include/rpc/bible/ptyk
/usr/include/rpc/bible/ptyp
/usr/include/rpc/bible/ptyq
/usr/include/rpc/bible/ptys

Jesus, its bloody freezing in here! she thought fiercely. *The air conditioner has never been so efficient before! Final check, then let's get out of here. I'll use command 'suvi' to the file ptyq....* And then her eyes opened wide.

    0 0
    1 212.100.5.100
    1 200.221
    1 200.232
    1 196.196
    2 epostol.ecb.int
    2 thyarc(I).com

It's not 'Apostol' but 'epostol'... probably to confuse any obvious searches. This is unbelievable!

While Francesca studied her revelations, the temperature in the room dropped to about 4 degrees Celsius! What was going on? Her fingers were practically freezing.

I think the thermostat's going crazy in here, her mind yelled, sensing another drop coming. As she stared at the console, Francesca became aware of a soft sound behind her. *What was it — it sounded like breathing...*

The boring drone of the switches seemed to dull and disappear.   Straining her senses, Francesca's ears moved a little in reflex and decided to ignore the sound as a figment of her imagination.

Suddenly an icy draft blew straight on her shoulders this time, sounding more like breathing but heavier this time. Francesca's mind finally caught up with her senses. *It is breathing*! her panicking mind screamed silently in dread, staying with it, focusing her attention at the screen ahead, pretending to herself that everything was ok, not wanting to turn around.

Steady girl, steady. Luke is fully functional. All green...complete! Get out of here, let's go...! Oh, fuck....

Francesca turned slowly and apprehensively... the breathing noise stopped. *Really, no breathing?* She felt a bit silly for her terror.

Christ, thank God it's nothing...but then, how stupid was that? What kind of air conditioning does this?

Francesca fearfully scanned the immediate area... everything looked normal — the only unusual thing was the temperature drop. There were too many metal cabinets in her line of sight to see clearly, of course. Still, she remained apprehensive about being here all alone.

'Is there anybody in here?' she shouted, but heard no reply. *I must be going mad,* she decided. *I'm out of here!!! – I've had enough of these bloody conditions, anyway!* Her logical excuse…

Francesca tried to keep calm although her mind was careening near the edge. The constant humming and drone of the switches and electrical fans seemed louder in the air as she made up her mind.

Halfway towards the door thinking… – *ten metres, now five,* si, *closer – good!*

The heavy breathing seemed to be following her once more, and not from far away.

Oh my God, don't look back! Keep going, keep going….

'Oh no!' she groaned audibly as she remembered her ID card! She fumbled, trying to pull it from her pocket, *faster* urging to go quicker!

WHOOSSSHHH! Cold air blew down on her!

Francesca jumped, her breathing becoming shallow and rapid. Strangely the hot breath from her mouth condensed visibly in front of her anxious face distraught in the icy cold breeze. The blowers switched full on on again and a mad rush of cold air flooded the room from above.

WHOOSSSHHH! It felt colder than the Arctic, biting into her face!

Francesca's hair flew about wildly around her face with the fierce air current pounding into the room, the girl shrieked — only one thing in her mind now.

Get out! Get out! Get out! It sounded like someone else was panting loudly right behind her, *get out now!* Was she going crazy? Reaching reached the door, her ID card grasped tightly in her hand. One accurate swish downwards, and....

"BUZZZ!" the alarm sound of the door signalled that the lock was now open.

Francesca pulled hard using both hands until the door flew open. *I'm OUT!*

BANG! The door shut tight behind her, and she rested her back against it. She'd done it—she was out!

Francesca pressed her ear to the door so tightly that it hurt—for a split second, she imagined that she could still hear breathing from behind the air tight door. That was impossible; the door was built for fire safety, and was soundproof—airtight! Then the breathing stopped suddenly, as if on the other side and at exactly the same time, the breather had realized the same thing.... Panic in her eyes, Francesca raced down the corridor towards the lifts.

****

Completely spooked, Francesca emerged from the lifts and quickly passed the commissioner's desk, which was still unmanned. The Swiss guards were reassuringly silent outside the front doors, although they must be bored to tears. One yawned widely as he looked over the grounds and the small car park.

St Peter's Cathedral was most visible that evening, soaring high into the sky not far off before them. The guards looked into the surrounding tall trees at the Church of Santo Stefano to their right.

The sound of tumultuous water from the crystal fountain brought a sense of normality back into Francesca's mind, helping to block out her horrible experience. The administrator entered the I.T. division, passing again the unmanned helpdesk. She wondered who was supposed to be on tonight. She sat down at her console and composed herself; Francesca was not easily scared—it must have been a very long day for her nerves to get so rattled, she decided.

She checked on the servers one final time, and things looked normal again: all disciples displayed all green lights with synchronisation checks of good health and good stats.

Brilliant, I'll check the logons just to make sure. She spent longer than normal viewing the log files, reading each line to line in sequence pedantically from top to bottom.

So what we have is someone gaining access to the system – how, at this stage, I do not know – and then creating a back door and Trojaning the server, but who? Is Michaelangelo Apostol? No, it's too obvious.... Francesca found herself caught in a fierce yawn. *Time to go home girl,* she reminded herself. *Tomorrow is another day. I will talk to Paulina in the morning.*

She logged out and picked up her expensive, brown-leather jacket with matching handbag and left at eight thirty, her shift over. As Francesca left the office, she was unaware that an e-mail from Michaelangelo had arrived in her inbox.

The weather seemed to be changing – the wind seemed nippier than usual, remaindering her that it was the end of autumn and much colder times lay ahead. Twisting her face into the cold wind, Francesca headed for home.

****

The sun rose early over Vatican City. Francesca looked towards the rear of the Administration Building and, above it, part of the magnificent St Peter's Basilica could be seen beyond the building. The sun peaked over the dome, silhouetting its crucifix against the blue morning sky on its rise. It was a lovely and warm morning for the time of the year and just about 7:20 a.m. on Friday — the last day of the week!

The Vatican gardens were rich and beautiful in the sunlight, every shade full of colour, almost like summer again.... Her senses were alive and Francesca seemed comfortable, almost happy.

The Vatican gardens dated back to medieval times, when orchards and vineyards grew to the North of the Apostolic Palace. However, the gardens had developed in many other areas beyond and around the Palazzo del Governmantorato since then.

A mass of vegetation surrounded Francesca as she walked inside the maze-like gardens, passing flowers of all colours, shapes and sizes. Red stripes, wild snapdragon and little blue flowers rose to the humble, bowing yellow buttercups. Tall *Cupressus sempervirens*, "Glauca", or Italian cypress trees, had grown up here over centuries, brought by the conquering Romans from Eastern

Mediterranean countries like Syria, Bulgaria and Turkey over two thousand years ago. These forty-foot specimens were branched with dense blue-green leaves, tapering at the top. Arizona Cypress, also known as *Cupressus glabra*, grew to about thirty feet in height and stood showing their fine textured, thread-like silver-blue leaves. It was always a pleasure for Francesca to sit in this area of the garden, while the sunlight made such beautiful shadows.

Forgetting about her work problems and friend for a moment, Francesca took a deep breath of fresh morning air. *It is great to be alive, even if it is the last day of October in Rome.* Francesca contemplated the lovely time of the year. She wore a nice red satin blouse with black jeans and smart brown flat shoes. Carrying her leather jacket in her hand and her bag over her shoulder, she walked slowly along the twisting paths; the gardens had small walls on either side of her, bordering the many varieties of flowers and high shrubs which grew well-above above her shoulder height, making it difficult for her to view anything above eye level.

An unexpectedly strong, cool breeze lifted her beautiful, golden-brown hair around her face. Francesca's natural curls lofted and swirled about. Feeling full of life, her spirit rose.

The path before her led to the Administration Building Offices. Getting lost in the garden was easy — she reminisced about the number of times she'd been lost inside this maze of mature landscaped gardens when she first took the job a while back, but she had quickly realized that St Peter's was always a good compass.

Sensing footsteps behind her, Francesca turned around to greet whichever colleague approached. Surprisingly, there was no one there behind her! No sound other than the chatter of birds and the noises of insects assailed her. The narrow path was empty. Francesca could not see beyond the bend behind her or the curve before her.

Very strange, she thought. *What a fool I'm being. I do not really want to be up in that server room again for a long while, but that's the job or I'll end up in a straight jacket.* She gratefully latched on to a momentary distraction. *I am definitely going to have a word with Mr Messy, Massimo, for leaving that junk food sitting around.*

Turning to leave, she began to walk again. Her brown leather handbag was now swinging a little faster on her shoulder. *This is ridiculous of me, getting spooked two days in a row. I must need a holiday or something.*

Some of the paths criss-crossed or joined in a "Y" shape, but most generally channelled in the direction of the offices. She looked up as a plane flew high overhead in the distant blue sky. Then she heard another sound, this time much closer but difficult to make out.

Whisper, whisper...her left ear twitched a little. Struggling to separate the new noise from the background noise, she heard it again... whisper... whisper....

Her immediate instinct was to instantly bolt. As fast as her legs could carry her, Francesca sprinted towards the Basilica. Before she knew it, she was running around one curve and then the next, passing an occasional empty bench. Her own breathing struggled out of control as she ran and her legs began to slow, drained as they were of energy. The footsteps were right behind her now — she looked back over her shoulder as she sped forward, and then...

WHACK!

She hit something!

'Oh! Bloody leave me alone!' she screamed in complete panic, her eyes tightly shut. Someone grabbed her as she tumbled in mid-air, both bodies falling hard to the ground. A scrap and twist of arms and legs ensued as Francesca struggled to free herself from her attacker.

Using a combination of natural instincts and incredible strength, she managed to tumble over and onto the other person. She was on top!

The man's arms held her shoulders firmly, and she grabbed the inside of his wrists although her eyes were still closed tight. His voice began to penetrate her stark terror.

'Francesca! Francesca!' a man's voice repeating her name over and over again, his song-like voice was warm and comforting as it broke through her fear, melting her iced mind. She slowly opened her eyes, *Ciriaco*?

'What is going on? What has frightened you, Francesca?' he asked, staring into her terror-filled eyes. 'Calm down, and here, I'll help you up.' They both rose together, but Ciriaco held her protectively for a moment, checking behind her to see if she was hurt.

His green eyes had a natural sparkle like emeralds as she looked into them. 'Let's get you tidied up, eh?' he offered her a clean white handkerchief from his breast pocket and dusted her face a little while she used her hands on her trousers.

'Ciriaco, don't think me mad, but I think that someone was following me,' she explained in a petite, frightened voice, looking back in fear. 'I'm sorry that I smashed into you. Are, are you ok?'

'*Si* Francesca, it's not a problem—no bones broken. Are *you* hurt?' he asked in a stronger voice.

'No, I am fine, really. Only my pride is hurt, I think. I am glad to see you.'

'Look, let's walk together and you can tell me what is going on.' He lifted her chin with his hand gently and smiled warmly into her eyes.

They were at the office five minutes later. After cleaning and tidying herself up in the powder room, Francesca entered the I.T. office. The office was bright but cool in the early morning air as the sun shone through the tall, elongated office windows. She stopped and looked down at Ciriaco, whose headset rested lightly over his spiky, short black hair. Gazing up at her, he finished a quick helpdesk call.

'*Grazie* Ciriaco,' she murmured. 'Thanks again for helping me. I really got a scare.' She smiled into his eyes. 'It may have been my imagination, although the sound of footsteps behind me at the time seemed real enough. Lucky you came down the other footpath... Oops, sorry again—it was not so lucky for you,' she giggled a little, holding her hand to her mouth and trying to hide her face as it became a deeper shade of pink.

'Here is your handkerchief back, *grazie*. Where did you come from?' Ciriaco smiled, folding his handkerchief back into the top pocket of his black pinstripe jacket, which was now lightly soiled on the arms and elbows. Usually he arrived quite smartly dressed for business, but by the end of the day he would be down to his waistcoat. Helpdesk work was more difficult than other professionals gave credit for.

Ciriaco stood up, bent over the side of his desk and touched Francesca's wrist tenderly. Looking deep into her sensual brown eyes, he said:

'I would not have had it any other way, Francesca. Indeed, it was my, uh, pleasure.' He squeezed her hand gently. 'Maybe we could catch a cappuccino later, after work?' his voice was like that of a little boy who had stolen a sweet and was caught by the shopkeeper: *What do you say, come on! For me, eh?*

'So, who was manning the helpdesk Wednesday evening, then?' Francesca said suddenly, avoiding his question and remembering her confusion.

Ciriaco's face changed slightly — he looked taken aback, disappointed. It was his turn to blush and he answered in a low tone. His green eyes stared at her somewhat boyishly.

'It was me, but I left a little early. Do not tell anyone, please Francesca.'

'Si,' she answered quickly, her heart racing at the thought of a new romance.

'*Grazie* for not telling anyone, Francesca,' he said, looking a little embarrassed.

'No, *si*,' she brushed off his gratitude. 'How about, 7:15 tonight, at Café Dabbruzzi's, it's just outside the city. You know the place.... We can talk about forgiving your absence last night then.' Francesca laughed.

'*Si, si*, I will be there,' Ciriaco said with a look of amazement; he almost fell back onto his chair. He watched her as Francesca walked confidently away from him with a light if not flighty bounce in her step.

There were a few helpdesk calls already in his call queue. '*Si,* IOR Helpdesk,' he said in a friendly tone as he fielded another call for the Vatican Bank. 'Ciriaco speaking, how can I help you?'

Smiling happily as she sat down at her console, Francesca began tapping in to the database.   She felt energetic and full of life. *Good to go, girl! Good to go!* She cheered herself on. Looking over to her right, she saw that

Jonathan had already arrived. Her smile disappeared as she focused intimately on her immediate technical responsibilities.

Still, she couldn't help but look over at the contractor from time to time. Jonathan's desk was unusually untidy — in fact, it was an absolute mess. Hardcopy lay all over the area, and a few sheets were scattered on the floor near his desk. He looked intensely busy as he read through reams of computer program printouts, scrutinising each character, head down and roving left to right quickly. Francesca wondered what had gone wrong.

****

Paulina's major responsibility was to maintain Noah and the Vatican's fire-wall. Noah was a critical and a sensitive server used for performing security checks on people. The Vatican spent serious money on security, believing that confidentiality and privacy was paramount to a successful organisation. Therefore, only Internal Audit (VIA) personnel and a few more senior personnel had access to Noah. Access was permitted only through the operation of a computer application called Prayer-Seeker, or "*PS*" for short.

The system unified various searching applications, engines and spiders, using inherent heuristic techniques in one user interface. By utilising artificial intelligence techniques with AI language Prolog 2010 processing algorithms and lightning speed multiprocessor threading, Paulina could find out just about anything about any person or organisation. Noah could probably tell you what colour of underwear a person is wearing, if you asked it to.

Probes and targeting Applets were sent out to interrogate foreign systems and discovered many things, most of which was rubbish, and then sorted the debris into a comprehensive collection, much like how trash that's been taken to the dump will be sorted through by people interested in garnering information from un-shredded documents. It was all perfectly legal due to new data protection legislation passed this year in the EEC.

The program could second-guess decisions made by individuals and company directors with an uncanny degree of accuracy; it would be a very powerful application if it fell into the wrong hands. Francesca looked around for Paulina, feeling her head being nipped at the mere thought of all the possible and dire consequences of any security breach to her system.

I will speak with Paulina as soon as she arrives, Francesca decided. *I'll do my morning checks first, but there is certainly a big security breach on "Noah". A hole in this ship and the arc will sink....*

If the server is really compromised, then the shit will hit the fan at all levels – personally, morally and politically! she groaned a little as she thought about it. *It will be difficult to keep it out of the papers... The wrath of God will smite this department with an iron fist, for sure. The Vatican Gendarmerie will need to be informed....*

Like clockwork, Francesca continued with her morning checks. To an outsider, she would seem perfectly nonplussed by the situation. And perhaps she was. *Ok, all lights on the "green"...a few switches on the "yellow", but nothing to worry about – just known problems scheduled to be sorted.* These types of jobs would normally be attended to by Francesca, Massimo and Michaelangelo.

All the disciples seem fine. Francesca had many systems to check and many checks within each system and subsystem in order to make sure that everyone received the IT services required for them to complete their work. Most people had come to rely on her support, but would not understand or even give a second thought to just how difficult a balance it was for her to keep things running smoothly. Francesca was a smooth operator, fortunately, and highly skilled—a far cry from the roboticism of many Technical Administrators. She had a natural flair when it came to the intricacies of Operating Systems.

Analysing her secondary console, she began pulling up the current network topology. This was a map that showed the locations and statuses of all the servers, computers, printers, switches, users and any other piece of equipment or hardware connected to the Vatican networks. The overall picture provided a three-dimensional plan of the old Vatican City, with various areas of interest highlighted appropriately.

Most buildings were on the green, but a few were in different stages of alert. These alerts were normal, of course, and did not necessarily represent a big problem. Possibly, the fuss was only about a printer going offline, or maybe a network card was switched off. If the operator drilled down into any part of the map, it would oftentimes open up a three dimensional window that connected to a CCTV so she could view the status remotely.

A thought came to her mind. *I must try to give Michaelangelo another call. Perhaps he is accepting calls now....* Francesca looked around the room and pressed his number. The phone rang three times before going to voice-mail, but at least it didn't send her to voice-mail automatically.

'Hello it's just me,' she said, after the tone. 'Are you all right, Michaelangelo? I am very worried about you. Please let me know where you are and what is going on. Please.' she set down the phone, resigning herself to the bland message.

I must try later, she thought, a bit upset and very disappointed. *There must be something seriously wrong...I cannot understand why he said*

nothing to me! We were close, I thought....
Annoyed, she looked over at the DBA.

Jonathan's still having a system failure, she noticed. *About time.* She giggled a little at his torment. *Now I am the bitchy one, although it's nothing that big head does not deserve.* She was still immensely enjoying his discomfort when Paulina entered and sat down at her desk. Gabriella arrived at the same time.

'*Buongiorno* Paulina, Gabriella,' she chimed. The girls reciprocated her greeting and sat down to logon. Giving them a chance to grab a cup of coffee and settle in, Francesca waited.

'Are you ok, Fran?' asked Paulina, made nervous by Francesca's impatient gaze. 'What is the matter?'

Francesca got up from her desk and walked over to Paulina, bending over and whispering in her ear. She quietly spoke for about five minutes regarding what she had discovered the previous evening. Paulina's eyes opened wide as she learned of the security breach on Noah. Paulina was not too happy that Francesca had been snooping around on her system—Francesca'd had no right to examine Noah without Paulina's permission, and her actions were strictly against company policy.

'This puts me in a very compromising position,' Paulina replied, speaking quickly and quietly. 'Look Francesca, are you trying to get us *all* sacked — you for accessing a system with no prior authority and me for not informing VIA?' Paulina was more than a little annoyed; she was nearing panic, unsure how to deal with the embarrassing situation.

Francesca was taken aback for a moment as she stood up. She had not thought her friend would mind so much. Francesca composed herself and apologised.

'I am sorry Paulina. I was only thinking of Michaelangelo and finding out the truth — I am very worried about him! Things are just not right, the way he left...the whole thing smells, and I must get to the bottom of it. Please help me?' she had raised her voice a little, since Jonathan was too busy to even turn his head.

'*Si*, then let me have a closer look at this. But I will have to report the breach, maybe I can say that I discovered it, which will make it not so bad for both of us,' replied Paulina in a softer voice. Paulina held Francesca in a warm friendly embrace for a moment, knowing that Francesca was frightened for their friend. Paulina then went into overdrive, looking at what Francesca had discovered.

```
0 0
1 212.100.5.60
1 200.221
1 200.232
2 196.196
2 epostol.ecb.int
2 thyarc(I).com
```

Francesca girl, you are right again, Paulina thought. Si, *nothing in the log file "syslogd", which is used to record file history security and system maintenance events as expected — only the number two entry shows that a log file was removed.* Si, *the ROOT_KIT_LOG_FILE to dev/ptys...very clever indeed, but who?*

****

Later that morning, Francesca looked over to Paulina with interest. 'Any luck?'

'*Si*, it looks like the shit is really is going to hit the fan here,' Paulina groaned. 'I'll explain once I know more. Di San Angelo will need to be informed." She sighed and then rubbed her eyes. 'Say, what's up with Jonathan?

Observing the DBA as he spoke intensely to fat Alfredo, another of the Application Developers, Francesca shrugged and returned to her checks.

Paulina studied the file "ptyq", knowing that this was the hiding file for the "netstat" command. *It will remove tcp/udp/sockets from and to specified addresses, uids and ports. So the meaning of the digits at the beginning of these lines are:*

Type 0: meant, hide the user identification (the user ID).

Type 1: meant hide the machine local network IP address.

Type 2: meant hide the remote network IP address.

Type 3: meant hide the local network IP port.

Type 4: meant hide the remote IP port.

Type 5: meant hide the Unix operating system IP socket path.

IP addresses are somewhat like street addresses. They are basically a unique way of identifying anything on a computer network, be it a computer, server, switch or person in the

Vatican community or any foreign computer system or network; all these restrictions were being used by the Trojan, which had now compromised vast areas of the Vatican's Noah System. Paulina worked intensely; her brow furrowed with worry.

****

Francesca remembered that she had not checked her personal e-mail, so she launched into her account using a smooth sweep of her mouse and a swift double click. The egg timer began to flip on her screen as the computer took its time. Unexpectedly, a small alert from "Mathew" appeared on Francesca's console. The message was orange in colour and was accompanied by a wailing siren sound, indicating a degraded state.

"Mathew" was failing over to "Mark"'s system and moving critical services, like e-mail, seamlessly over. This backup ensured that the Vatican's many clients would remain in peaceful ignorance of the potential computer crisis occurring at IOR.

If "Mark" failed, then the services would move onto "Luke", and then to "John". However the chances of all the servers failing like that were negligible. Immediately opening up the computer plan on her screen and viewing the problem area, Francesca drilled downwards until she would see a computer simulation display of "Mathew".

She saw that one of the managed switches as also malfunctioning down in that area. CCTV had not been installed down in the LG areas because it was too dark to see anything and the benefits would only be marginal, or so the accountants had advised. Mathew was down on lower ground basement area 2 (LGB2) — the Dungeons! Clearly, the accountants had never had to visit LGB2 before...

'It looks like we'll have to check this out, huh Fran?' Massimo spoke to Francesca, his calm voice seeming indifferent or complacent. She reminded herself that he had seen this sort of failure occur many times before and knew exactly how to sort out the problem.

Massimo is on the ball, thought Francesca appreciatively. He was already scanning the communications side of things inside LGB2 area. She decided to let him deal with the problem so that she could attend to her e-mail, happy to pass the responsibility over to him on this occasion. Francesca cast a glancing eye from top to bottom of her inbox. *What... one from Michaelangelo's pseudonym, his nick name - Pope!* It had been sent last evening, just about when she was leaving for the night. *My God, I hope he is all right!* She quickly opened up the message and scanned its cryptic contents.

Fran,

You are in serious danger! The phone is not safe. I cannot explain in this message so be very careful from now on. Leave this place if you can and do not come back! Watch your back and take great care.

I will be in touch soon...

POPE xx

P.S. **Do not let anyone...** – *VIA or the Police know that I have contacted you!*

CHAPTER IV

ROOT OF THE GODS!

⌐•⌐> ⌐⌐>⊓⊔ ⅂•⌐∨

Cardinal Giovanni Dalla Gassa logged onto the super computer system. *The super slow computer system, that is,* he thought to himself. *As usual, the system is pitiful again today. Those technical people need to get their act together and speed things up – the system's about as slow as one of the Pope's prayers!* He snickered good-heartedly. *Pardon me, Lord. I was only thinking in jest.*

In the last week he had made many preparations and set up numerous dangerous missions, some of which he'd been plotting on for years, going to numerous parts of the globe in his attempt to find the three ancient relics of power called the "Root of the Gods".

The "Order" had come of age. They had heard a rumour of the whereabouts of two other Reliquiae in relatively recent times. Their knowledge was kept secret and safe for years by the chosen few. Whispers passed from word of mouth, and although none of the relics were yet in his possession, the cardinal already knew when and where to find the first one. He would have to wait, however.

Over three hundred years had passed since a Reliquiae had been discovered, and several different faiths were responsible for spilling much blood for knowledge of its whereabouts. This knowledge descended from one Order to the next in near-complete secrecy. Despite his high office, Dalla Gassa was not above risk of exposure. Acquiring such sanctified knowledge and power did not come without a heavy toll.

Distant rumours told about all three Reliquiae, that once were spoken in legends long ago and told in tales, which were in part chiselled in tablets of stone that had been eroded by decades of wind and rain, and were later written in ancient languages on paper scriptures and scrolls, on vellum, and in the minds of the secret-keepers. The story had been in existence for millennia!

And so the rumours of the relics endured death and deceit, for the most powerful of the three had been mentioned again and again, suspected to be travelling with a holy bearer who brought a great gift to a promised land in the mid-sixteenth century and almost rediscovered in the seventeenth...

The mystery and elusiveness remained. It had only been in recent years and with the aid of many billions of dollars that vast sums were channelled from countless sources in the cardinal's quest for this great knowledge that would give him absolute power. New technology made it easy for Dalla Gassa to obtain the required sums essential to fund his holy quest. With great manipulation and care, collecting funds from sources all over the world was child's play if one knew how to tap in. The cardinal was one of those few who did.

It was said that possession of the links to God would be enough to tip the cosmic and spiritual balance in favour of the holder. Truth was difficult to distinguish. What was fact and what was fiction? Most likely it was another twist of fate. Stories scribed in lost languages and etched pictures had ether worn away or lay decayed and had then been forgotten somewhere long ago, *until now*. The expedition had made the discovery and had found his dream.

It was said ominously by shaman that the relics were hidden in a distant land in *"Nowhere to be found."* The men who might have remembered what this message really meant were since long dead. Whether silenced or killed by curse or disease, the legend and the rumours had become blurred and almost forgotten. What would become of him? The cardinal cared nothing for the sacrifices he would be asked to make, because the knowledge and power of these celestial objects would bring him more than enough glory to compensate.

The man painfully opened the e-mail sent from Amazonia, already a few weeks old, and read the correspondence. Studying the latest detailed scanned images and roving his fascinated eyes over several ancient manuscripts became engrossed in every part and detail of their complex codices. Furrows deepened in his forehead, corrugating with intensity as his passion washed over his excited mind.

The interpreted codices...

>П□< ⱱΓᏞᏞ ᏞᕮƎ□ ᏟΓΓⱱ> ᒍ□ᒍ ⱱƎΓ
>□
ᒍᏞᏞ ⱱΓᏞᏞ ⱱПᒍⱮ□ Γ□ >□ΓΓᕮΓ
ᏞᕮᏞᒍ Γⱱ >П□ Ꮮᒍ□ᒍ
□ᕮⱱП□Γ□ >ᕮ ПΓᒍ□

**They will come first and smite
All will shake in terror
Cold is the land
Nowhere to hide**

Is this really the legend? What do the messages mean? What does it mean? His eyes then widened suspiciously, observing the date that the e-mail had been sent. The date did not correspond with the date and time the images were taken! The images were much older.... Giovanni Dalla Gassa suspected foul play; he knew that someone was holding back. Now all contact with the relics had been lost!

If the sacred Reliquiae were hidden in *Nowhere...*, then when and where would they appear? It was obvious to the cardinal that the information was only a puzzle... Like a marathon runner paced his mind narrowing his mind on to the finish line. A set purpose marked brow, pulling his thin lips hard together. With renewed determination and focus, Giovanni would find an answer in these runes and follow his dreams!

Now, in these days of ours, a great mystery was beginning to unfold....

CHAPTER V

THE VATICAN DUNGEONS

>⊓□ ∧⅃>⌐⅃⅃◧ ⊐<•⊡⊓⊓◧•⊡

Francesca reeled back in shock when she read the message. The expression on her face said it all as her visage transformed from that of a lively young thing to that of a pale ghost. She stared blankly at the message from "Pope".

It's from Michaelangelo — he really is in big trouble! What's he talking about? How am I in any danger? He's finally cracked. What does he mean that I should not let anybody know? My God, when will he contact me? Oh shit.

Francesca began to panic, and her heart raced to beat hard in her chest. She quickly sent the e-mail to print, and then sent a copy to her own personal e-mail address before deleting the original message from the system, just to be safe from the auditors' prying eyes.

The last thing she wanted was for anyone to read the message, and especially not VIA. Without looking at the hardcopy, Francesca quickly folded it up and put in safely in her handbag. It was morning, about ten o'clock by now, and the office was in full swing. Busy, busy, busy. Francesca's phone was ringing when she sat down once more...

'Hey, Francesca, is the server going down again?' Francesca felt the shock and horror flooding over her features but could no longer hide her emotions. Massimo sunk below his desk until she could only see his stupid-looking face. The young man had always been a bit of a comedian. 'I was just looking at your shocked face, honey. Ha! I wish I had a camera!' He'd noticed that she had been acting peculiarly for several days, and wanted to cheer her up a little.

Picking her head up, although still reeling in dumbfounded surprise at Michaelangelo's message, Francesca tried to manufacture an appropriate response. 'The only thing that's going down now is *you,* clown features!' she joked, half smiling at him.

'Touchy, Fran, touchy! Come on, pal, give us a laugh — you're looking so *serious* today.' Massimo urged her to lighten up. Francesca knew she seemed distant, but wasn't sure how to behave normally anymore — she wasn't sure what normal felt like, anymore. 'I'll make a deal with you, gorgeous,' Massimo proposed. 'Let's both go down to LGB2 later. That data switch badly needs to be replaced and I'll need a hand.' Unfortunately, he was right.

'*Si*, handsome, we will go down later, after lunch?' Francesca tried to sound bright and bouncy again, although nothing could be further from the truth. The last place she wanted to visit was the recesses of the Dungeon!

'We will go down hand in hand then, baby.' He laughed with no more enthusiasm than his co-worker at this gloomy thought. It was always good to have company in the Dungeon — the room was cramped, with narrow walls and a low ceiling, all roughly cut out of the stone. It felt like being buried alive.

****

Francesca had keen eyesight, and something caught her attention as she looked past Paulina's shoulder, through the glass entry door and towards the commissioner's desk that was just visible beyond the white rush of water crashing down into the crystal fountain. Two people had just arrived, and were standing at the desk in dark corporate suits, speaking directly to Mario, who turned to stare at the glass security doors into the office. Both people were wearing dark sunglasses that obscured much of their faces. Francesca ducked behind Paulina a little as the people were led to the entrance of the office. The commissionaire swished his ID card through the soundproof doors and, for a short moment, the crashing noises of the fountain flooded in from the polished foyer as the man and woman entered.

The man was slim, about five-feet eight inches tall, and was accompanied by a much taller woman. Both appeared to be very healthy, with fit bodies and sun-kissed skins. The man's dark brown hair was perfectly parted to the side and he wore a white shirt with a multi-coloured tie and soft, expensive, black leather shoes. The slender, blonde haired young woman scanned the office. Her hair was styled up with mousse, which made her appear taller than the man. Her smooth, shapely legs and sculptured face made her seem too perfect to be real. Wearing a white and tight-fitting blouse beneath an open pinstripe jacket, there was a disturbing sexuality about her personality as she strode through the male-dominated office.

The commissionaire led them further into the office. Both people had scarlet purple badges shaped like crosses with gold lettering clipped onto their hips. The cross-shaped badges swung like swords as they walked between the desks. *Is that VIP?* Francesca wondered. They each carried a small leather briefcase with a minute papal seal crest glistening between the combination locks.

By now the office was in a riot, at the peak of morning, phones ringing irately and people speaking in various languages and all exasperated! Sunshine radiated through the tall windows, because most of the blinds were fully open. It was bright outside and blue — a heat haze could be seen forming in the distance beyond the gardens, and tourist masses already were beginning to mill around the building aimlessly. Francesca couldn't be bothered and thought that this moment would be the perfect opportunity for her to slip out unnoticed.

The business-like pair headed towards Jonathan's desk. The distraught DBA looked up when the visitors arrived at his desk.

Paulina spoke quietly to Francesca. 'Look at prime bitch walking in..., by the way, *who are those guys?*' the women watched the two corporate suits strolling towards the DBA. 'Anyway, I'll have a new "Confessional" box set up by the end of the day with an updated operating system and the latest security patches,' Paulina said, looking back at her monitor. 'Di San Angelo will need to know about this security breach. He'll be in a right flap over this one and he'll make sure that someone else is to blame. Expect the e-mails that cover his ass to begin—'

'Have a look at this,' Francesca interrupted. She pointed to the next three entries of code in the computer log, which looked like data someone had wanted to keep hidden. 'I'm going to run a few traces on them to see what they bring up. Look here, the Apostol entry again!' she highlighted the login with her mouse. 'This is really odd...it looks like they have gained entry on this box and then attempted to jump from here onto

"Luke."' Francesca was now beginning to think that it was Michaelangelo who had disabled the logins, although she didn't know why. Who else knew their system so well?

Yet something still is not right, I feel it. Why would Michaelangelo leave and not come back? There is still a fucking big piece missing...

'Did you not say that Apostol disabled the logins the other day?' asked Paulina. 'There are no more entries in the file, I checked earlier... Anyway, I must take "Noah" offline in about thirty minutes, after I advise the boss.'

'Thank you Paulina. I am as confused as you are right now — this whole mess will take more time to work out. Can you keep this issue to yourself for the moment, at least until I find out a little bit more? Please Paulina?'

'Hey Francesca, I have visitors that need to speak with you!' a voice shouted across the busy office. 'It's about *your network!*' She turned her head; it was that pratt, Jonathan. The man was trying to make everyone think that Francesca and her team's operations were badly run, when he'd been the one buried in panic all morning!

'Seems like you're passing the buck to me, Johnnie boy,' she replied with a wry half smile. She stared at the two people with VIP badges as they headed over. Her smile did not change. Francesca remained calm, although her heart almost stopped when she spotted their identification badges approaching closer. They did not read VIP, but VIA!

Oh shit, it's the cardinal's office! Francesca felt quite sick as she realised what a mess everything was about to become. Struggling with her best smile, Francesca stood up from her console as they reached her. Francesca extended her hand in friendship.

'*Ciao*. Signorina DeRose, *Si?*' the man asked rhetorically and opened his palm to hers. 'VIA. *Mi chiamo es* Agent Zito. and this is Agent Schiavone piacere di Conoscerla. We are pleased to meet with you,' his eyebrows lifted charmingly above his dark sunglasses. 'We would like to ask you some questions if that is ok, *si?*'

The man's grip was light and felt somehow peculiar, although Francesca couldn't place just what was so strange about it.

'Si.' Francesca nodded.

'I know you are busy, but can we sit down with you for a small moment please?' he asked, 'This should not take long. *Grazie.*'

The man spoke in a natural and friendly roman accent. Francesca shook his hand and nodded, gesturing for him to draw up a seat for them both.

He seems nice. Francesca smiled awkwardly, taken back a little by the man's consideration.

'*Ciao, come sta?*' Fran responded. Agent Schiavone sat down behind the man without saying a word.   She did not extend her hand. Francesca could tell that the woman was trouble from her hands, which were absurdly large for a female and had two huge knuckles each. The systems administrator took an immediate dislike to the girl. Trying not to seem unnerved or suspicious, Francesca showed an air of indifference and suavely pressed the button to turn off her computer monitor.   She sipped mineral water from her plastic cup as she turned back to greet them. 'Hi, I'm at your service. How can I help?' Fran sighed, smiling at both visitors.

The two sat patiently, their dark glasses firmly planted on their noses. *It must be a VIA thing,* Francesca decided. *Here we go*, she thought as the girl agent crossed her long shapely legs and pulled out a respectable notepad.

'We require some information,' the man began. 'You are aware that there has been a major security incident. Si? We would like to clear things up. It is important to keep all this in-house, you understand, and so your strictest confidence is essential in this important matter.' he smiled, although Francesca sensed no humour in his tone.

'*Si*, I understand.'

'I must remind you that Vatican policy requires every page to be turned; nothing must be held back or else it could result in serious breach of discipline. Your full honesty is essential. And er,' he lowered his voice, 'you must *not speak to anyone* of this matter, as doing so would open up another disciplinary matter. No disclosure to anyone — am I clear?' he looked about cautiously. No one was in earshot.

'Crystal,' she stated soberly. *Little shit head,* she thought angrily. Her first impression of the man was completely wrong. Francesca suppressed her rage at being treated like a child.

Agent Schiavone then spoke to Francesca. 'As do The Vatican Gendarmerie — Police, we have control and authority over security matters within the City. I am sure you understand the gravity of the situation. If this information was exposed, then there would be repercussions for his Holy Office worldwide in terms of confidence, to say the least. We have already spoken to your manager and he has given us a summary of what seems to have happened. We now need more specifics from you, Signorina DeRose.'

'Can you to tell us everything you know about the *Apostol* account?' Agent Zito smiled politely at Francesca, knowing that she was in no doubt of the full implications and gravity of this security breach and their absolute right to question her.

Francesca took an instant dislike to being threatened with reprisals in this manner. She well knew about privacy and confidentiality, as they were the focus of each day of her working life, and certainly didn't need to be reminded or coerced. These two meant business, however, and Francesca didn't want to make trouble for herself just because she felt miffed. The next hour past slowly, very slowly for the systems administrator as she disclosed as much information as possible while making sure not to compromise her or anyone else's delicate positions.

Everyone wanted to find out what was happening, but she needed to protect Michaelangelo first and foremost. He was not going to be made into some kind of a scapegoat! Francesca knew that she would have to watch out so that she did not become a scapegoat, either! She knew that eventually everything would be disclosed, including the breaching of Noah. Absolutely everything, that is, except the e-mail.

Francesca had long thought the Vatican had given VIA far too much power and the arrogance of the two agents proved it. She glanced over at her co-worker. Paulina was not at her desk and Francesca had not seen her leave, and so Francesca surmised that her co-worker was likely looking for a spare server to use as a replacement box for Noah and as her new "Confessional Box".

Agent Schiavone was silent for the rest of the interview, giving only a cursory nod from time to time, mainly listening and making notes on all Francesca's responses — from body language to any hesitation in speech. Francesca felt that the electrodes would be out next!

She is so rude, thought Francesca, *even though she is wearing a lovely crucifix around her neck.* The agent also wore a fine, small-faced silver analogue watch with fine Roman numerals and a small symbol that looked something like a setsquare and compass replacing the XII. *Too perfect,* thought Francesca, flushing with female jealousy. *Huh, "looks" are only skin deep, especially with her model features, sensual full lips and blonde hair...what a cow. At least the guys have somebody new to look at today.* She smirked, feeling little more vulnerable than usual. Agent Schiavone spoke at last.

'I have listened to you with interest, but I feel... there is something you are not telling us, *Si?*' The woman paused and licked her lips slowly, as though tasting Francesca's discomfort. An answer did not come, and so the agent studied the girl carefully. Francesca recognised the woman's look as the same one given her by the contractors every morning. She felt naked and disturbed at the close attention as the woman continued her questioning. 'Was this Michaelangelo something more than a colleague, to you, more than a friend? Are you in an intimate relationship with him?' the woman asked with clinical clarity.

'I don't think you should be speaking to me in that way, Signorina Schiavone.' Francesca felt herself growing red in the face with a suppressed wrath, 'I am a good friend of Michaelangelo, as I am with all my team members, and his departure has come to me as a complete surprise!' Francesca retorted sharply.

'*Agent* Schiavone,' the woman corrected the girl. 'Come on, Signorina DeRose, do you expect me to believe that? What do you know about his substantial financial debts?' Schiavone looked down her nose at Francesca, her dark glasses slipping down the bridge of her nose a little. The agent edged closer to the girl...

'He is a good friend, *si*, as I said before, and I do not care what *you* think! What has his finances and my personal life to do with VIA, anyway?' she shot a glance directly at her adversary, her composure lost in outrage. 'Who do you think you are speaking to?' She then looked at the male agent for support. 'Signore Zito, put your cat back in a cage! I will not put up with these insults any longer.' Francesca was up for it now, livid and with good cause!

Agent Schiavone seemed unperturbed, almost as if she enjoyed baiting her subject. The agents were about finished. This was what she had been waiting for...this moment, when Francesca was at her most vulnerable.

'*Si*, I know he only dropped me an e-mail — nothing else!'

'Did he?' the woman focused in.

'Er, *si*, before he left last week. To say goodbye?' Francesca had made a mistake and quickly tried to cover it up.

'We might like to see this e-mail next.' Schiavone licked her lips once more.

'Ladies, ladies, come on please. Let's not get too hot under the collar. It's a marvellous day outside and it's been a long morning—let's not spoil it. I think we need a spot of lunch, Agent Schiavone. I have to apologise for my colleague, Francesca, it's just a simple misunderstanding,' he said politely to Francesca while staring with a little disapproval towards Agent Schiavone. She had overstepped the mark.

The female agent apologised in a sympathetic tone, her mouth curving upwards a little at the same time. Francesca's life meant nothing to her. Then both agents stood up and looked towards the exit.

'*Arrivederci*, Signorina DeRose, or can I call you Francesca?' Agent Zito excused himself politely. 'Maybe I can speak with you a little later this afternoon?' Giving her a mildly warm smile which made a few lines around his forehead and jaw noticeable, he turned. 'We will see ourselves out. Speak with you later'.

Francesca watched as they walked up the middle isle, through the door and past the commissionaire. They did not exit the building, however, and instead entered the elevator.

My God that was terrible, I mentioned the e-mail... they will definitely inspect the mail logs now. Shit! She caught me out! What are they all about? Totally out of order! I'm going to speak with Anatolio about their outrageous behaviour. She stewed silently for a minute. *Surely there must be more to this... I need to keep one step ahead of them and find out just what Michaelangelo is mixed up in. It only is a question of time*! Francesca felt low, knowing that things were going from bad to worse. She had lied to VIA!

Pope was her pet name for Michaelangelo. It was always funny because he was not religious in any sort of a way — born catholic but also a complete atheist, and he just liked to take the piss out of the Vatican at any and every turn. Francesca could see why, considering how she had been treated today. There was never any justice in the world. *I hope that tart walks in front of a car or something. Although she does have a good taste in perfume for someone with too many male hormones. Gucci, it's my favourite.* Francesca smiled, attempting to make light of what had happened.

Francesca worked through her lunch, knowing there was now a race against time before the two Gestapo agents would be back. There was no doubt in Francesca's mind that the VIA agents were deadly serious. Francesca *did* want to keep her job and help Michaelangelo get out of trouble, but where would this all end up? She thought that things needed to be put into perspective —

It was not as if anyone had died!

****

There were about a hundred and fifty to two hundred employees inside the building at the time, which meant that there were quite a few cars parked securely not far away. Outside the Vatican wall a silver Alpha Romero was discreetly parked in a side street outside and its occupant sat still, observing the people as they went about their business. The change of guards was at nine in the morning and at five in the afternoon, and then another watch occurred around one in the morning. The observer watched the tourists mix and meander aimlessly all day approaching the Swiss guardsmen at the gate entrance occasionally to take photographs, usually to the Swiss army soldiers' amusement.

****

A little later, Francesca had come up with nothing but more questions. She headed towards the powder room, passing Mario on her way. The man greeted her as she passed him, his portly belly wobbling like a jelly. He was spending much more time behind the desk here at the Vatican than at his previous job, walking the Rome beat.

Massimo came back into the office just after lunch and created a few new user accounts on the system.

Bless you all, you simple and naive employees. Grace is to Massimo the master who has created you. You'll soon regret it this time next month – you will see that God can get blood out of a stone...they don't know nothing yet, Massimo thought, amusing himself with cynicism.

The Vatican computer system was a complex of all kinds of computer objects representing users, containers, printers and servers, to name but a few. This was the way things were organised and collated logically together in the Vatican network. It was amazing that there are other administrators in different geological locations that were still part of the same directory tree. This was made possible by using a quick, wide-area data network and satellite links. This network gave the Vatican flexibility in its design—the directory tree structure was scalable and could easily expand all over the world, into Europe, South America and a few other locations in the USA. God worked in mysterious ways! The wide-area network was an ideal system for the Catholic Church.

This system is normally secure, even though this guy Apostol is kicking about. The account did have administrator privileges, so he could have done much more damage...

Apostol may even have been a "test admin" user for Michaelangelo, who knows? Surely Francesca had thought of that, though? If the rumour is right and he has been caught up in the Casino and owes money to the Sicilians, then he is in fucking big trouble! That would explain why he has taken a low profile. Massimo conjectured and then grew tired of thinking of other possibilities. Turning round to look at Gabriella, he spoke.

'Hey Gabriella, I have to go downstairs and fix some faulty equipment, me and my bosom pal, Fran. She is supposed to be coming with me.'

He emphasised the word "bosom" because he liked to annoy Gabriella just for the hell of it. The young man was attracted to all the girls in the office, but he knew that with his slim frame and nerdy looks he was unlikely to catch an admiring glance from any of them.

The girls did not mind Massimo too much, feeling sorry for him, rather — he was quite a lonely boy, good at his job and sometimes could be quite funny. Mass only needed a little understanding and sometimes required them to have a thick skin. They girls knew when to put him in his place if he got a little out of hand, of course.

'When she comes back, let her know where I am. I'll do what I can myself, but I will need a hand to position the new switch into the cabinet downstairs in LGB2.'

'Have you filled in a change control form, Massimo?' Gabriella asked rhetorically.

She knew that he had not done so, although it was standard practice in the Vatican for I.T. people to fill a form with any special instructions and back-out procedures when changing anything on the network. This documentation would help other people know what was going on with the project if anything bad or unexpected should occur and provided a backup plan or work around. Focus would come directly to Gabriella's front door at any point of failure — she would then fan out appropriate resources to compensate any short-comings, keeping the helpdesk informed.

'No, it'll be fine. They'll not be a problem — I can fill the form in later.' *She needs to lighten up,* Mass thought as he unlocked a short metal cupboard and pulled out a bunch of cables of various sizes and lengths. He dumped this hotchpotch in a pile on the floor, giving himself room to see inside. Taking out a spare keyboard and placing it next to Gabriella's desk, and he fished out a tool kit, a spare comms switch and a head lamp.

'Hey Mass, I hope you don't expect to leave that rubbish down here next to me, you messy pup!' Gabriella quizzed the technician.

'Stop gabbing on, Gabby,' he dismissed her comment with his usual blasé.

'Oh you look so big, so tough, Massy my dear,' Paulina jibed a little. They all laughed loudly as the others in the office looked suspiciously at the three-some, jealous of their good hearted banter. Massimo looked around at the contractors.

'Well, what's wrong with you lot now? Better watch yourselves or I might disable all your accounts again,' he raised his voice and then laughed heartily. 'Permanently!'

The contractors, who could not stand Massimo to begin with because he always spoke out loudly against them, grumbled at his joke, not understanding that it was only a game. Massimo made light of recent events in the office to overcome their continual moaning and whispering of rebuke.

'I should be downstairs for about an hour. Let Fran know where I am.'

'I will tell her, handsome. Oh, by the way, remember that both Paulina and I will be leaving early this afternoon, at about three thirty. Fran should be back by then, though.'

Massimo nodded, and then headed away along the aisle past the contractors.

'*A domaini*, ladies, *arrivederci*.'

'*Arrivederci* Massimo,' they replied.

'What a man,' Gabriella said, shaking her head a little at Paulina in jest. 'A hero, what can I say?'

Massimo passed the VIA agents on their way into the office without acknowledging their passing. He descended the stairs outside the office towards the so-called Dungeons that lay far beneath the echoing sounds of the crashing waters of the crystal fountain.

****

Francesca looked at herself in the mirror of the powder room. *I look a real mess. What a start to the day so far and it's only half done.* Resigning herself to another interrogation, a much worse one, she groaned. She had lied! Yes Pope had sent her an e-mail, but not last week! Her response had been a panic reaction. They would insist on scrutinizing her account, the mail logs, his e-mail account...they would see that she had deleted the message he'd sent last night. That would be seen at least as a breach of discipline and would maybe cause her to lose her job. It was much worse that Michaelangelo had warned her not to speak to the police or VIA! Why didn't he trust them?

This is insane!!! Why should I be worrying so? But that blonde! I'll end up smacking that bitch in the face.

Francesca inspected her complexion in the mirror, her face changing to a pinkish red tone. *Oops, a little more makeup I think*, she said as she brushed on some more. *At least there is something to look forward to... Ciriaco is treating me later to a coffee tonight and maybe it will lead to something else, who knows? I can't wait to get out of here!*

The young woman's heart raced at the thought of a passionate embrace as she pencilled in a little additional eyeliner, extenuating her beautiful, large brown eyes and naturally long lashes. Fixing her hair, Francesca smiled at herself as she pulled the long red corkscrew curls away from her face and back into a pony tail. Francesca looked at herself with renewed confidence.

She entered the office just as Ciriaco had finished a call. She walked past slowly, smiling a little at him. He stretched out his arm and held her wrist lightly.

'*Ciao*, Francesca! Not so fast.' The young man looked shyly into her eyes. 'What's the story with those creeps with the glasses earlier? It looked serious....' He nodded his head to where Francesca had sat earlier that morning with the two agents. 'More importantly, Café Dabruzzi's at seven tonight; are we still ok?' he smiled sweetly.

'*Si, si,*' Francesca said, her face glowing. '*Arrivederci*, I'll see you later.' Francesca walked slowly towards the T&O section near the back of the office.

Business was in full swing, and so Francesca's mind began to de-mist a little as she quietly informed Paulina Toscano of her good news. Her friend smiled wickedly at her.

'You are a naughty little girl, aren't you? That boy could pass as your little brother — baby snatcher! Though...he *is* kinda cute... maybe I could get a shot after you finish with him?' Pauline asked tentatively, looking at

Francesca with a mixture of good humoured wit and envy.

'Not a chance, you jealous thing,' Francesca replied. 'Have you set up a new system yet?'

'No, not yet,' Paulina grumped at Francesca's power shift. 'It should be ready by tomorrow. I tried to inform the boss, but he has slipped away to a meeting and will not be back today, so that gives us a little extra time to play with,' replied Paulina with that same wicked smile. She laughed a little and Francesca grinned with her. 'Well then, back to it girl,' Paulina commanded herself. She turned her focus to the work at hand, installing a new "Confessional" box on Noah (II). 'Noah's Ark will not sink this time!'

'Oh, before I forget!' exclaimed Gabriella from her desk as Francesca turned away. 'Massimo is away fixing something downstairs; I thought he had bumped into you. He said you were going to help him. Oh and, by the way, Mr and Mrs Stooge from the VIA came back to... to cross-examine you again. It was around forty minutes ago, they did not hang about once they realised you were not in the office. I don't think that they will visit again today. They're probably writing their report or some crap thing like that.'

Gabriella spoke with disgust, remembering the ill treatment Francesca had been subjected to earlier by the auditors. Vatican Internal Audit agents were intensely disliked by everyone in the Vatican, with the exception of the cardinals for whom they worked.

'I'm out of here — going downstairs ASAP to catch up with that boy Massimo. You don't know where I am, ok?' Francesca felt weary and fed up with the whole mess, Gabriella could tell by her dispirited tone. 'I hoped to have got rid of them earlier, but I guess it was wishful thinking. *Si,* you are right. They are probably scripting my last rights, or my marching orders, at this minute.' Francesca resigned herself to more questioning and possible disciplinary action.

'Lighting a candle for you, more like,' Gabriella added.

'Someone has to take the blame for this and I am sure it will not be Anatolio.' Annoyed by the latest witch hunt, Francesca picked up the hardcopy of the script she'd printed earlier that displayed details of the hacked off Noah (I) server and put the paper inside her briefcase-like tool kit.

Francesca attempted to assemble together the gathering complexities of this enigma. Strapping the small briefcase containing her tools, headlamp and various testers and abandoning her desk for the server room, she ran up the stairs to the fifth floor in order to avoid the busy lifts. She needed some private time to think.

Francesca's dedicated workstation for interrogating the network topology was located in the server room on the fifth floor, and would present to her an up-to-date picture of the current network. A piece of equipment was identified by its IP address, like the 212.100.5.60 server, which showed up as nothing the last time a search was carried out on the network. Francesca continued to juggle the issues in her mind, and then gasped as she was hit with inspiration. She had a new lead!

There might be something obvious in this room...Unlikely, but somewhere else... another location on the vlan, I am sure. This will take a little longer to find, but find it I will! I must have a quick look before I join Massimo....

Sitting down at her dedicated workstation, there were still a few leads to follow, some areas still to quickly pursue at her desk before the VIA returned. She used the familiar network tool called "ping" and *pinged* the unknown address again to see if it was switched on and working the 212.100.5.100 address. 212.100.5.100 was possibly a computer address somewhere on the Vatican internal network rather than outside of the organisation, unless a hole had been well and truly punched in the firewall!

No reply, destination unreachable.

Francesca reaffirmed that the IP was at least hidden from normal view on the network. It could be switched off or unresponsive and hidden to her analyses; it could simply be sitting waiting to be switched on and to burst into some kind of secret activity on a single instruction. Francesca knew she had to find out more.

Trying the telnet and rlogin proved ineffective. *The External Firewall might give me the answers I seek, but that creep Jonathan is in charge of the firewall and would be immediately suspicious even on a good day if I asked for access to it. He would not ever lift a finger to help me, anyway.*

Just the thought of Jonathan made her feel sick, let alone the prospect of sweet talking the Englishman.

She studied the numbers on her screen.

0 0
1 **212.100.5.60**
1 200.221
1 200.232
2 196.196
2 epostol.ecb.int
2 thyarc(I).com

The three sets of numbers and were known as octets. 212.100.5 suggested that the device might be located in the server room within the Vatican, since 212.100.5.anything meant the equipment would normally be found on the fifth floor, corresponding to the number five, and was on a virtual local area network, or vlan 100, for short .

Great! Francesca shouted silently to herself. *Unless it has been moved, the first thing is to find it!*

The other addresses did not follow the same conventions and seemed likely to be from the outside world. The numbers 200.221 and 200.232 had nothing to do her network! Studying those addresses again, the girl knew that they could be from anywhere—anywhere in the world! It was impossible to find out anything much; the best thing she could hope for was to block intruders at the firewall.

Francesca was worried that a door to the network was still wide open at the moment, and that anyone with the right technical ability could wander freely through the Vatican City network without even a by your leave. No wonder the auditors were sniffing about! Nothing was safe. No system and no secret...

She could not tell how long the door had been open, but she hated Apostol a little for opening it. He had allowed other hackers the opportunity to have a field day at the Vatican; anybody could have been piggy-backed inside after the first breach of security. But this was all nothing new. What really mattered was whatever Michaelangelo had wanted her to find…

A bit more time on the other external 196.196 address is required, I think. Francesca used a simple Domain Name Space (DNS) tool to look up information on epostol.ecb.int. She needed a little more time to be able to see where the attacker lived or if he had been in any way sloppy. She would find him, she knew it... she waited for the results... Nothing!

DATA WITHHELD BY ISP, No Authority

Let me try another similar tool, she decided. Si, *my favourite – the Hunter Seeker.* Downloaded from Michaelangelo's own private hacker website in the United Kingdom that she'd found recently with some of her latest updates, Hunter Seeker was a multi-system utility with the ability to probe firewalls and manipulate past security policies using advanced heuristic techniques that allowed a hacker to open foreign systems. It was totally illegal to use, of course, a risk taker and clever little utility that would cover up its own tracks.

It was not fail safe, so Francesca was, as always, very careful.

Francesca remembered the third rule from the hacker's code book: "A hacker's purpose is to seek knowledge. This knowledge may come from unauthorized or unusual sources, and is often hidden."

So be it....

She launched her special unique port-scanning tool, Socks, a backdoor strobe with stealth analysis and tracing utility. She then typed: hunter-seeker epostol.ebc.int

Waiting flashed on the active window. About ten seconds passed, and then...

RESULTS

Start of Authority Record SOA [TTL=86400]

Primary name server frankfurt1.ecb.int
Hostmaster e-mail address mail.ebc.int
Serial#20091025
Refresh 10800
Retry 3600
Expire 7200
Default TTL 3600

All these numbers were normally not hidden and would be a typical result, except perhaps the ISP, if the DNS administrator chose to hide it. Looking at the results, Francesca could tell that these were not the parent servers.

The parent name servers came next.

nsVIVIVI.de.uu.net   **200.221.101.5**
nsIVIVIV.de.uu.net   **200.232.101.9**

Francesca studied the results closely.

Ah, a bit of luck for once! Si! *So out there somewhere, possibly in Frankfurt, there are two responsible "name servers" that should hold a clue!*

nsVIVIVI.de.uu.net   **200.221.101.5**
nsIVIVIV.de.uu.net   **200.232.101.9**

Francesca's thought processes sparked wildly! In tune with the numbers like a blood hound on the trail of an escaped prisoner, she knew she was about to find her answers.

Now where might I find our devious hacker? she teased herself with the data. *The domain is ecb.int and I can definitely find out more about this! The master name servers at the bottom...these don't mean much to me, but it does confirm their overall authority. The ISP is in Deutschland because of the suffix de. Yep. Definitely hosted in Frankfurt.*

The Internet Service Provider could be totally unaware of this potential hacker was on their systems. I cannot blame them directly for this breach of security. I must be very careful before making any such accusations or pointing any fingers...

Her mind slid quickly through the data like a well-oiled machine. She was going in for the kill. Another minute passed as she waited for the computer to retrieve her final analysis. *What next, another dead end?* Francesca felt her anticipation drop a little, had she failed again...?

WAITING...

RESULTS

Epostol A 196.196.66.6

'Eureka!' Francesca blasted out as her result appeared on the screen.

Here we are! This explains all the hidden entries in the file. Anything with 196.196 or 200.221 and 200.232 will not appear in any of our

*own logs! When my friend Apostol was in his own
account or in the epostol logs, this is his real internet
address – 196.196.66.6! Who the hell in Frankfurt
belongs to this? And what is the "ecb.int" domain?
Let me see if they have a website, first. That'll be
easy.*

Francesca used her internet browser and
typed in the following website uniform
resource locater (url): www.ecb.int. Her screen
filled quickly with a picture of a large blue Euro
symbol imbedded with a picture of a
skyscraper—the Euro-tower!

*Wow! Handy tool, that. Hang on girl, this is
it – it's the European Central Bank! We've been
hacked by an account holder known as "epostol"
from the ECB!!!*

Francesca slowed down her self-
congratulation as she realised what this meant.
*I might never learn who epostol is! Maybe someone
at the ECB can help me find out, though.... Christ,
this is big – much bigger than I can handle. I don't
get paid near enough for this shit! I'd better inform
Anatolio – this is a definite lead and something we
can stand on for our investigation. He should be
pleased with this and get those blood hounds off my
tail! How the hell Michaelangelo got mixed up in*

*this, God only knows...unless he found out
something else?*

Francesca had another moment of
inspiration as she tried to unravel the mystery.
*Si, I'll ask Ciriaco tonight over coffee. I think the
helpdesk guys have some dealings with the ECB.
Oh, what time is it? Bloody hell – Massimo will be
cursing me now!!!* Francesca, realising that she
had neglected Massimo, tight for time she was
flooded with guilt.

*I should be with him downstairs! But I'd
better send this e-mail to Anatolio, first, with some
details to cover my smart ass. It would be best to
keep this stuff from the others at the moment for
now, until I speak with the boss. No point in
involving them, for their own protection!*

****

Massimo had entered a long, curved
corridor — a passageway winding far beneath
the Plazzo del Governmantorato building. He
crawled like a rat under the earth as most of his
co-workers still slaved in the office, oblivious to
his wanderings. The grimy passage descended
slowly and then spat him out at a dusty

plateau. It was more dark than light here, and a dim orange glow cast uncanny shadows on the rough walls that surrounded him.

Power and communications cables passed along this passage, sunk below the stone floor, while the communication data cables ran along a shielded trunking along the tunnel's ceiling. Its white protective trunk could be seen easily above, secured to the surface of the top of the ceiling arch. The low arch above Massimo was near head height. The ceiling then began to gradually lower and the walls narrowed as the man progressed slowly along the dingy passageway.

Massimo was unaware that this corridor was also part of the old catacombs that continued onwards toward the Church of Santo Stephano and then on further to St Peter's Basilica. The main corridor trailed far below St Peter's Basilica and beyond in a complex subterranean mesh. This was an old and relatively well-used main route for communications, estates and computer personnel like the T&O team. No grim discoveries would be found here, since archaeologists and clergymen had discovered everything there was to find many years ago and had removed any macabre reminders of history. The lack of dead bodies did not make much of a difference, however — the tunnel was still a lonely place with an unhappy atmosphere.

Any deviation from the main tunnel was prohibited by locked grilled-iron doors with signs. The thick iron bars were old and pockmarked with rust. Some catacombs were open to the public, but these were few in number and required guided tours. Historians, archaeologists and men of the faith were the only people who would visit the more remote areas of the city. Not many found these places comfortable, so hardly any visited. It was cold and quite literally as quiet as the grave...

Massimo always felt that he never wanted to speak much when he was down in the catacombs, even when he was in company. He did not want to disturb the slumbering silence.

The only sound right now was that of feet walking...his. Sound did not travel well through the tunnels — it seemed to be absorbed by the spongy and porous rock that formed in a calcium carbonate incrustation on the walls.

The passageway trailed the main communications fibre channels and power cables under the city and extended out to various spots all over the old Vatican City, feeding off the essential technological services and main electrical power throughout. There were many other such pathways underneath the city used for this type of thing, and so several times a year someone was required to descend to perform routine maintenance of equipment and infrastructure expansion — usually a communications company or T&O. These tunnels were usually dry, cold, and dimly lit to save on electricity costs. One thing was always true about anyone that worked in this remote place. No one would hurry back!

The technician had been walking along for ten long minutes and was only half-way along the low and narrow subterranean passageway. He had to crouch like a soldier on the battlefield for a few minutes at this midway point, where the ceiling dropped for no apparent reason. Being careful not to bang his head on the stone above him, Massimo stooped further, feeling his laptop and tools weigh heavily on his back. The man was finding his journey quite burdensome; his breathing became heavier as the walls closed in around him.

Bugger this for a carry on, he thought, exasperated. *I drew the short straw on this one.* His thought changed direction quickly. *It's bloody tight down here and fucking freezing! I'll be suffering from hypothermia soon!* The air was very cold below ground level, with no sun to warm the rock. Mass was a young man, used to the hot and pleasant Italian weather. He hated the cold!

Stuck down here when there would still be some gorgeous and good looking tourists walking about in the gardens to gaze at topside? Come on Massimo boy, let's hurry up and get this crap over with. The place was beginning to drag him down, so he turned his attention to Francesca.

It would be nice if Fran was with me right now. Mmm.... Not only for her looks, but she might warm me up a bit...if I was dead lucky! His mind twisted direction again, ping-ponging from one subject to the next, and finally again...*do not think of the dead, not in here!* The oppressive atmosphere affected him more than he really knew.

What a stunner she is...Francesca. His mind refocused back on the right track. *She is good company,* he tried to cheer himself up, expecting that the girl would be following behind him very soon. The technician rounded another slow bend and then found he was peering along with outstretched and aching neck to see a distant alcove. That was where the communication cabinet was located.

His bent back ached but, still crouching, he managed to unlock the heavy wooden door, which was about chest height and four feet wide. He used a special large key that the T&O team used to open similar communications and power ducts throughout the city. Massimo tugged a few times at the door handle; it would not move, so he used both hands and pulled again at the door. The door finally opened, making a horrible creaking noise as it came towards him. *Not a good sign,* he thought. Obviously, the door had not been opened for some time.

He entered the dark room, which was lit only by the eerie orange light splashed in from behind Massimo. He was able to stand upright again inside this large area, which had apparently been carved out of stone and earth a while ago. The technician stretched his shoulder blades, easing his stiff back, and gave a sigh of relief.

This area had been acquired unofficially by Anatolio's team in the man's great wisdom, because it was useful to have a small communication room for switches and servers down here secure and out of the way. Access to LGB2 was difficult. The domineering, heavy atmosphere was more difficult to handle; it was cold and dry; dust coated everything! No wonder the equipment was going faulty!

A familiar small set of flashing LEDs lit up brightly in the dark room from the switches in the dull area. Mathew stood by himself on the left side of the fixed cabinet on the wall, like a guardian keeping watch over the room. Massimo switched on the main electric light next to the doorway; a single light bulb burst brightly into life. After walking along the dimly lit passage, the bulb caused a momentary blindness.

'Hello Mathew, my old friend. Feeling lonely?' speaking aloud, Massimo sat on an old stool next to the Mathew server. 'Not as lonely as me.' *Let me login to you.* The technician typed in his login name and then his password. Waiting for the system authentication to let him in, he looked around the room. As his eyes became accustomed to the brightness, he became a bit bored and disinterested with the view during this long logon stage. He couldn't help but notice a small, white-painted metal door just behind the server, which he thought might lead to a maintenance duct onwards and up to the nearby church above.

Turning his attention to the electronic data switches in the small metal cabinet, Massimo could observe that the bottom switch only had a few cables running from it. One led to another second switch just above it, and a few cables trailed away underneath the space below the small internal duct door at the far wall, sandwiched into the corner next to the duct's hinge and easy for any observer to miss.

Massimo noticed that the power light of the data switch was on the green, but the rest of the small LEDs were not flickering! *Might be goosed. Typical, and just as well I brought the spare.*

The other data switch above, installed in the comms rack, was fully functional. Its lights flickered madly, rejecting the darkness of the catacombs. *Good connectivity on that one,* he thought. A patch cable ran off from the switches, trailing and joining to another patch panel, which in turn fanned out to a variety of rooms, where individuals could connect their computers almost by magic to the network. A computer or printer could then be attached physically to some wall point elsewhere from here, and a technician could trace an individual person right to their desk, if need be. One could trace this physical route to locate potential problems, and Massimo had just the tools for the job.

He was now logged in and began a quick analysis of Mathew before his planned shutdown and restart of the server. Checking the current health logs, the technician confirmed the reason for their current problem. 'Yeap,' he drawled. 'This shit is still losing its logical memory. As well to sort this out now and then look at the data switch afterwards. I'll probably need a hand with the switch anyway.'

'Ok, then let's restart you,' he said to Mathew as if the server was a person. He typed the command at the console. *Bouncing you now, Mat, come back up boy.*

Time passed by and, an hour later, the server had decided not to come back up immediately. This meant that Massimo had to repeat the same start-up process many times and, just when he was going to give up, the server came back online! Massimo was eventually able log in and checked the server's status.

All right! Mathew has finally joined the other disciples in the cluster. Smashing! Job done, now what next? Si, well, Fran is not here yet.... Massimo was now at a loose end and contemplated killing a little time until Fran arrived. Checking his watch and his patience, he saw that it was about now about five o'clock!

Fuck, where is she? The man thought, really wanting to get out of the catacombs before dark.... *What about this broken data port on the switch, then? I'll just attach my laptop and have a look at its system status. It seems to be ok just now, except...that the port seems down and not connected? It is attached to the cable which is going beneath that duct door. Odd... I'll just bring up this crap port.*

Massimo Rossi used a secure telnet session and logged in as administrator to the data switch showing VATGPLG02 as its description. Expertly, the technician typed on his console window commands to make the switch work again. Interface fa1/0 followed with "shutdown" and "no shutdown". The port on the bottom data switch burst into life again! Green LEDs began to flicker frantically as data moved madly across the computer network.

Well done! I might not need to change the switch after all. That's so cool – I can go home now! Satisfied that the data switch was working fine again and could leave without replacing it, however, something else was still bothering him. *Where is that grey cable going? And is that power?*

There were two cables covered in dust and difficult to see lying under the thick layer of floor dust. A data cable and a power cable.... For Massimo, these cables were an impasse that ate away at him. He needed to know where they were going, so he decided to move the server carefully out of the way. This allowed him clear access to the small duct door.

The floor around the door was completely covered in dust. The young man stared at the mysterious cables with bewilderment.   One was attached at one end to the data switch, and then trailed down and disappeared beneath the duct door next to him. His large, iron key fitted perfectly in the small, internal metal lock, and then he pulled open the door. Unlike the outer door entrance, this one glided easily out to meet him. Not even a squeak was heard.

It was dark inside and, in the dimness, he saw the cable stretching along and disappearing inwards far into the tunnel.   Once the door was opened, the tunnel did not look much like a duct. Massimo's curiosity got the better of him and he decided to find out where the cables went.

Nothing else for it...

Waiting only for a brief moment to put on his head lamp and switch it on, Massimo resembled more a coal miner than a technician.

Torch blazing full power, he cut through the dark tunnel with his narrow beam. Massimo gauged the size of the passage to be just below head height at the top of the arch, observing the white surrounding walls to be about five feet wide. Further up, the passage bent sharply left. The ground was uneven with a crumbly dry surface, unlike the flat, dry-bricked stone floor of the main passage way. The air inside was desiccated, still and lifeless. There was also an odd smell... perhaps the memory of rot or decay....

Massimo's trailing eyes followed the thin grey cable as it twisted up the partially illuminated passage. He followed it like a bloodhound, swivelling his head left and right, lifting his gaze upwards and down in a smooth motion. The sandy arched ceiling was low and closed in around him.

Darkness pressed just beyond his beam and Massimo adjusted its brightness to see the walls. The technician's mouth was dry like the environment, and he began to feel on edge going deeper inside the passage as his light cast weird shadows off the uneven surfaces. The technician soon reached the bend and extended his neck to see more... he could just barely see around the shadowy passageway...

There was something in the gloom — a box or piece of equipment sat there...maybe an old computer and a stool?

Shit, this is so crazy. Nothing should be here. What the fuck...? Who would be stupid enough to put a computer in this place; I was not told about this... trying to make sense of the hidden computer, Massimo's mind racing, working it out.

Anything is possible, I suppose, especially working for the VAT. It might have been here for years and was forgotten about...maybe it's been chugging away for ages.

He looked down at the equipment, which was also completely covered in dust. There was no keyboard or monitor attached to the computer. He examined the back of the computer as a green light flickered on and off, transferring data to the hard drive. *It is possible that, by opening up the switchport a few minutes ago, its active connectivity sparked this box into action and somebody or some program or user is accessing it right now. Could it be Apostol?*

Massimo looked back in the direction of the entrance as he heard Francesca's footsteps echoing in the small alcove of the communication room, where the switches were located. He walked to the edge of the curve and saw Fran stooping a little as she entered the passageway, her female silhouette providing stark contrast to the hard walls.

'Hey Fran, it's about time you turned up! You can stop looking for Pope — he has run off on holiday somewhere. Anyway, you are late and I am ready to go home.' Although he chastised her, he could not wait to tell her of his find. 'Come up here for a moment, I have something to show you! Up here and around this corner. Follow me! You'll need your light on, have you brought it?'

She moved inside. 'Come on gorgeous, hurry up!' Massimo dashed back down the passage. The girl followed, her steps crunching against the crumbled dry ground. Massimo was still astonished by his discovery. He looked along down the passage way and saw that it seemed to fork into the gloom beyond. His beam would go no further, and he presumed that one channel went upwards and to the right, probably towards the Church, the other probably back-tracked to the government building. It was not important. Rubbing his dusty eyes, the technician could not see any further. He was still standing partially upright because of the low ceiling, and he stared above the old computer and then sat down onto the old wooden stool that had probably been brought in from the storage room. Who put it there, the boy would never know.

From the corner of his eye, Massimo saw Francesca coming around the bend with her head and shoulders crouched a little, due to the low arch. Fran did not have her head lamp switched on, and had been following the glow of his lamp. Massimo examined the flickering lights at the back of the busy computer and decided that someone was accessing it at this moment for sure. All he would need to do was connect his laptop and then determine who it was. It was so simple.... Distracted by this task, Massimo encouraged Francesca to come over as she opened her small briefcase taking out her headlamp.

'Hi Fran! Mmm... you smell nice, your perfume is a pleasant change from the rotting odour of this place — I think it is a dead rat or something. What kept you — it's bloody freezing! Oh, and by the way, look what I have found! It's the system that you've been searching for.' Massimo grinned from ear to ear, his teeth white in the darkness. The young man filled with delight now that he had company. He angled his narrow beam at the concealed system. She approached slowly and stopped.

'Hello, is it working again?' she asked, clicking on her headlamp into his face.

'*Si*, and I think that Apostol is accessing it right now. Who else could it be?'

'No one,' she agreed.

CHAPTER VI

THE FREEMASONS
>⊓◻ ⊏⸋ ◻◻⸋⌋V⊏ ◻V

Before she joined Massimo, Francesca was sitting in the main computer room on the 5th floor typing furiously to Anatolio.

The hums and whines of numerous servers and data switch fans. Adding to the din was the air conditioning, which switched on and off, maintaining a low temperature of sixteen degrees Celsius. Like soldiers on parade, the servers stood stock upright within the many metal racks positioned along the middle of the floor. The disciples Servers sat preaching the Vatican's bureaucratic doctrine at the far end of the long room.

It was a noisy and untidy area, with long grey, red, and yellow network cables lying precariously across the floor surface, waiting to trip an unsuspecting technician. There was never enough time in the day to tidy up the place. Numerous patch panels connected the servers to switches from here to everywhere else in Vatican City. Most of the Vatican's vital services were provided by the data that travelled from this central location.

Francesca sent off her email but needed to scan all the electronics end to end for any unlabelled or out-of-place computer equipment in the room. *A few more checks…* as she walked back and logged onto the specialised computer terminal. She immediately brought up a top-level design of the Vatican network. This design launched her protocol analyser.

Concentrating on multiple screens, the systems administrator drilled into the virtual server room area, examining the spot where she was sitting. An image of the server room was displayed online. There were many computers and data switches in various states of operation. She had done this before, but this time Francesca knew what to look for. It must be hidden somewhere in here...

After spending several minutes analysing the detailed data sets of information in the active computer display, disappointed she concluded that this room did not have any suspicious equipment.

She sighed, slightly demoralised, realising that her search would take some time; it was like looking for a needle in a haystack! Hunting for a clue, any clue, Francesca searched for the computer with the unique address identification by the numbers 212.100.5.60. Maybe it was hidden behind something else, like a smoke screen, communicating only so far? *Maybe that something is not working at this moment...where is it, where is it?*

Suddenly, there was an explosion of air into the room. The noise was incredible!

Whoossssshh!
Whooossssssshh!

Air conditioning fans came on madder than ever, sharp and Baltic thundering into action right above her head, blowing away the loose papers like feathers along the floor while wafting her long auburn hair like a witches!

Bloody fans again! They are so annoying! Francesca pulling her hair down and under control, dismissed the rude interruption as the cold air pressed down on top of her neck, although she was trying at the same time to shake the rising and unexplained trepidation inside herself that she had experienced the other night. There was no logical explanation for the growing fear, this feeling of dread, but she felt already that she was not alone in the room....

Fully focused, Fran continued her examination, searching the lower floors where her colleague was working. She watched in real time as Massimo was in the process of taking Mathew server to off-line status.

Mathew's icon on the screen was shaped like a tall computer which had transformed to a wobbly and misshaped image. It then turned to a different colour from its current state of yellow alert, which suggested that attention was required, moving to an unstable yellow colour and then to red. Finally transitioning to a black solid colour, the icon indicated that Mathew was now completely powered off.

There are two switches downstairs in the small comms cabinet, and only one was suspected of malfunctioning, Francesca guessed. This was why Massimo was there in the first place.

The top data switch in the dungeon was the main communications switch that connected most users via a fast link to St Peter's Basilica. She could see its status from where she presently sat. The dungeon was therefore a critical link to the rest of the old city — the second data switch in the dungeon room was linked to the top switch as a redundant backup.

No one should really be using the backup, it was just for a spare. However, it has malfunctioned and so still needs replaced. No good keeping a flat spare in your trunk.... Francesca looked at the switches remotely from where she sat.

Mmm...I see. There is an individual data port which indicates that data switch two on the gig fibre channel is faulty. Something has caused it to malfunction and disable itself.

No sweat, she shrugged. *It should affect no one, since the main top switch is functioning perfectly. The dungeon seems to check out okay once Massimo is done with the server.*

Francesca felt guilty about not assisting Massimo at this moment, although she thought he might have been comforted by the fact that she had checked in on him. Still, time was passing and it was getting quite late. Sighing wearily again, Francesca logged out, fearing even more where she was going. Yet, it was unfair to leave the boy down below by himself to remove and replace the data switches — it was a two-man job!

I'd better go and help him....

****

The sunlight set unusually early; the building was in darkness as clouds gathered overhead. The weather had been gradually worsening during the latter part of the afternoon. The time was approaching ten o'clock on the eve of the last day of the month. This meeting was going to be one of the most important of the year!

The building was a light-coloured, two storey house with dark-green wood shutters closed tight against the chill. Above the doorway, roman numerals were etched into stone, reading: MDCLXXXV. A little below this was a small stone eye, set within a small triangular shape. The lidless *"All-Seeing Eye"* stonily watched everything that approached the house. Worn by the centuries, the esoteric insignia was no longer easy to perceive. But those who knew it knew it well.

Two solidly-built bald men stood outside on the worn, bevelled stone steps at either side of the entrance to the old stone hall. The men were as massive as body builders, and they easily blocked the closed doorway. Dressed in light faun chinos and smart casual light brown blazer jackets with black- and red-peaked, spotted handkerchiefs, they spoke casually to each other and laughed a little while keeping vigil on the premises. Anyone brave enough to leave the busier roads might wonder why these giants stood guard in an empty, dead-end road. But they would not stick around to wonder for very long. Both men were armed and very, very dangerous.

A solitary, small man wearing a pinstripe suit entered into the quiet lane and began walking towards two harden men as they studied his casual approach. Both burley men bowed slightly as he shook their out-stretched, monstrous hands in a mutual bonding. The henchmen's hands were immense compared to the man's delicately sculpted fingers. The visitor's grip, however, was uncannily firm, surprising both giants. They greeted him, then, with much respect.

The handshake was the first sign of their ancient and secret fraternity. The man was the Grand Master of this and many other Holy Orders of Italy. This was a very special and meticulously-planned visit, and the man knew exactly who would be in attendance on this eve.

The responsibility of the Worshipful Master and every other Freemason is to uphold the craft and the Grand Master with a reverential attitude — not for the sake of the man in that elevated office, but for the maintenance of the office's absolute significance.

When the Grand Master visits a lodge, it is not he, the person, who should be honoured, but the nobility of his title. The honour that is paid to the Grand Master is to this office, the highest that freemasonry can impart upon any of its members and yet one which carries with it the heaviest responsibilities.

The Order was assembled inside, waiting.... The man in dark pinstripes moved slowly inside the open entrance as the doors shut behind him. He moved into a large, empty hallway. It was a bare and inhospitable place, lit with many flamed torches that were periodically anchored into the stone walls. The building was a dim and deserted shell with a peculiar, colour-shifting stone floor. The place appeared abandoned.

He changed in a private anteroom near the rear of the hall, pulling over his head a long gown made of black, coarse material and strapping a leathern girdle about him as an emblem of humility and poverty. The girdle was distinguished with the initials GM engraved in a black metal square, accompanied by a compass medallion. His chest was strapped with a red sash, covered in esoteric symbols. He carried a staff, hung with rosary and cross, in one hand, and a scrip in the other.

The Grand Master descended the rainbow spiral stone stairs at the far end of the hall. Beneath him he heard the low muted noises and distant murmur of voices and whiffed the strange smell of incense.

Everyone in attendance was dressed in black as they bowed briefly in recognition of his status, moving apart as the Grand Master travelled between his brethren. He seemed to glide like an illusion moving smoothly along the floor as if on a bed of air, travelling towards the altar.

A large Masonic symbol was oil-painted above, covering the whole ceiling in this lower level of the building. Every faith was represented inside the symbol — even some members of the Catholic Church were freemasons, and this lodge meeting tonight was no exception to that. Some of the members attending had no faith at all beyond the "only faith" — the "fraternity of the brethren".

The Worshipful Master of the Grand lodge MDCLXXXV was already in attendance and watching intimately as the Grand Master approached. The Grand Master Mason soon stood up beside the Worshipful Master Mason on a light marble altar.

The early part of the Worshipful Master's ceremony was finished, and now he welcomed this distinction with the Order's unique handshake and greeted the Grand Master with his extended hand and the real grip of a Master Mason.

Anyone watching in ignorance would think the grip to be an odd practice. More peculiar on this night for the brethren was the realisation that the Masters were not using their right hands to grip, as would be expected. The Masters interlaced the thumbs of their hands, and the Worshipful Master pressed the top of his fingers against his fellow Master as it united with the left hand. The Grand Master simultaneously pressed his fingers against the other Mason's hand and fingers in a similar fashion.

This strong Lions Paw grip was also given at the graveside after a candidate had been raised. The men gripped with their firm strong hands and held each other in a strange embrace of the five points of fellowship, with right arms embracing over the fellows' left shoulders.

Left foot to left foot
Left knee to left knee
Left breast to left breast

So it went on to left hand gripping left hand and the Worshipful Master's mouth to left the ear of the Grand Master's head. In a low voice, while the audience looked on in worship of these strong men, the Worshipful Master whispered.

'Mah-Ha-Bone,' he said steadily, meaning, "What a Builder". 'I do promise and swear that I will not give the substitute for the Master's word in any other way or manner than that in which I receive it, which will be on the five points of Fellowship, and in low breath.'

Both men released their grips after about twenty seconds, and then the Master turned to his gathered brethren with both hands above his head and arms bent at ninety degree angles with his shoulders and wrists, almost as a soldier would surrender to an enemy.

'Let God stand before us in judgement day, the eve of our new beginning! Let us all welcome our fellow brother the Grand Master to this Order!'

The Worshipful Master then lowered his arms in three definite movements to his sides in standing of the Distress of a Master Mason. He then stood down from the altar and positioned himself to the rear of his superior, the Grand Master. No further words were spoken between the Grand Master and the Worshipful Master of this lodge.

The Worshipful Master copied the movements of the other Master and, at the same time, spoke the words....

'O' Lord my God, is there no help for the Widow's Son?'

These words should never be spoken at the grand hailing and would be deemed as disrespectful. The Grand Master stood erect now with his left hand positioned horizontal across his abdomen.

The Lodge acknowledged his signal.

'Amen, my God. We are your servant and builder apprentices.' The brethren all chorused together in a monotonous, low voice. Raising up their left hands horizontal to their throats, they symbolized their throats being cut and their tongues torn out by their roots and their bodies burned in rough sands of sea at low water mark, where the tide flows and ebbs two times in a full day.

All the members of the Masonic Temple except the Masters appeared in strict Masonic dress, consisting of a suit of black clothes, black necktie, black apron with red silk border, black silk hat and white and blood-red gloves. The Worshipful Master dressed in a heavy, dark brown gown with a green and a sash intricately embroidered with symbols, as well as a black medallion of the square a compass with the letters RWM embossed upon it. The Grand Master was all in black, with his red sash and jewelled compass medallion.

There were also both sexes in the company; men and women dressed formally. Standing and looking in awe at their spiritual leader, they waited. Freemasons dress differently all over the world, and each lodge dresses appropriately to the formal dress of its homeland. This was no ordinary order of freemasons, not recognized by any respectable order…. Oh, no, these were special, a very special kind. Each of the brethren was a member of a more ruthless and fanatical fellowship.

The altar and the three lights above it represented the Sanctum Sanctorum or Holy of Holies of the original tabernacle in the wilderness. Draped as a mark of respect to a dead brother, a black cloth was displayed beneath the three Great Lights. Black candles inserted in black metal iron candelabras above uncannily gave out very little luminescence, an

almost pitiful dull light that caricatured each
member of the lodge. The brethren wore black
cloth masks over their faces made of material
similar to that of the drape on the altar, in order
to disguise their true identities.

The cold flames from the torches that
were secured on the walls gave out an eerie,
shivering effect, casting weird shadows over
the dim, subterranean room. The site was
sobering and heavy, and yet was marked by an
atmosphere suppressed and pregnant, with the
potential for hysteria and excited anticipation of
some pending fate or unquestionable destiny....

Chapping the altar with his gavel, the
Grand Master began the main ceremony.

'Tauta o bios!', or "such is our life!" he
shouted powerfully to his audience.

'Gerusale, civitas et ornamentum
martyru(m) D(e)I'! or "Jerusalem, city and
ornament of God's martyrs!" they yelled back.

'These inscripted in the plastered walls
of the Pope's crypt.' He projected while raising
his left hand.

'There is much left to be discovered and
much still unknown. It is now time for they
who will lead us to the beginning and to the

root of immortality.' His immoral tone building up, 'We will touch absolute power of our most revered Relic Smite!' the Grand Master bellowed. A short pause ensued as the lodge felt their Master's soul deepen softly with lustful ecstasy.

'A great secret has been kept. It has been this way for hundreds of years by the silence and blood of our enemies. My brethren, we have all taken solemn oaths of the fellowship. Tonight we are nearing the end of our long journey — the journey that began before even time. Once these forces are unleashed and in motion, no man will be able to stop us. A new dawn will be seen by all, and a new beginning. These things cannot be undone...,' screaming energetically, 'It is a *new Genesis!*'

The Worshipful Master then opened a great book and read from it, grave esoteric words of black magic. A silver pentangle was embroidered onto the black book, which was bound of human leather and had pages yellow with age. Written in scarlet were the immortal words of magic and scratched in mortal sacrificial ink. Gory teaching dipped in from the well of blood. They were unfathomable and heart-rending esoteric *teachings of the fellowship.*

A large stone vessel was then passed between the thirteen members of the lodge, and each fellow member took a deep sacrificial draught. To the palate the drink was bitter and to the lips and tongue it brought a taste of sweetness.

The thick, slippery red fluid felt warm and burned their innards as it touched the stomach wall. Their minds became hazy and numb and the members became almost drunk, transformed into an insane state although though their minds and eyes were able to focus on the Worshipful Master's drugged and Godly words.

The lodge had almost gained possession of one of the three Reliquiae. Its whereabouts had been discovered after divine direction was given in the olden scriptures. A Reliquiae dwelt secretly below, inside the bottomless catacombs, they knew this. And yet no one in the lodge had ever physically seen it, not even the Grand Master, although he knew of its hallowed presence. Oh yes, he knew it was there! A hidden energy brooded within.

The man had seen it in his dreams, and he shared these dreams to the fellowship. The time for its appearance was so close, and nothing would stand in their way. Far beneath, the Reliquiae lay undisturbed and unseen at the bottom of the deepest and remotest tunnel of the ancient city. Something they had not calculated for or foreseen, it was the exact whereabouts of *Smite*. Was "Smite" a power or something else… darker. The prophecy told the story. A tale of other dark powers was at hand.

Old walled and forgotten passages ran in all directions, joining into a warren of dead tunnels. These lonely, subterranean paths ran from the lodge and on through a complex of derelict caverns and clerical crypts. Evil, over the centuries, had readied that dead way. The passage led into the dead Catacomba and beyond that, further in and deeper they would have to go to find the gruesome *Cubicle of Colpo*. Dark and abandoned are those places…

****

descent. She had not seen anyone from her team. It was about five o'clock, and most people had gone home, "No more money? No more work," was the contractors' motto.

It was silent here, in LGB2. The room was half the size of the previous one and surprised newcomers with its breath-taking interior design. Entombed in deathly quiet, the room was a surprise indeed. It had a fine sculptured Roman cornice ceiling high above with many detailed small Angels stretched around along the cornices. A rich, large Fresco of the twelve disciples gazed downward upon her from the old cracked ceiling overhead.

The floor, in contrast, was a mosaic of colourful small triangle-shaped tiles forming a depiction of the Coliseum and, looking around at life-sized wall carvings of a gladiatorial battlefield showing men in mortal combat, battling each other for existence, Francesca couldn't help but suppress a shiver. The gladiators' eyes were wide and life-like, each fighter anticipating the other combatant's final and fatal move. Their blood poured bright red and scarlet onto the ground for the entertainment of the people; even after all the centuries of wear, the atmosphere felt exciting and macabre.

The building was so old that some of the walls had thin tributary of cracks like that of some mad root structure making its own picture images to shadow those figures as they gasped their last breath. And now these men remained immortal....

Anyone who came to this room felt shocked and awed by the life-like images and somehow felt drawn into the arena's struggle for life and death; the sounds of the arena were dead, although the passion still shouted out loudly from the past, as did the barbaric crowds in the background who viewed the glorious spectacle. Francesca found it all too disturbing to enjoy and walked quickly through.

Rome was Christian when this room was decorated. The Government building had been built atop the room before it was discovered. Light came from small, dull electric lamps on the sides of the granite pillars next to the walls in each corner, providing supporting structure for this part of the building. Amazingly, the room was not used except to give access to the passageway leading towards St Peter's Basilica.

It was a magnificent piece of artwork in its own right, but was sadly hidden from public view. The pictures must have really been something to see in their day!

Francesca exited the room and descended a final set of circular stone stairs that wound round and downwards for another twenty feet until eventually she reached the bottom of the lower building. The girl found herself staring with dread into the man-sized tunnel that would lead to where Massimo would be. Ahead was gloomy place, lit only with an eerie, dull orange hue of diffuse light. None of the team members chose to spend time down here—the only one who seemed willing to volunteer was Massimo. Francesca suspected that his bravery being so young had always been bravado. This place was an unnerving place, a cold environment and most inhospitable.

With a deep sigh, she disappeared into the long passage hastily scurrying along the tunnel, peering into the gloom ahead. The orange light strained her eyes in a different way, and when she reached the part of the passage where the walls and ceiling closed in, she slowed.   Now Francesca was forced to crouch, bent almost double for several minutes, finding it hard to breathe. Why the corridor was so small here, she never knew. Bumping her head a little off the stone-arched roof, she cursed sharply.

'Oooh!' *Bloody sore,* she agonised. I'll have to speak to estates about this tomorrow.' She continued on the best she could along the imposing corridor, holding her aching head with one hand.

The passage began to widen again and Francesca was able to walk more upright. She approached a long bend, noticing that the orange hue had given way to a lighter ambience. A low, humming noise began drifting to her ears as she rounded a bend and the light grew brighter. It was at that moment that Francesca saw the white florescent light shining like a beacon out of the open doorway at the alcove. The communications room!

'Thank God. Here at last!' she spoke aloud in her relief.

Francesca looked through the open doorway, screwing up her eyes as she emerged from the darker tunnel. There was "Mathew"!

Sitting alone on the floor next to the cabinet and stool, the server was still busily providing the essential redundancy and backup required to keep all the other disciple nodes healthy. *But where is Massimo?*

Francesca entered the small communications room, which, long ago had been dug out of the wall of the main passageway. The familiar electronic sounds of small fans whirred continually from the two comms switches and the server; these were the only sound other than her breathing. A light dust coated everything inside.

Massimo must be somewhere.... Francesca scanned his earlier handiwork and his footprints, which were impressed into the dust. She also saw smaller, female footprints which were probably her own from the last time she had entered this remote place.

What was that? Francesca asked herself, looking at a small, partly-open doorway on the far wall. She had previously thought the door to be some kind of fire exit and wondered why Massimo had decided to open it up. Perhaps he was still inside?

Why? Oh Jesus, tell me he did not go in there, she prayed a little. *There is no way I am going inside! No way... I just can't do it.*

Francesca approached the entrance slowly, the stale air motionless and... there was something else — something that subconsciously alerted her. Against her better judgement, the girl focused on ahead and into the dark tunnel.

'Hello?' her voice fell dully without any resonance; she raised her voice again. 'Hello, Massimo?' she spoke tentatively and cautiously, seeing only a light glow reflecting off the wall surface beyond a curved wall. *That must be Massimo's head torch shining not twenty metres off! Massimo should be around that curve!*

Francesca had entered the passageway without thinking, almost like being pulled by a magnetic attraction to the darkness. She was in! Although she'd always hated dark places, Francesca maintained her leadership without thinking or hesitation — she could not let her fear rule her head when one of her team might need help.

Inside, the floor was uneven and fragmented, making it difficult to walk. Her steps crunched and crumbled as she walked.

She made her way between the data and power cables, following them along the passage where she could see a light up ahead. Francesca tripped and stumbled as she approached the bend. *No one should be in here...* she thought. It was too quiet.

The young woman began to round the long curve. *What's this?* She wondered and quickened her step and there was Massimo! The young man's headlamp was resting on top of what looked like a computer tower, silhouetting his thin frame, which sat in front of the lamp. His head turned downwards, staring at the place where the cable run appeared to end.

'Mass, I am so glad to find you. What are you looking at?' Francesca was still spooked a little at being inside this awful place, and yet incredibly relieved to have found her co-worker and friend. Massimo seemed disinterested or preoccupied with his find, however. Francesca drew closer to him.

'Mass? Massimo, you know, we should not be in here.' Francesca touched his shoulder lightly. 'Thank God I've found you. Mmm...hey! Is this? My God—you have found the hidden computer!' she shouted with excitement, then began coughing a little while catching her breath in the airless and dry atmosphere.

Massimo's head turned sharply around as she shook his shoulder again. He did not look well. His face appeared ghostly and white as he twisted his head to look upwards at her then his whole body fell suddenly backwards with a jerk, striking the ground hard with a heavy muffled thump.

'Massimo!' Francesca shrieked, jumping back instinctively in fright. The young man's head wobbled on the ground like a jelly for a brief moment in the shadows. He was badly hurt!

'Mass, what's wrong with you, where are you hurt? Mass!' but Mass did not reply…

Francesca felt helpless at that moment. *Has he fallen in a bizarre accident? No that was fucking stupid. It must be his diabetes!* Si! *That was it!*

Quickly the girl searched his pockets, looking for some kind of sugar or chocolate bar or just anything sweet, and then squatted down next to the fallen man.

Putting her hand on the ground, Francesca felt something sticky as she tried to feel for a pulse on his neck.

Nothing, God...surely not! Oh Lord, don't tell me, he must just be unconscious? It can't be true. Oh, help! The girl screaming inside shone the torch directly onto his face with a dreaded realisation... Massimo's eyes and pupils were open wide and staring at her. He wasn't hurt... *he was dead!*

Oh shit! You poor, poor boy, Massimo – not you...not you... Despairing, she began to sob and, in the darkness, the girl gradually became aware of the red treacly wetness on her palm.

Its blood! Fixing her eyes on his right temple, she saw that it was swollen with... a star like hole into his cracked forehead! This revulsion instantly turning her stomach, she retched onto the ground in disgust.

'Oh my God!' her eyes bulged wide in disbelief as she tried to shout for help. Nothing came out from her voice but a pitiful squeak, while wiping her mouth burning with bile.

The girl's shock caused her to drop the headlamp. With a mixture of utter nausea and stunned astonishment, fear began to rule her.

Reflexively she stood up and stepped back, her face contorted in terror.

'Oh. Oh...oh...' covering her mouth with her hands, she suppressed the urge to scream aloud. In a state of shock beheld the cold brutality of his death. Francesca had never seen a dead man before, let alone one that had been murdered!

Her mind kicked in like quicksilver as her eyes darted around in the restricted light. *There was no rigour, it must have happened not too long ago...* she thought. There was one other thing... only of one other thing, on her mind, now. Survival, her own!

Francesca looked around nervously, although she was unable to see well in the dim light. Something else was bugging her that she couldn't quite put her finger on... she had subconsciously noted it already on her short journey...

Yes… the foot prints in the dust – the small point marks and round dents! I never wear pointed toes unless I'm going out to a night club! It must have been another woman who killed Massimo! Who would wear heels down here? Nobody. The

****

In the meantime, Francesca's assailant had just come around the first bend and noted the dead man. He had been easy, clinical work. The gun fired again several times as she shot in the direction of the next victim! Massimo's torch beam was shining directly into the killer's cold eyes, making accurate shooting impossible. The girl was escaping! A few minutes later there was no sound along the tunnels — not a scream or a footstep.

She had been here only moments ago thought the cold blooded killer! Massimo's lifeless eyes looked as a woman stepped over him. Cursing quietly, she grabbed the head torch that sat on top of the computer tower, quickly scanning it and walking forward, the killer wildly fanning the light across the passageway its beam showed two tunnels, both going in opposite directions…

****

Francesca knew that she would be pursued, and followed a right bend in the passageway, which curved in a long decent. She began to slow down, her mind quickly sobering and forcing her panicked body to a stumbling walk, for fear of hurting herself in the utter darkness. Francesca knew that she had panicked and run away blindly... She was very lucky to be alive!

Unexpectedly, she tripped on the uneven and crumbly floor, landing heavily on her knee. Feeling her jeans tear as her knee scraped the floor, the pain of friction assailed her a moment later.

'Oooh...' the hot sensation nipped sharply, something she had not felt since a little girl and had run away uncontrollably in a thunderstorm and fallen and hurt herself on the ground. The image of herself as a frightened girl came flashing back, as did the pain. Her grandmother had come to her rescue then — *who will rescue me now?* Francesca was alone and afraid.

I hope that bastard goes the wrong way or at least finds it difficult to follow me here! Who is that person? She smelled the air, finding it was clear of scent. *Why is she trying to kill me?*

Francesca began feeling her way along the wall of the passage again, getting to her feet slowly using her right hand while probing the grainy wall next to her with her left arm outstretched in front for protection.

With the coordination of a drunk, the girl staggered warily, moving as best she could while trying not to smack her head on anything else, especially the low ceiling wall. Hidden dangers were everywhere!

Little by little, Francesca moved further and further away from her assailant. Darkness had been her ally, at first, but darkness now threatened to tip her sanity. The blackness completely engulfed and enclosed her mind, strangling and numbing her senses. The only sounds she could hear were her own. Gently feeling and patting her way along the dry, rough walls, Francesca's footsteps crunched loudly and her breaths came shallow. Like a blind person without a walking stick, arms outstretched, she moved through the catacombs.

After some time had passed, Francesca stopped to listen. She heard breathing and tensed... and then realised the breathing was her own! Her heart began pumping adrenalin quickly through her aching body.

Where am I? Where am I going? Straining her ears and eyes for any sign or sound of pursuit, she tried to hold her panic at bay. There was nothing. Was it coincidence then — had the killer stopped walking at the exact same moment?

****

Standing alone next to the inside passage divide of the rock where both passages forked, the killer switched off the dead man's headlamp, listening carefully in the darkness and concentrating, like Francesca, waiting carefully for any sound. She experienced her first moment of indecision, waiting there in complete silence, conscious that with every minute that passed the girl would be getting further away. The girl would raise the alarm!

The murderer knew that tourists would be in the church above and suspected that the technician would run to the church. It was quite close and once there she would have the safety of the crowds.

She is getting away.
She must be stopped – she knows far too
much.
She must be rescinded....
The church passage?

****

In the darkness, Francesca imagined a sound far away... then nothing. Her senses heightened more exploring out into the a graveside quietness that threatened and enveloped around her; she almost tip-toed away, holding her breath and feeling with one hand, inch by inch along the wall with the other outstretched arm in front, probing nervously the complete darkness.

Downwards the passage descended. Francesca could feel the change, the temperature dropping colder the deeper she went. Down and round the passageway it led travelling in a slow and steady decline. She had not dared reach into her tool-case, which she had still strapped onto her shoulder. It contained her own headlamp and a few other tools — the light would have been welcome, but she was afraid of revealing her whereabouts. *How long have I been down here?* It might have been ten minutes or ten hours... time had become an illusion to the girl.

Francesca's progress slowed as she scraped and banged her hands and fingers again and again off the walls, which seemed to have become rougher to the touch. She occasionally toppled to her side, her arms flailing about like a mad windmill. Then an opening would suddenly present itself, and she would move on. Progress became dangerous as she allowed herself more and more to realise that she had no idea where she was... or how to get back!

Uncannily she intuitively gauged the ceiling's change in height. Occasionally the ceiling became so low that she might have hit her head if it wasn't protected by her outstretched arms. Her mouth was dry as a stick and felt sore all over. Francesca needed water... She was alone, and lost.

The wall in front of her disappeared, and the girl realized then that she was standing on a precipice of some kind that opened into a wide, black void.

The girl stopped, peering blindly over the edge. There seemed to be a step or ledge directly below her. Edging forward, bit by bit, she almost lost her balance on the first large step!

'Oh, fuck! What the hell is...?' she exclaimed out loud before taking another step. 'It's a step... a fucking step! There must be more… I'd better be very careful here, or I'll break my neck!' her voice fading quickly into the darkness like water in sand.

The wall then came into her sonar like senses and then felt its closeness and comfort of touch once again on her right so began to feeling her way down, one step at a time.

It felt worse than being on a tight rope with a blindfold — she did not surrender to her strong feelings of vertigo struggling to maintain her fragile balance.

Step by step, she precariously descended, steadily down thirty or more large, smooth, stone steps. Her blood-stained hands on the wall helped her keep her steady. Then, suddenly, the wall disappeared!

She fell forward and off the step and away into a chasm on her right! Panic was complete in her mind.

'Aagh!' she shouted out with anguish, anticipating a broken bone or worse.... She unexpectedly landed... on the last step!

'Shit! Shit! I don't believe it!' Francesca stood up, feeling more surprised than hurt. Luckily there was no damage. 'Whatever the fuck is coming next?' she cursed for more courage. Standing up, Francesca staggered a little in anguish—she stumbled onto a shorter stone wall about waist height and began quickly probing the top surface like a blind person without a stick with her lacerated hands, thinking that it was like the flat surface of a balcony.

Fumbling fingers moved carefully across the short flat surface which felt cold and frosty, surprisingly touching something different upon it, something round and smooth. It was not stone.

What is this? Then suddenly realising what it was screaming quietly when her fingers inserted into an empty, smooth eye socket, lower jaw bone and broken teeth—it was a skull!

She shrieked even louder this time, her anguish all too much! Instinctively, the systems administrator jumped backwards, away from her instant revulsion, and hit her head on the opposite wall.

Its hard impact made Francesca feel too dizzy to stand, forcing her to sit on the cold floor, terrified and trembling. Swallowing a groan of defeat Francesca breathed heavy with exhaustion against the low wall.

The girl began to sob a little with fatigue and shock, and then hope filled her as she suddenly remembered her mother's kind face as she caressed Francesca's forehead long time ago, softly saying kind words to her. Francesca's mother was always in her mind. She had died a long time ago, when Francesca was very young. The darkness mixed and blended inside her rattled mind and her shadowy surroundings seemed to smother her when everything swirled around inside her throbbing head and then went black

****

The young man sat waiting with eager anticipation, sitting alone on a tall seat at an intimate round table by the large window, drinking a small café espresso. Ciriaco was early. It was a quality coffee of that brisk type and snappy taste that made the hot liquid so refreshing.

Where is Francesca? She is late... a woman's prerogative, his pleasure of this new romance excited him. The young man's view, however, was somewhat restricted by where he was sitting— he stared out the window through the large brown italic swipes of the 'D' in **"s'izzurbbaD effaC"**.

Where was his beautiful colleague? Ciriaco felt like a school boy again as he gazed onto the street towards Ponte St. Angelo bridge; next to the River Tiber. Doubt began to creep into his mind—would she looking out the window unsure?

The Café was just outside the Vatican City and his date was still nowhere in sight! The brown, circular stone structure of Castel San Angelo stood in the distance. Ciriaco watched the familiar light-coloured clothes of

the castle's many tourists as they meandered
around aimlessly. The road outside was
cobbled and led back through Borgo Santo
Spirito, onwards to the Vatican and then further
on through tall lush herbaceous trees lining the
streets to the city.

A family came laughing across the street
opposite, a girl about fourteen and a boy of
thirteen, with their mother and father close by.
It was early evening, although the dark had
come early tonight. Ciriaco turned his head
around to the sound of the café steamer.

HISSsssss.

Burble.

Shhhhhhhh, shhhhhhh....

The smell of fresh coffee was strong and
aromatic. The attractive Barista behind the bar
caught his attention.

'Would you like another espresso,
Signore?' she asked with a friendly grin.

'*Si, grazie*. The last one was delicious.'
Ciriaco responded, looking a little lost.

'*Si*, it is,' she agreed. 'Did you know
Signore that if any of the stages from the bean,
grind, tamp, and pour is not perfect, then the
espresso will not be correct?' she replied,

teasing him a little with her judgment and skill. She had been trained by the Maestro himself; the Barista was used to making the perfect espresso every time!   She spoke in a young and lively melodic voice.

'The sharp quality characteristic of high-grown coffee is tasted mainly at the tip of the tongue, is it not?' Ciriaco offered in kind.

'I'm impressed, Signore, you obviously know your soft coffee bean.' They both laughed loudly.

The attractive girl had naturally shiny short black hair that she tied back in a bow. She smiled at him softly and moved her slim body with graceful agility around the bar.

I don't believe it, I was so charming earlier with Francesca, Ciriaco moped a little. Then, coming back to reality, he realized that it was 7:50PM, and almost an hour past when Francesca had agreed to their rendezvous. He could not believe it, she had stood him up! He really, really liked her....

She would be trouble, Ciriaco knew it. He was a professional, and he knew better than to mix work with pleasure. The fiasco was certain to compromise his position at work.

However, as much as he wished to be relieved at her no-show, the young man's mood was becoming gloomy at his missed opportunity.

Si! *She was going to be big trouble, all right!* Ciriaco stood up, smiling at the Barista. *I thought she would come, pity. She seemed keen enough to meet with me... she must be too good a catch to be true. Why is she not here?*

'Your girlfriend is late Signore?' the Barista prompted 'I hope you don't mind me being so inquisitive, I could not help but see you looking far out and over to the Tiber. I am sure there is a good reason for her not being here.' The pretty young girl smiled at him as she secretly wooed the handsome young man for herself. She smiled softly at him with a hint of... *was it innocent wickedness? He knew that expression....*

The girl lifted the empty coffee cup from his round table and placed it on her tray, replacing the empty with a fresh one as Ciriaco looked up at her.

'Would you like a piece of cake or, anything else?' Her body held the suggestion of warmer delights as she handed him the menu.

Ciriaco smiled, knowing that she would be much more pleasurable than the delightful coffee. The light yellow menu was covered with wine-coloured Palatino fonts displaying a mature menu with all-day breakfast. The café sponsor was displayed at the bottom left with a red wine-coloured *VSS logo*.

'What is your name?' Ciriaco asked as his pulse quickened.

'Jagbir. I am delighted you asked.' and giggled a little.

'Mmm, the Panini looks good.' He smiled. *She is fun,* thought Ciriaco.

'I recommend the spicy Panini, Signore,' she winked, suggesting yet other hot delights not on the menu. She served a good cup of coffee, but not the best. The best was yet to come.

'No, no thank you, no Panini.' Both of them laughed a little, teasing each other. The pretty Barista eyed him passionately as she moved back to the bar, rubbing a glass with her cloth. Sounds of light music could be heard drifting from the other side of the café. It was Luigi Boccherini's famous minuet, from his String Quintet in E major.

A few other clients were laughing lightly inside Café Dabbruzzi's, all tasting the culinary treats of their exceptional menu. Good hearted banter and friendly conversation echoed from a small group of women and men drinking wine and eating fresh Panini bread sandwiches. The Maestro of Dabbruzzi's was chatting genially with his patrons. A couple gazed at each other, a mature lady played with a tall, slim glass. Cappuccino frothing at the top, the woman stirred her glass slowly with her long spoon, almost with orgasmic delight and then sipped it down slowly, looking deeply into the eyes of her husband. Their romance was still real, running still deeper than the deepest ocean.

Ciriaco could only imagine such devotion and passion with... there she was again, Francesca. Her face, the girl seemed to be haunting his mind.

Reinforcing thoughts of self-preservation, something warned him not to get involved with her. But unknown to him, he was not in control any longer. *Where is she*? His thoughts were undecided: his heart or his passion? There was the Barista, what about her infatuation? In the small café, Ciriaco was changing from boy to man. He stood with a sigh.

'Are you leaving, Signore?' she said, sounding disappointed. 'Can I offer you anything else?'

'Sadly, I must go,' he gently declined. 'Thanks for the company and the coffee.' The man had made his choice.

****

A soft voice spoke quietly in the darkness. "Francesca, my dearest daughter, it is time to rise and get up! Come on, dear, come and see the new-born foals running in the field. Please waken, my dear, my daughter. Please wake up... please wake up... please wake up." It was her mother's voice, speaking to her in a dream....

Francesca finally sat up, groaning as she held her head. *Did I fall asleep?* She quizzed her own sanity, trying to clear her mind. Had she imagined hearing her mother's dissipating voice, convinced of still hearing it echo further away and drifting further into the still darkness? The void surrounded her.

The woman's mind became clear and sharp again. Bodily she was exhausted, however. Francesca thought that the possibility of the killer following her was very slim. It was too easy to get lost in this God forsaken place. For the first time, she wondered if maybe she had a chance.

If the killer was here, right now, I would be dead already. Her mind warped into a familiar spiral.

Why the hell am I being hunted, and why is Massimo dead? Is it because of the secret computer back there? Have we stumbled onto something else? Something to do with Michaelangelo...? He warned me! Bloody hell, the others must also be in danger! Shit, I need some light if I'm going to survive this fucking place and live to warn them!

Francesca opened her technician's side bag, which was strapped to her shoulders. *Let's get this thing on*, Francesca thought as she positioned the strap of her headlamp onto her forehead and switched on the light.

The lamp lit up and blared like a beacon; the piercing brightness hurt her eyes! Panning her headlamp left to right and then up and down, Francesca's hopes for water were dashed. The systems administrator could not help but note the enormity of this place – it was a vast dumping ground... for the dead!

****

The Catacomb walls were of a dirty yellow colour with algae encrusting the internal grey cut stone Loculi. Many rectangular holes were cut into a system of galleries, sliced out into rows of rectangular niches at even and regular points alongside and above her. Macabre was the site, and organised like a stack of death crates – one stone row upon the other.

These stone containments were known as a "Loculi", and each held the bones of the dead. All of these dead holes had skeletons hidden inside, away from direct view – the bones lay in their last resting place. Francesca's face was one of sheer horror and complete revulsion at this underground cemetery. Inside the Loculi were other, unnamed things that the girl could not see – there was much, much more hiding inside these dark resting places....

Oil lamps and small vases containing perfumes would often be placed beside these open tombs, to hide the evil and rotting odour within. It smelled... as if this place was still being used. That would account for the reek earlier in the Catacombs — it was strongest here. She had found the source!

Unknown to Francesca, she had entered The Dormitory of the Dead!

'What time is it? Where the hell *am I?'* she asked, almost as if expecting someone to answer her. And why not — after all, she had plenty of company!

Looking at her gold wristwatch, she saw that it was 7:30 P.M. *I've been down here for hours!* Then she realised.... *My God, the second hand isn't moving!*

Francesca was sore all over, but at least her cheek had stopped bleeding. 'Steady girl, try to keep cool,' she reassured herself while looking back up the way she had come.   She tried to bottle her growing fears and observed the stairs she had nearly toppled down. The stairs rose up high and high into the darkness. The place was freezing.

Taking a screwdriver out of her tool case, Francesca scraped and grooved a letter "F" into the right side of the frosted Loculi wall, in order to prevent her from going round in circles. The tiny scraping noises resonated eerily up to the high arched ceiling. She was being listened to....

'My God, there must be hundreds if not thousands of dead people down here! I cannot go back. *This is my only way out!*'

The girl looked upwards and around submissively, then, turning to the way ahead and trying not to look too closely at the Loculi that enclosed her on either side, Francesca slowly walked through the long dormitory. She progressed further and further into the cruel dwelling place without an end in sight. Eyeless sockets watched the girl with all the patience of eternity....

Francesca's pace quickened along the stone passage, her lungs breathing fast in the cold, rotten air, she seemed to be losing it! Then a muffled sound of a click or a stick hitting another stick sounded in the echoing cavern.

'What was that? Shit, its bloody cold down here.' Francesca pulled her shoulders together automatically as another shiver travelled up her spine. She watched as her

cold breath escaped into the still air and drifted
for a moment. 'What was that sound?' she
asked herself again, talking in order to keep her
sanity.

She heard nothing further, not even the
popping or muffled slapping noise of the
killer's Silencer. That would have been easier
to explain. The cold intensified as Francesca
continued through the surrounding dead.

On all surfaces of the narrow dormitory,
floor and walls, a heavy frost had made
progress more precarious. It was unnatural.
The floor glittered and glinted with the many
particles of ice as her headlamp beam crossed
over it. An increasing frost coated every
surface — it was forming more thickly every
moment that passed. More and more white
crystals expanded across the void as she
continued further and deeper into that ghostly
gallery.

Her hands were, by now, freezing, as
was her face. Everything felt icy cold from
head to toe. Francesca moved as quickly as
possible. Her thin garments were no
protection, her movement should have created

some heat... she was shivering, but it was not enough.

****

The killer reached the top of the stone stairs. Most annoyed at taking the wrong bend, she had backtracked swiftly. The hunt was now over for this one.

Through her state-of-the-art AN/PVS-9N scope and night vision gun sight with its short scope, darkness was converted into day view; with the improved sensor technology, other surrounding effects were becoming obvious as well. Multiple motions could be detected all around the area, and something else was being picked up by the low frequency sound sensor.

This specialised assassin's tool was located on the barrel of the killer's gun and could see the girl perfectly, ignoring the other unexplained interferences and strange noises. There was unfinished business to take care of, and the systems administrator's luminous image was sharp and clear as she came quickly towards her assailant, walking back towards the stairs.

To the naked eye, the girl's figure appeared small and distant and completely white in colour, she was shivering and encrusted by a light frost that grew all over her body. The killer was waiting. Standing elevated overhead and magnifying the night scope, the executioner saw Francesca in a blue luminosity, and pulled the girl's image tight.

She must be lost. This is going to be easy, after all! The environment must be causing the damn interference... it won't matter because the idiot is nearly at the end of the corridor. It'll be a one shot kill. The assailant readied, but then....

What's she doing now? Looking at something... on the side of the wall? Rescind her now she said to herself, *and I can get out of this stinking place....*

Suddenly the girl below slipped on the ground, which was covered in ice and frost.

Tricky, she slipped... what's caught her attention? Wondered the killer?

The killer seemed more curious than deadly as she observed the technician's sliding reappearance. Other signals were strong, but the killer ignored the major warnings and vibrations all around her. There were also sounds inaudible to the human ear, waves that showed up as luminous patterns of moving hashed greens and yellows. These waves were instantly converted by the smart electronics into a shifting and shaky movement within the killer's scope controller unit.

The equipment sensed movement everywhere, too much for it to process. The uneven motions were closing in from high above where the killer stood. Shapes were undefined, interfering and difficult to focus on. It was impossible to target the girl. By this time, the whole corridor was by now completely covered in thick frost.

That is a massive movement! The assassin was confused and cold. *Some kind of shifty motion is occurring everywhere,* swallowing a groan. *It must be a malfunction of my scope in this crap temperature.*

Looking around suspiciously, lifting her eyes from the scope for a moment, the killer observed only darkness and the odd clicking sounds above. The killer raised the scope again to see the image of the girl below, who appeared to be surrounded by a new and bizarre, luminous phenomenon. The assassin attempted to refocus on the technician.

On target, the prey was again in the crosshairs. Taking careful aim and holding a deep breath, the killer tightened her finger on the trigger. The hunt for the girl was over... *say goodbye!*

****

Frost in Rome? Not usually if ever at this time of year, although perhaps in January or February...but never underneath the city! This is fucking crazy....

Francesca attempted to make sense of her white and icy surroundings. Frost coated the yellow algae that grew on the walls.   She had travelled maybe half a mile, she was not sure; the journey seemed to go on and on...

Is that the end of the corridor over there, in the distance?   Si! Francesca began to run, so excited that she slipped and slid in her desperation to leave. She nearly toppled and fell, but somehow managed to keep her balance.

Getting closer now… Francesca could see the high steep steps ahead growing near. *It must be the other end. Great!* Relieved, the girl began to march more quickly, slipping more as she came closer and closer to the stairs. Unexpectedly, her keen eyes caught something—it was a mark….

A spot on the left wall as she walked closer, she saw that someone had scraped a letter familiar to the one she had made. Closer she saw it was the letter "F"—it was her sign!

This mark was on the opposite side of the staircase, although identical in shape and size. That did not make sense—confused; she had scraped hers on the right!

Francesca's eyes were drawn only a moment from her direction of travel and then she violently slipped on the ice! She fell so hard that it seemed like she was being pushed backwards by a giant bully. The girl felt herself flying bodily through the air coming down heavily. Her lamp flew off her head on impact, sliding along the icy stone ground! Everything went black once more....

****

Frantically, Francesca groped around in the darkness for her headlamp, in fear for her life. She could not believe her ill fortune. She was lost, perhaps concussive and someone wanted to kill her! Francesca scrambled on all fours, reaching out one way and then the next in a crazy circle, searching for her light. Frantically, she remembered the gasoline fuel lighter she had collected from Michaelangelo's desk. She flicked the flint to fuel with a grating noise and the lighter sparked to life. Not far away in the shimmering dimness lay her torch. *Got it!*

Thank God, the second bulb works! Directing her beam to the wall to confirm what she saw earlier, Francesca's eyes widened. It was true!

I was here earlier – my sign, my letter "F"! How could I have ended up back here? I have not turned around or gone around in circles and I have kept my view mainly ahead... how can I possibly have gone the wrong way? Who...what is that whispering? Am I going crazy?

Still on the cold ground, Francesca hysterically began to question her own sanity. Something gripped her inside—an unexplained trepidation came upon her as her internal alarm bells began ringing noisily inside her head!

Get up, get up, GET UP! A deep fear gripped the girl's mind and body. In her shock, something stirred—her stubborn willpower, she would not to give up. Francesca pushed herself wearily upwards from the floor. With sheer grit, she checked her direction and dug into her deeper self she about turned and headed back the way she had come. FAST!!!

Dazed Francesca heard unexplained whispering all around her, they frightened Francesca. Her eyes bulged in suppressed terror at clicking noises came from dark places she could not see into as she walked.

An area of flesh just below her neck grew hot until it was burning her. At first unaware of this unknown heat, due to her panic, Francesca soon felt the heat of this pain coming from her charmed necklace but could do nothing about it. She ran and limped,

frantically traversing back through the long
Dormitory of the Dead.

****

They were now awake and among the
lying dead; they sensed her fear... and the girl
was moving at a fast pace. Ghostly
whisperings were floating in the icy darkness
fuelling her quickening steps, Francesca
fearfully sliding through the icy darkness.
Hidden somewhere in the lofty heights above
her, disturbing noises, lots of them, uncanny
sounds like the drums of dry bones continually
knocking together, they kept on following her
with an increasing fervour. It was as if… the
dead were chasing her from one dark place to
the next! They waited, hidden for the moment.
Bile rising in her stomach, Francesca's heart
banging hard, when without thinking her
Olympic dash for freedom began!
'Aaaaaaagh!' Screaming loudly and
uncontrollably, her mind dislocated from all
logic, the girl running blindly and slipping all
the way, but what could she do against skeletal
athletes! Her nerves shredded and no wonder,

because, this place would test even the bravest of spirits.

It was observation, they existed among the lying dead, sensing her fear... *'The Abaddon Clerics'* detecting her every move. All hooded and about the size of dwarves, ancient and awful, *curse their rotten souls.*

Cursed things from another world.

Cursed to be here and cursed in an unending search.

Cursed to do their masters bidding and cursed to find the lost *Links to God.* Their lord and master cursed their servitude. A great and evil lord, a superbeing that controlled them from another dimension in spacetime.

Something about this one is different... they considered blackly, not really wanting her to pass through but because of the prophecy and her charm they had to allow it, *the time is not right for this one,* the unliving clerics watched, brooding over her, speaking in strange gruff evil tongues among the breathing of the dead...

'Allow her passage.' One said coldly.

'Then let us encourage her to leave this place...' another gnarled quickly.

'The other human, will not pass so easily.' Came a thorny tone rasping from another Cleric with gluttony in its mind as they allowed Francesca to continue.

'Yes, the other… *will stay.*' A deep and wicked voice joined the whispered breathing of the dead as its long razor-sharp tongue licked around dry bones.

****

About half way along the towering Loculi, without any indication, the dormitory suddenly opened up to display additional and adjoining dormitories to either side. Francesca looked around, using the powerful beam to light up the distance. Presented by high vertical and horizontal stone structures, these vast corridors were higher and deeper than the one in which she stood. The site was... breath-taking! It was a truly macabre spectacle to behold. In the surrounding darkness, the whispering continued and Francesca pretended to ignore it.

The blackness seemed to get blacker – to close in around her. Her view was diminishing rapidly, almost as if the headlamp was losing power. What would she do, without her light amidst all these bones?

'Do not look down there, Francesca! Don't look anymore! Keep walking! Please God help me!' Francesca pleaded to God in utter despair, completely terrified. She was lost and knew that she needed all the help she could get.

The darkness was heavy and the corridor was long, so long. Francesca began to slow down her pace and eventually ground to a halt. The cold was so intense that crystals were thickening on top of her body as she moved less and less. Far away, the stairs again came into her cold beam of light. It was her way out!

The frost permeated into every muscle and sinew. Francesca walked and slipped towards the end of the dormitory, her mind slowing in pace along with her limbs, although she still had enough wit to check for her markings. Survival was instinctive — another mistake would prove fatal.

No sign! This is the way, the right way! Francesca stumbled onto the first three or four steps, feeling weary and exhausted, her body completely frozen. Her plight was desperate and this would have been the finish for most people, but somehow Francesca was given one final boost.

'Come on girl, move it! Come on, get up! Lift yourself now! Up!' She screamed defying failure as a surge of adrenaline instantly injecting throughout her body.

Her heart began pumping strongly enough... and Francesca started crawling up the stairs two and three at a time. Eventually Francesca reached the top.   She had made it!

Her teeth chattering uncontrollably, her body also shaking. Completely frozen, covered totally with white frost Francesca's hair stiff with ice, her face and eyebrows covered in crystals - she came to rest, lying on the cold floor, resembling more like a thin snowman on a white field. The girl's pallor gone, she lay down on top of the frosty hall, her marrow frozen solid. Francesca fell asleep, her body shattered from overuse.

As she lay, time passed. Eventually the frost began to melt from her shoulders and hair, the temperature rising a little; her cold white skin and blue complexion thawed, and a blush started to flow once more in her cheeks as she remained still, slouched and unconscious to the sound of someone screaming from below. Agent Schiavone's.

****

Francesca slowly became aware of her body lying there in the darkness — some light appeared to shine in this solitary place. Aware first of her toes and then her fingers, she imagined in her mind a golden colour flooding around her body. Her bruised and battered self, she began to move bit by bit, wincing at sore muscles.

'Ooch, Ooooh,' the girl groaned long and hard, raising her head a little. Her clothes were wet with melted frost. The corridor was still and silent. The light from her headlamp was still shining, shining the way ahead, down the hall and into a smaller passageway. The temperature was cold, although not as extreme as before. Slowly, Francesca raised herself up to a kneeling position and, with a great effort, stood.

'I must look a right state. What a trivial thing to think about at this moment — at least I don't have hypothermia! Ooooch...my body is killing me.' Holding her head, her face felt pained, her bloodied knees scratched and skinned from falling on the ice. She must be black and blue all over, but at least she was still alive!

The reality of her immediate danger began to return, or was it even real? Real or unreal, she had to deal with it. Somehow, she had gotten lost in the Catacombs....

Francesca refused to look backwards to the void below the stairs — it was quiet and brooding down there, imbued with a feeling of a hidden menace. Something lurked down there in the darkness, not human.

Then, from the frozen depths, came the sound of a blood-gurgling subterranean scream! It echoed up rudely from below and was followed by another resounding scream of sheer terror. *Is that Human?* She wondered. The sound died instantly, and there was again silence....

Shit, what the fuck was that? Francesca's mind jolted in fright, decided she was not staying long enough to find out. *A woman's scream, that's what it sounded like! I am losing my mind?*

Francesca jumped up and sprinted as fast and as far from those sounds as she could. Further she fled into the dark catacomb, scanning left and right as the tunnel began to twist again on a flat plane. Just to get away from the cavern of bones seemed like the right thing to do.

Francesca soon became aware that her battery power would not last forever — the beam of light was beginning to yellow, losing its sharpness.

Bloody great, that's all I need. It's going to be really bad for me if I don't get out of here soon. Although her initial stiffness was gone, she felt desperate and very thirsty. Francesca prayed for help.

I hope I am not going to be the next skeleton down here! Looking ahead, Francesca found another fork in the passage. Again, it was a fifty-fifty choice.

Shit, which way! Which way, left or right? I went left the last time and ended up here...I know that this is a different place, so I'll take the other fork this time and hope that it's right.

Francesca knew that a wrong decision here would mean the end of her lamp and her life! Hearing her laboured breathing and looking despairingly in both directions into each dark passage, she tried desperately to make the right decision.

There was a greater urgency than even the darkness, though. Instinctively, the girl knew that something would follow her. This thing was not over yet. If she did not keep going, whatever that awful sound was would find her. It was not human.

Unknown to Francesca, people went about their businesses as usual far above on the city streets, unaware of the girl's battle for survival way down in the depths beneath their feet.

Francesca stumbled or was pulled towards her right side as the weak light beam struck something darker farther down that right hand tunnel, it appeared to be a darker place, or was it... a different surface?

Whatever it was that she saw, it did not seem to be like the wall of solid rock that spread before her down that subterranean passageway. It appeared to have a strange effect on the light. The beam could not penetrate this substance! It was difficult for Francesca to even establish just how close the substance really was. *Is that a mist?* The substance appeared to be constantly shifting its shape, making the light beam alter the shade and depth of the outlandish surface. With no definite pattern or edge, there seemed to be a heavy, ominous atmosphere that exuded from the place.

Francesca began to move cautiously further in the passage as she descended downwards into this right-hand divergence. To her, it still seemed like the correct way to go.

Unaware, the girl was being attracted by a type of invisible force—it was a pull or magnetic attraction within her own mind. She then became aware of a pungent odour that caught the tip of her nose. Alarm bells sounded in her mind—a warning! Francesca felt quite sick—this was all wrong! *No, this is not the way to go!!!*

Francesca struggled with herself. The malevolent blackness might have been one foot or ten feet distant, and its slick, thin protrusions, its wispy tentacles, became visible to her as some nearly broke away from that outlandish opaque surface. The substance had changed its wispy properties and then quickly stretched out fully, like a thin, light cloud being blown out by the wind, its strings whipped around, trying to catch her with its light tentacles.

Francesca could not see from where she stood that inside the mist were tiny capillary-like needles with cruel, curved barbs in this gruesome mist.

Beware, child, a soft voice within her head spoke. It was her Grandma's voice, a warning from the grave....

Francesca's fatal march instantly stopped, and she became anchored to the floor with fear, struggling so hard that she almost fell forward! The bottom of her neck had begun to feel hot again. She heard Grandma's voice again in her mind.

It is something evil, child, great evil is down there! Francesca's eyes were completely fixed in terror at the sight of the undulating darkness directly in front of her. The girl's eyes stared at the wriggling dark mass. Her will was strong, and her cross charm burned as she began to slowly walk backwards, a bit at a time, slowly and gradually willing herself away. She had come without knowing and backed out, still transfixed, staring into the horror as many thin, evil fingers of long tentacles protruded out and up the passage, gradually moving further towards her...trying to touch her!

Go back, move, get away, run, do anything...MOVE! Francesca's mind told her to run, but her body could not—she wanted to get away. Terrified, Francesca again stopped. The girl could not move she was so frozen with fear!

Each second seemed like an hour as her cross burned more hotly. Her skin seemed to burn near her neck, where her cross touched the skin. The cross had been given to her by her Grandma. Small, penetrating coloured rays of light shone out of the various inset precious stones that were fixed into the golden metal; the rubies blazed red as laser-white light shone brightly from the diamonds inset on the left and right of the horizontal.

The stones shone unbelievably brightly, and yet Francesca was unaware of the miracle because of her numbed mind and her terror. With a slow half-pace step backwards, she moved again, spurred on by the heat on her neck. It was a holy power, divine protection....

She took another small step and then another; the outlandish mist was still gaining on her — she had not got far enough away, and now it was only a metre from her!

Inside those tentacles were thin, white and dark-blue veins! The narrow long tubes were never still, changing and convoluting all the time, organised into something like spaghetti in constant motion, wriggling wildly around inside the indefinite and evil composition.

Curving this way and that, the substance was in view for a moment and then out of sight the next, forced along with some evil, fluidic substance enclosed within its tubules and being pumped from nowhere in particular. The protrusions had small, deadly little barbs on the ends that seemed to be evident not only on the surface but inside the putrefied fluid, as well. The monster with its evil hooks wanted to grip and tear at her...tear her apart!

Francesca took another half pace backward...and then a pace or two more. Finally, she was again moving backwards at a rapid pace, with her eyes still fixed wide in terror as the blackness continued to follow!

Her stomach felt filled with sickly butterflies and, near retching, she eventually reached the junction. Unexpectedly, an invisible force let her go and she was suddenly able to run. The girl ran in great haste away up the other subterranean passage. She had escaped the creature's cruel barbs! The dark cloud pulled itself instantly back down the black passageway to where it was first seen and waited again. Prey came seldom, but the creature could wait...

Francesca's clothes soaked in dirty sweat and terror, speaking out her anguish to herself as she jogged quickly upwards.

'What is that fucking black stuff? I have turned into a raving lunatic! It can't be anything else — this place is driving me mad, it must be a hallucination.'

She then realised that maybe she had been drugged, at some point... her nightmare was not over.

Running along the next dark passageway, for how long she did not know. The endless catacombs seemed fairly level in this area; the light from her headlamp still had strength enough to reflect off the walls of the pale stone passage.

The cross that she wore had, by this time, dimmed to nothing. Had she really imagined it all? Francesca couldn't have imagined the pain at the base of her throat where the cross lay touching her soft skin—the area it was burned and blistered... sure to leave a brand.

Francesca became more aware of her dingy surroundings as she fingered her cross and finally noticed that there seemed to be something different up ahead, coming into her view. It was thin and vertically laid, with horizontal lines going up the wall. The girl slowed as she approached.

'It is a ladder! A bloody ladder! Oh my God, it's a way out!' she almost cried. Francesca wept with utter relief. She had been given yet another chance! It was the first sign she'd had of modern civilisation in hours, maybe days.

The iron ladder appeared secure and firmly attached to the wall by long metal bolts from the bottom rungs that were driven into the stone, although the ladder stuck out a little from the wall. The metal rungs rose upwards, losing themselves in a hole cut through the ceiling. The hole was about four or five metres wide and would take her out and above the catacombs!

Francesca strained her neck backwards and shined her headlamp upwards; staring as far as the beam would go.... It fell flat before she could see the exit. Francesca began to climb and could only guess where it would lead to, but as far as she was concerned, up was good. She resembled a worn miner as her head peeked through the large black aperture above the catacomb ceiling. There was nothing else for it. Francesca immediately ascended the chimney-like structure, up and into the black hole, leaving the subterranean catacombs below.... *Why is this place here?* She wondered. *I don't care...thank God it's here. I've found a way out!*

****

CHAPTER VIII

DEATH IN DARK PLACES

⊐⊐⊐⟩⊓ ⌐⊡ ⊐⊐⌐⌐ ⁊⌊⊐⌊ ⊐∨

Hand over hand, Francesca began her long climb. It was going to be hard one and God only knew where she would end up! One rung at a time, she was morbidly careful to keep at least three limbs in contact with the ladder at all times. Her headlight would not last much longer, and Francesca was conscious that precious time was passing as its luminosity was depleted on the cool façade. A waning, dull yellow orange glow washed over the inside of the smooth circular stone shaft. Francesca maintained her long climb without rest. She was just about all in, but somehow her body kept going. So desperate she had become to live that the thought of eventual escape from the catacombs had given her fantastic strength. Yet in time her body weakened and her climb slowed down to a crawl. Francesca knew that she must be already quite high up the chimney-like structure — gauging her treacherous predicament, she began to panic a little. *What happens when the light goes out…?*

Certain that she'd left the killer far behind, Francesca sang to herself to sustain her shredded spirits. Her thoughts were abruptly broken by the image of the rude Englishman, Jonathan! Her mood instantly changed when she saw his arrogant image, a stuck-up look and smug smile. And that was enough!

Keep going, girl, keep going! she cheered herself on. Her anger gave her the boost she needed to keep on climbing.

Another twenty minutes into the climb, Francesca was resting more regularly and not daring to look down. After all, what would she look down for? There was nothing to see down there except the black hole below.

An uncanny feeling came over her during a resting period; she felt a bit like she was swimming in a great ocean, above the Mindanao Trench. So deep it was… and that thought was freaking her out, a spooky sensation of an unknown depth. More than that, a dread of unnamed dangers lurking inside the subterranean dungeons stirred up fearful emotions.

Looking up again, Francesca was surprised to see the top! Si! *The ceiling!* And not too far away, either. Francesca was excited to see her goal before her! It was already much closer, although the girl's thighs and calf muscles were aching severely. She ignored the screaming pain of her muscles in her forearms and legs. There was no going back — she had to go up...

'Oh!' she shouted in panic, as her foot began to slip. Her hands gripped firmly onto the two rungs of the ladder as both feet quickly disengaged from the rungs. It all happened so fast that Francesca had no time to think. She was at once fully stretched out, dangling by her arms and desperately scrambling to regain her feet. A few long seconds passed and, her heart racing, she somehow managed to pull herself up, hugging the ladder close to her chest as she regained her balance.

'Whooooophfff, *shit*. That was close!' Francesca blew a hard long sigh of relief... telling herself that the ceiling would still be there if she climbed slowly. It mocked her, only four metres away.

After regaining her breath, Francesca slowly scaled to the top and...and...well.... Nothing.

The systems administrator looked around in complete dismay. Gob smacked and totally taken aback, the girl mesmerized at her ill fortune. She began to hyperventilate as her breathing becoming more and more rapid and out of control. Her heart paced madly with dreaded excitement. She could not believe it—after all this, the ladder went nowhere? There was no exit? She had only found another dead end!

'Where the fuck is the way out? What the hell am I going to do now? This can't be happening. Gods help me!' she yelled at the ceiling, knowing that this climb had been her only hope. 'The last thing I want to do is go back down to that hell hole!' It was a horrible thought. Looking around in worry she clung with one hand to the rung and gazed around wildly, searching for escape. It was becoming harder to see—the light was nearly out! Things could not get any worse...and Francesca's spirit seemed broken and utterly demoralized. She had run out of ideas! There seemed to be no other way to go except down.

Twisting her body around, Francesca searched frantically above and to each side of her. Although the torch beam was ebbing by the minute, she refused to give up, gritting her mind vainly as she searched for escape. She looked up again in disbelief; had she come all this way for nothing? She strained her neck backwards to look for some secret exit, anything, *anything at all.*

'Shit,' she muttered, confirming that there was no way out and no escape. Her heart sank as low as it could possibly go. It was at this last dreadful moment that she lost her grip on the ladder, this time slipping off and away from the ladder for good. She plunged straight down, falling fast though the rushing blackness of the deep mine shaft.

Francesca gave out a last and loud scream as she fell. It was true! She was uncontrollably falling down the shaft.

'Eeaaghhhh!' she cried, picking up speed as she plummeted. Her body reflexively twisted in mid-air to a nearly horizontal position. Terrified, she stared downwards, watching her approaching fate coming at lightning speed! *What's that?* was her last thought....

THUMP! BANG!

In reality, only a split second had passed slipping... Her body struck something hard and somewhat resilient, violently knocking the breath out of her!

A loud, springy noise and vibrating sound could be heard as her body bounced like a ball, springing off a light and thin metal plank or gangway that appeared to be suspended straight across the chimney's diameter. This short platform was only about eight to ten metres from where she had fallen!

'Mmmph' she groaned as the air blasted out of her lungs. It was the last of her last breath puffing out wind her…

Hurt and in agony from her fall. Only a second had passed in this instant, her eyes wide and transfixed, focusing as much out of desperation than survival.

The girl's body bounced again above the gangplank and dropped back down like a rag doll onto the same flat metal structure. Instinctively grabbing out, Francesca continued to bounce up and out of control! Her mouth opened wide to take a deep breath. Contacting the tensile platform once more, she found herself partly hanging off again, and seized out in the dimness for her life!

Fate found Francesca once more dangling high above the inside the stone shaft! Her grip was putting immense strain on her spine, her legs moved freely and frantically in mid-air!

Pulling herself up took an immense strength and effort—lesser men would have faltered. She affectionately hugged the top of the metal surface, terrified of letting go! The girl's body weight still threatened to pull her down—her arms and sockets in agony, her shoulders screamed. Gravity was killing her!

The metal gangplank's surface was cold to the touch and had an odd, dented feeling about it, which helped her grip. Francesca, with one last effort, managed to lift her leg with a reserve of energy... digging deep into her soul, with a last surge of adrenalin pulled up.

'Aaaghgrrrr!' she screamed like a weight lifter. Both her arms and chest managed to get on top on the metal surface — she struggled up the rest of her body by raising one leg onto the surface of the platform and levering it. The girl rolled over and Francesca was up. It was a miracle!

Her battered body lay bruised and exhausted, her arms outstretched and wide and hanging over the precipice. Francesca could not move, lying almost crucified in the darkness as she was. She lay there for a long time, a very long time; time passed because it meant nothing inside that black hell! Still, there was light, the sharp beam from her headlamp. It still shone... enough....

Eventually the girl began to feel the force of her life flowing back to her limbs. Francesca's spirit stirred and gradual energy moved first through her toes, then her fingers and then her arms and she began looking around from side to side, taking an interest in her surroundings. There was a metal pipe or a safety barrier or railing directly above her. Luckily for Francesca she had missed it by inches. Striking the barrier with her full body weight at that speed would likely have broken her spine. Relieved realised how damn lucky she had been to be still alive!

Lifting her heavy arm held on to the barrier, pulled herself up until she was standing unsteadily on top of the platform. Balancing herself on the waist-height railing, Francesca let out another loud release of air as she with disbelief wondered where this platform led.

My God, it really is! A... a door? A door is...over there.... I climbed right past it, stupid! In her desire to escape and, given the darkness, it had been very easy for Francesca to miss this exit, especially in her state of metal degradation and physical exhaustion. Holding tightly onto the metal railing, she walked unsteadily, soon reaching the small square doorway, taking extra care in the dimness not to step off the platform by mistake and finish the job for sure!

Francesca recognised the painted door, made of metal — it was a standard-sized duct entry door. She had no idea where it would take her but felt strongly that anywhere would be better than here. Francesca turned the stiff lever and pulled it.

It won't move – it's ceased! She thought in horror. 'Open!' calling at the top of her voice. The door was proving too difficult to budge. Panic-stricken, the girl began frantically pulling and pushing at it until it reluctantly gave way. The girl stooped a little and did not hesitate; entered through and into another dark place. Utter relief washed over her cut face—at last she was out! The catacombs brooded far below her...

****

This new exploration, too, was pitch black, pitch black with a distant noise... the sound of a dull and muted hum, like an engine reverberating from her left. Looking towards this noise, she observed a light switch on the wall—what luck! In complete disbelief, the girl flipped the switch. A light turned on and she cheered for joy that she would soon be out of here.

Scanning the area several times, unsure where to go, Francesca noticed that the place was dust-laden, dirty and very enclosed—a straight, vertical grey wall appeared directly in front of her, straight up to about ten metres. Overhead was what looked like a steel platform. There was nothing to her right other than a dead end, a blank vertical stone wall. The corridor was only one or two metres wide, tight and very claustrophobic.

A channel led away to her left, to a corner close by where she was standing. The lighting was bad, as it was supplied by a single light bulb on the left wall just above the doorway. The bulb was protected with a heavy, transparent-ribbed plastic front facade, allowing only enough luminance to see her immediate vicinity.

Francesca turned ninety degrees at the stone corner and saw that the high vertical walls continued and extended upwards; ahead the dirty and dusty floor was covered in rubbish and many pieces of discarded junk. The strange humming noises were much louder here. Where in the city she really was, the girl could not guess. With the catacombs behind her, at least the girl rationalised that she must be closer to some place good!

She ran her bloodied fingers though her long hair, stuffy and very warm inside this place inside the innards of some strange building, Francesca shook her head in dismay at the total contrast to where she had been earlier.

The technician found herself staring at a myriad of metal pipes, large and small and on either side, all travelling horizontally and vertically up and along the stone walls. To her right, red painted pipes were boiling hot to the touch; on her left, they were black and cold. All were travelling along in parallel and in pairs. There was no other way to go, so the girl followed the trail among them, hoping it would lead her to safety.

Francesca walked only two hundred metres before she came to a dead end. Here, the humming noise was much louder. The sounds were more distinctive at this end.

'Ah! A ladder!', Francesca said excitedly. This would give her access to the level above, which would certainly bring her closer to the outside world she knew and loved. Francesca switched on another light on the wall, and the level above instantly lit brightly!

BANG! She jumped. *What was that?* It was only the electricity kicking into action from somewhere, maybe a "trip switch" or something like that, banging on its power. As electricity fed the lights above, their brilliance flooded down!

A split second later came another loud noise, which boomed from behind her. Francesca jumped again. The loud echo, now silent, had come from... back where she had been only minutes before?

Shit, what was that noise? What have I done? The girl tried to make common sense out of rising primal fear. *There is nothing wrong with the switch to cause a sound like that – the noise came from the catacombs below.*

Her nerves on a knife edge she strained all her senses again to listen... the girl had not expected any noise, not any bang at all and especially not from where she had recently emerged! With bated breath she remained waiting, for that noise *had been* different; it was not electrical and more like a door, closing

There must be a generator somewhere, which means that someone comes in here, Francesca reasoned. *It's not part of the catacombs. Maybe I'm being… followed! Christ I must get out of here!*

Francesca tried to hold her composure together despite her true feelings of impending horror.

The bang had left quite a distinctive echo resonating around the large structure, which she had picked up above the regular humming of electrical generators and distribution boxes and crazy water pipes. Dismissing this intrusion to the back of her mind, yet all she wanted to do was run away — to just get out!

The environment was unpleasant and extremely warm inside the man-made structure. Like a sauna, it became gradually worse as she moved up from level to level. Now Francesca was presented by another complex set of pipework left, right and above her. She was completely surrounded in metalwork. The platform walkway ahead was again made of a dull, silver-welded metal that had a flexible trampoline-like movement about it and an unusual, slightly raised pattern of points providing extra traction.

Francesca followed the path, which ran parallel as expected the length of the passage underneath and, although it seemed safe enough, her footsteps made a light dull clanking noise with each step. Predictably,

Francesca came to another dead end further along and yet another ladder to ascend. Climbing up and finding another light switch at the top, she flicked it on. There was no bang this time, and the light was duller, illuminating a scene of much more twisted architecture and poorly lagged pipes of all shapes and sizes. There seemed to be plenty of shadowy hiding places among the twisted metal. Continuing along, in the dimness and without any warning, she stumbled....

'Shit! My God, where did that come from?' the girl was taken completely by surprise by the disruption, and she stopped immediately. Taking extra care, Francesca slowly swept her foot across a square hole in the platform.

It appeared to be a small area and roughly cut out from the floor. The hole was a hidden danger! It had probably been made some time ago as a "through pipe", cut out by some engineer and then abandoned. Whoever had done it had been negligent, leaving it open like this! Anyone's leg could easily fall through, breaking it a bone or cutting an ankle and leg into shreds with its vicious ragged edges!

Not losing much time, the girl passed another fuse box on the wall and then, like before, she began to climb up to another level. *This is a big building,* she realized. She could be anywhere in the Vatican City. *How much further is there to go?*

Stuck inside the guts of this building, the hot environment became increasingly noisy. More gurgling noises and the sound of something new, something massive and heavy and in motion caught her attention. A loud rushing sound or a sliding away noise, up and down it went... ascending quickly upwards behind the wall and beyond, high above her current position, and then back down somewhere underneath.

Pipes surrounded her, hot and cold, large and small, in diameters of all colours; this place was just a total burrow.

Who is looking after this shit place? No doubt the Estates Department. She passed a stone brick ledge in the wall, where some old light bulbs were sitting on their own, completely covered with the dirt and grime of years.

Nobody has been down here for quite some time, surmised the technician, believing herself to be on a fourth level somewhere. Her mind was also keeping a keen eye on the increasing number of precarious and ragged metal holes in the floor that weakened the walkway!

The girl sensed more danger than she could see through one of the holes in the floor, however — upwards about two floors, she spotted a familiar sight. It was that of the communications cable runs that extended the Vatican data network throughout the old city; they stretched up through mid-air, hanging between floor levels!

Relief came over her face and Francesca's heart immediately lifted, she knew that it would be only just a question of time, and soon she would escape this filthy place. Then it came again... that periodic roar and sudden rush from somewhere behind the solid wall. It seemed now more like thunder, going up and then down.

That must be on the other side, it's a lift shaft or something. She listened and followed the sound, tracking it, Francesca again felt the floor become springy beneath her footsteps, too springy! Then saw to her sudden dismay another large gaping hole in the centre of the corridor. The closer she moved towards the precarious precipice, the more like a trampoline the floor became... Observing that it was a long way down, there was no other way to go, and *back was not an option.*

Francesca would have to jump—and it was about four feet to clear the gap!

This would be more difficult than any leap she'd ever tried. At the approach, her balance would not be good for jumping, because of the springboard effect of the floor. The jump would be more dangerous the closer to the verge she got, but she could only jump so far.... It was going to be very close!

Fucking hell... She snorted, viewing her immediate and apparent peril, testing the ground a little and rebounding precariously from the hole, judging the risks while balancing on the very edge. The floor squeaked uncannily on the bounce.

Come on, girl, you can do it, she bolstered her courage. The light was not good here— she was looking down through the large hole when something underneath unexpectedly moved and slowly caught her eye...

Whatever it was, it seemed to be sluggish and deliberate, a movement which attracted her attention, far away and near the bottom level. *What is that?* She fixed her eyes onto the distant object—it was slight and almost indistinguishable. She anchored her view to a movement far below, narrowing her eyes and refocusing, readjusting her viewpoint.

Eh? Francesca tried to focus on something impossible to differentiate. Just as she began to get a clearer view, some of the lights in the lower levels clicked off!

They're probably on a timer, she thought, hoped. It was no good trying to figure it out, even with her excellent eyesight. It bothered the girl because there was something down there, hanging on the ladders below... *I didn't pass anything like that down there; it must be something new. Oh God...*

It was a dark brown or black sack. The material seemed to be attached onto one of the metal rungs of the ladder. She stepped a little closer to the ledge. Had it moved?

Did it move? Surely not... Since she'd first seen it, the object appeared to have changed shape, a little at a time; Francesca narrowed her keen eyes as the platform below her feet bounced perilously.

'Si!' *There it is again, and it is fucking moving*! Failing to comprehend exactly what she was seeing, her nightmare continued. Everything that had occurred since she entered the dungeons was totally unbelievable! Maybe it was a nightmare, a dream that she would awaken from? She had completely lost her mind, yes that was the answer!

Whatever that thing was, it did not have a definitive surface. It slowly and continually changed its contour — at the moment it resembled a dark sack. Had it moved little since she last looked? Leaning a bit closer, Francesca was not sure....

'Mmm... What is that, *that thing?* It's like a large potato sack or an old bag? Maybe it has fallen down from somewhere and latched onto the ladder somehow... *maybe hot air eddies wafting inside this place, might do it,* she tried to make sense of the illogical. Talking to herself around her trepidation, 'I've been down here far too long, I'm losing it,' she insisted. *It can't be moving, not really...stupid...it's all in your imagination, girl! There is no other explanation.*

The sack twisted again. …*looks like it's higher than halfway up the ladder, somehow is nearer…* self-doubt crept back into her mind.

'That's it. It is fucking moving!' Francesca continued to stare hypnotically at the strange object for what seemed like two or three minutes more until it seemed to sit about two-thirds of the way up the ladder. Just when her mind seemed to be relaxing, the bag moved again!

'Ah, Si, there it is again! *Si*, a definite shift in form… the shape, it's changing—my God, it's moving up!' The top of the sack-like object protruded a little and formed the shape of a pointed hood.

Her eyes bulged in true horror as she recognised the head-like movement and, as it turned, the thing looked up… at her and projecting pure hatred!

Evil glared from its obscene, saucer-like eyes the creature began instantly pulling into her mind!

Its face hidden in darkness of the hood— only its wide eyes could be seen. Francesca's psyche was being attacked! The luminous white blind saucers transmitted abhorrent thoughts of wickedness into her straining mind... she knew it wanted her to fall.

Francesca felt like screaming. *Have I gone off my rocker? I'm not going to fly! I'm not going to fly!* She fought for control, grateful that whatever it was had not fully paralysed her wit, not yet.

The thing could not see her standing above, but rather it could taste her presence with its sensitive antennae, which wafted around in the air, its wet tongue drooling like a dripping tap. The antennae slithered above and around in the air and then back on to the metal and back into the air again. She was being tracked!

The artificial electric light in the area did not help with its short-sighted vision, apparently. The creature stopped its ascent momentarily, looking at her or staring blindly in her general direction, almost appearing to be listening carefully for the slightest sound. Her increased breathing rate might be giving her away. The thing seemed frustrated with the surrounding overall noise inside the building as it paused significantly before moving slowly upwards.

Can it hear my racing heart? Can it hear me think? Get out of my mind! Then the thing stopped, as if making a decision and, reading her thoughts again, stared up and opened its mouth as wide as possible. When it came, the long maw that emerged was huge… and wide. At first no sound almost like it had travelled to some great distance to be here from a land beyond, like transmitting sounds from an older transmitter from the other side of the world, the creature's sound proved to take a few seconds more than its own physical being.

Then it came — it came, all right, and with an all-powerful hideous evil laugh, full of hatred and intense wickedness that made her skin crawl.

Its eyeless and macabre white holes stared relentlessly upwards, capturing her attention. These eyes never slept. Its tongue seemed to become more excited in anticipation of a coming feast!

Inside its foul orifice, it displayed a nasty set of red-stained and unevenly pointed teeth.

"Destruction awaits your soul. Come to me…" it said icily, and then a blood curdling scream followed…

It took great will power from Francesca to break this nefarious bond apart, managing to tear her gaze from that things depraved and hypnotic stare.

Completely horrified, the girl wasted no more time quickly turned, sprinted and flew towards the gap taking it like a long jumper, leaping it high and long to the echo of the heinous scream behind her!!! She understood without any question that something much worse was hunting her and it was not human!

The girl's landed with a spring on the other platform with considerable room to spare! Francesca began blindly running along the precarious metal platform heading to the end of the walk then catapulting bodily up onto the sixth wrung of the ladder, fear in her mind scrambling like a crazed maniac up another ladder!

How long will this go on? How much further can I go! Her legs ached and a feeling of heaviness overcame her; abruptly, she lost her footing and slid perilously down the ladder. Panic might kill her, and it gripped her more tightly this time than ever before. Eventually, the girl reached the fifth level, and not a moment too soon!

Francesca hurriedly located the wall switch and noticed straightaway that the gangplank was different from the rest and, surprisingly, made of wood. The sound of her feet pattering fast along its light surface followed parallel to the floors beneath her.... Francesca tried to stop her intensifying terror and trepidation from overwhelming her senses.

Oh, down there, that awful thing! What is it? I have lost my mind completely this time! It's a devil or a phantom, a demon inside my mind. Certainly not of this world! Oh my God, it was inside my mind, talking to me.... What is happening? It's coming, coming, coming for me! The girl was right about that....

The diffuse lights created uncanny shadows all around. Some of the air ducts were old and opened so wide that they could easily be used as a chute, easily snaking downwards to lower levels— and a quick ride to hell! This was not the way Francesca wanted to go. A fearful thought came into her head just then.

What if there are more of those things and they are already here, climbing up this hollow pipe? I'm trapped, oh fuck no! I'm trapped! She kept on going anyway. When she came to the end of the platform, began frantically looking around for another ladder to climb, anything just anything to escape!

Where is the fucking ladder? She cursed, quickly despairing 'Ah, there it is!' then sighed with utter relief.

She found it. Francesca started climbing for survival, determined not to let the thing to catch up.

'What's that?' she wondered, looking underneath her and towards the facing wall.

'It's a, do... door? A fucking door?' she stammered in disbelief and immediately jumped off the ladder, landing on her feet like a cat.

Francesca began trying to open the small duct door, crazily feeling the metal edges with her sore fingertips, gliding them along its thin edges, amazed by just how easy it would have been to miss her only escape!

Desperately, Francesca threw everything out of her satchel onto the wooden floor, looking for the duct door key. Unfortunately the key flew out with a bundle of cords and bounced fast across the wooden floor, as if it was being pulled away by an invisible force! Francesca screamed loudly in anguish and propelled herself through the air like a goal keeper.

With outstretched arms and fingertips falling along the floor, Francesca was conscious of being hunted by some unspeakable monster that crept towards her, not far away. Her mind focused entirely on the escaping key landing heavily on the floor and sliding forward, she screamed

'Got it!', catching the key only just before it fell out of reach and down the gap. Other bits and pieces of cable and screwdrivers were not so lucky. They clattered down the vertical heights, from platform to platform inside the building internals, bouncing off the walls and levels until they fell out of sight.

In her nervous hand, Francesca taking no chances gripped the key firmly, too firmly — there was no time to lose.

Sweating in desperation, her hands began shaking uncontrollably with anticipation and excitement as she approached the door. The shaft or duct door was about shoulder height and made of solid metal. Not daring to look behind her, she inserted the duct key solidly into the lock. Francesca felt that the hunter was very close...

'Ok, ok, come on girl,' she muttered, turning the key. 'Come on... come on...' A rotten smell seemed to permeate the air around her…

Click! The lock turned. 'There! Now push!' she encouraged herself, experiencing only short relief, which quickly disappeared from her face to suppressed panic. The small metal door still would not open! Her head shook and neck tensed with fear and fatigue.

What next? The door having no handle, the girl could only tug with both hands on the large key head, like someone possessed. Suddenly the door opened and Francesca blindly sprinted through the door with a yell into a small, dark area smashing hard into something just below waist level!

'Ahhsh! Ooch, what's this!' Francesca said, looking at some kind of flat-surfaced, two by two foot air duct that was bent, barring her from traversing over the passageway…

The only light inside the duct came from the entranceway, and she could feel the air becoming colder. Her headlamp by this time had lost all power. Something unseen was approaching, she smelled it, she felt it, she knew it!

That thing is on me, thinking frantically, staring into the lonely dim passage behind her.

But nothing happened, shocked Francesca flicked on the wall light at the side of the door. *Lock it! Lock it, quick...quick!* Francesca banged the door shut behind her, locking it tight.

Would a locked door keep that thing out? Probably not. Francesca felt her grandmother's cross heating up once more...

Running like an athlete she quickly vaulted herself like a hurdler with one hand over the curved pipe. The small duct entrance foyer resembled a small room; it was hot and very stuffy, unlike where she had come from down in the dungeons. She felt a little more secure, enclosed in this place.

Gurgling sounds could be heard all around as she walked along the narrow room, making sure not to touch any red pipes while observing the many grey data cables that trailed along the floor for about twenty feet and then disappeared up the wall into more ducting. *Surely they lead somewhere?*

The noises all around her were mixed with what sounded like "sparking", or the sound of water dripping from a great height from somewhere onto a flat surface. Francesca remembered again how desperately thirsty she was. She tried to locate the source of the sound, but it proved too difficult.

Strange, I cannot see what's causing that noise... perhaps it is behind the wall? This place is filthy!

The area was filled with old cardboard boxes covered in dust, discarded coke cans and pizza boxes left by a contractor a long time ago...

No, this pizza box looks too fresh. Somebody has been in here recently, but who? Well, at least I am going in the right direction!

Observing a large power box fixed firmly onto the wall with large yellow

"PANIC" and red "TRIP" buttons, Francesca also found an old metal shelf, on which an antiquated "Digital VT420" monitor sat alone, covered in cobwebs!

Jesus, they gave up making these things back in the eighties. Francesca could not believe that the old computer kit, forgotten and discarded, had been left inside here for such a long time!

She walked on, struggling through large chunks of polystyrene packing that made it difficult to move. She eventually reached another squat metal door at the far end. It was a familiar design, another small duct door and similar to the one she'd unlocked a few minutes ago. The room was shorter than the last and more enclosed — the girl wondered where this one would lead — to another passageway, another tunnel? Where was she going. Francesca turned the lock and pulled the door back. It opened easily…

She was out and emerged into a brightly lit and very noisy comms room. Hearing the familiar and familiar humming sounds of electrical fans coming from the numerous central data cabinets and servers, the girl looked relieved.

There again was that awful air-conditioning that haunted her so much, blowing hard as usual. She was inside *her own* communication and server room!

Standing upright, Francesca stretched her stiff and aching limbs. Never had she been so thankful in her life to find herself inside the fifth floor communications room of the administration buildings!

Mixed relief and anxiety all came together in the turmoil of her mind. Her face was a pathetic sight — of cuts and bruises, she appeared more like a dirty rag doll than a human. She was exhausted, but she had survived!

In the past, the girl had barely noted this indiscrete duct door that blended quietly against the walls of the room, never giving it more than a perfunctory glance. Never had she gone inside — there was no need. It had always been locked shut, and painted the same pale green paintwork as the rest of the room. Yet, disturbingly, it was evident that someone had been inside here not too long ago… *The pizza boxes, who was here, who could it have been?*

Complex computer and data network diagrams hung on the walls, as did pictures of high performance servers. A few humorous cartoon characters cut out of computer magazines that poke humour at I.T. management or just management in general had been stuck on the wall. Francesca, for the first time in ages, grinned with happiness. Her heart lifted. She was safe....

Francesca was about to go for the exit to her right, through the sealed, metal security entrance. Unexpectedly, something dropped loudly near the back of the room onto the floor, where the servers were located.

She stopped in her tracks, looking perplexed. Her view was restricted by the large communication data cabinets, which stood in the way.

What was that? Maybe someone is up there – someone who might be able to get help.

'*Si,* is someone there?' She walked slowly and cautiously on the left side of the room, keeping the cabinets on her right as she headed towards the server area. Francesca passed the many large communication cabinets which stood open, with their cables hanging out and mixed like spaghetti in all directions. She could not help but look at the humorous cartoon cut-outs from a newspaper affectionately called "*The Popeye Chronicles*. A tongue in cheek view at the Vatican and was one that Michaelangelo had subscribed too. She smiled a little, remembering when Michaelangelo had stuck it on the wall a year or so ago. He was always laughing at it. *I am surprised he never got the bible thrown at him!*

Thinking again of Michaelangelo, Francesca's smile was short-lived as the reality of her own situation came flooding back. She listened gravely to a familiar voice....

'Hello, Schiavone," a male voice spoke aloud from the back of the room in response to Francesca's earlier greeting only moments ago. 'Taking your time getting back here, then? Has the girl been "rescinded"?' the man paused waited for a response without turning around, concentrating his attention on the dedicated computer terminal.

Agent Zito, the VIA guy! They have the access rights to do just about anything inside the Vatican City! Oversized auditors with big sticks, that's all they are. But what did he mean by "rescinded?"

She crouched down with great caution, creeping up slowly to see what he was doing.

'Look here,' he said, sensing the female presence behind him. 'Those guys downstairs are transferring e-tender documentation onto another secure server and, better than that, they are using *different digital certificates.*'

For a moment, Agent Zito still believed that he was speaking to his younger colleague Schiavone.

Francesca's eyes widened in dismay as she saw his gun, a stainless steel "Beretta 92FS Inox", sitting there, originally designed for the Italian Army and Police. It rested on the desk next to the keyboard.

Not exactly a computer add-on! She thought. *It's time I got out of here, and... Fuck, I'm too late!*

The man suddenly turned around on the swivel chair. His eyebrows lifted up in complete surprise from behind his sunglasses, and then disappeared quickly below the dark frames.

'Ah, Signorina DeRose, I was wondering about you,' he began, and she felt certain that that part was true. 'Have you seen my colleague, Agent Schiavone?' and smiled in his pleasant way.

Agent Zito seemed too friendly and too collected for having just received an unexpected guest. Sitting there as if he owned the place in an unruffled pinstripe suit, and acting as though everything was completely normal....

It's wrong, it's a bluff. He can't really be thinking that! Zito is playing for time... she decided, distrusting the agent's overly familiar and forthcoming manner.

Studying the girl's shocking state, he sensed her antagonism and so extended his hand almost without Francesca noticing. It was a complete and smooth movement. Zito could so easily have been picking up a cup of coffee... instead, he lifted his silver Beretta!

Francesca did not flinch and, without thinking of the consequences, automatically brought down a heavy metal cable management arm that had been sitting close by on a shelf. She had been holding it inconspicuously where it rested on the data

Because assistance would soon be on the way, Zito knew he had only about five minutes to deal with the girl. The question was, *how?* She had already proved to be a very slippery and a more able opponent than Zito had first judged.

The agent stood back from the small door and shot at the lock. His bullet had no effect. Zito's breathing was beginning to cause him a serious problem, as the fire-retardant escaped from the massive Halon gas cylinders at each corner of the room. *What is that gas?* He wondered. In panic, he tried to inhale, finding nothing... *nothing!* to breathe. His lungs moved in short, start-stop movements.

The man's mind screamed as the oxygen was pushed out of the room. There was no air left in the room—everything was being forced out and replaced by this inert gas. Zito was beginning to lose consciousness... *smart ass bitch!* He thought. Zito's survival instincts were still working strong and, as a last ditch effort, the man unloaded his magazine into the side of the wall next to the door. He was not stupid. He was emptying his clip and creating a large hole, hoping that more air would come back through into the room for him. Perhaps it would choke the girl and save his life at the same time. To Francesca's horror, the trick was working — some air escaped from the duct and went back through into the larger room as the Halon gas displaced where she sat inside. She had hoped that the man would collapse.

Catching his breath again at the hole to her duct, Zito began to recover, his head clearing fast. Francesca had taken a deep breath and looked back through the hole, into the room. Immediately, Zito's sunglasses were looking back at her! He saw Francesca's frightened face.

Now that Zito knew the female's location, he aimed his silver Beretta at her with malice! As fate would have it, another full gas cylinder kicked into action immediately above him.

"HISSSSSSSsssssss," the strong loud noise burst into action! The system integrated an additional super-pressurised rush from a double large gas cylinder. It filled the room completely in seconds! Estates had done a good job of protecting their expensive equipment.

Zito's body could not find any more oxygen. He had lost a lot of blood, and there was no air left—none! His body screamed in agony. Impulsively turning his head up to the right and dropping his weapon, he stood and used his good hand in a failed attempt to stop the gas from escaping...

The room was by now completely saturated with the inert gas. Falling to his knees, the man could not even gasp for life—he held his throat frantically as froth began to exude from his lungs. With only a matter of seconds for him left to live, his final thought was one of disbelief: *Beaten by an amateur*....

Agent Zito collapsed onto the ground and inhaled no more... the deadly, inert gas polluted his body. Zito was dead.

The sound of the hissing Halon gas eventually seemed to fizzle out. Despite the hole in her hideaway, Francesca was still alive!

She tried to stuff the puncture with part of her shirt and then waited for the right moment to go, for she too could not breathe!

Taking a final series of shallow breaths—there was not enough air for deep breaths—she readied herself. This was it! It was time to move fast! Francesca knew that the gas was her saviour and might also be her undoing.

Unlocking and opening the duct door, she entered the server room and saw the man lifeless on the floor, white froth around his mouth, his face blue. Not wanting to waste precious seconds, she ran past him towards the security door. Francesca did not give the VIA Agent any more thought than she would a dying snake.   So much had happened that her nature had changed. The girl had become different, ruthless.

When Francesca reached the security door, she typed her code quickly and then realised with a heart-wrenching surge of disappointment that she'd dropped her access card somewhere. It could be anywhere between the dungeons and the catacombs....
My God, I do not have it! Oh God, I will die!

Frantically banging on the door with her fists, she was a woman possessed, though dying. There was nobody to hear her, unfortunately. In that last moment, she looked over at the agent, realising that she would join him in death... when abruptly she fell backwards against the wall as the door burst open! Wearing her dark purple *Proxima Eco-Cleaning Utilities* overalls, the cleaner woman Agata sprinted into the room!

For all her size, this little lady packed a punch — she picked Francesca up easily, with the strength of a fireman!!! The small woman quickly put the girl over her shoulder. She recognised that the man lying down was dead, and was willing to leave him so. There was absolutely no air left in the room as both women escaped, and the security door banged shut behind them!

Agata sat Francesca gently down outside against the outside wall to the comms room, and Francesca looked up at her friend wearily, struggling still to catch her breath. Her senses recognised the woman's smells, realising once more that the old lady smoked and liked to take a secret drink from the executive offices every now and then. No one would ever know... Francesca would make sure of it. The woman's old, scaly skin was rough on Francesca's cheek. How nice it seemed... to be still alive!

CHAPTER IX

SECRETS BEHIND
THE VATICAN WALLS
VⱢLᵣᐅⱽ ⱢⱢⱢ·ᐁ
ᐅⱢⱢ ᐱⱢᐅᵣLⱢ· Ⱝ·Lᵣⱽ

Sitting with her back against the wall, Francesca heaved deep, ragged breaths, still struggling to fill her blood with oxygen. She still could not move, feeling intensely cold and light headed. But she was alive! For a short moment, the young woman reflected on all that had happened.

Thinking of how she'd proved more than a match for the dead agent, Francesca opened her eyes. *Why was I to be "rescinded"?* It baffled her...

Rescindition was the clinical term used for the assassination of an individual, and that term had held deadly consequences for poor Massimo. What about those apparitions she saw behind the Vatican walls, what were they? Shaking her head in incredulity Francesca tried to convince that she had imagined these creatures were hallucinations brought on by being drugged. She knew it would have been too easy for VIA simply to drop a slow-acting drug into her water. It did make complete sense, it had too.

Francesca's mind had begun to clear, and her breathing much easier. Air flowed back into her lungs joyfully and then her mind jolted into reality!

'What is happening, Francesca, what is going on?' The old woman Agata asked frantically. Her voice panicking at her close involvement at the site of the mayhem!

The cleaner lady had had no time to think on hearing the alarm and the frantic banging on the inside door! Having the required security access to designated areas to clean and tidy, the woman rescued the girl. She was confused about what had happened and needed some answers.

'I... I don't know.' Francesca gulped copious amounts of air as her mind began clearing, she felt vulnerable and defensive as her breathing heaved.

'You don't look well… I'll get you an ambulance, wait here,' Agata said, running off quickly.

Francesca thought it was odd to see the woman as she picked up her bucket and ran off to a nearby office to phone for help.

That was too close, the girl thought, still shattered when a great urgency came upon her. *I must get the police and the commissionaire's help; Agata will have to catch up later!* She realised.

Standing up unsteadily at first, Francesca started running along the corridor towards the elevators with the claxons still resounding behind.

As she fled the elevator on the first floor, the girl quickly scanned the area — the crystal fountain dominated the foyer with its crashing water, which plummeted and splashed into the round pool. The clattering noises resonated off the polished marble walled interior and reflected from the clinically clean floors inside the main foyer.

Francesca passed the commissionaire's desk, observing that the electronic security alarm dashboard displayed a red alert flashing madly on fifth floor! There was no fire, she knew this. But the commissionaire was nowhere to be seen.

It was late evening, and Francesca could see only some of the fine gardens beyond the front doors. The floral arrangement, engineered in all its holiness, had been grown in the shape of the papal seal; the Swiss guards were preoccupied at the far end in the car park, checking a suspicious vehicle!

They are too far away – they will not hear me! Turning around and looking into her office from the commissionaire desk, she wondered if somebody was still in there, working late.

'Great!' Francesca said out loud when she spotted someone. *Oh, it is Jonathan!* Her face automatically sneered. The man was standing over Guielletta as the girl typed some program coding instructions into the computer.

They must be working on another system upgrade. They just did one last week! Still, I never thought I would be so glad to see them.

Francesca knocked on the door frantically, having lost her card entry. Jonathan stood to the right side of his colleague with his arm and hand over her shoulders, almost embracing his subordinate – both contractors looked up and turned around, surprised to see Francesca banging at the office door.

Jonathan saw her evident distress and anxiously ran over to help Francesca inside. When he opened the door, the girl collapsed in on top of him! Catching her in his arms and holding Francesca up, he stared in disbelief at her distressed state. She looked awful — totally shabby! She had dirt and blood all over her face, knees and hands, and every bare patch of skin was cut and grazed. Her dirty jeans ripped at the knees and her top was torn — her hair was bedraggled and matted.

'Francesca! My goodness, look at you — are you ok? Have you had an accident or something?' Jonathan spoke to the girl with genuine concern. 'Come with me along here and sit down at your desk.' He led her away from the door. 'Now, let me see, I will fix you up here and now. You'll be just fine.'

Guielletta watched closely as both stumbled into the office. A few moments later, Francesca was sitting and resting on her own chair. Jonathan offered her a cup of water from the dispenser. Francesca declined, although she was dry as a bone.

'Guielletta, phone for an ambulance and bring me a first aid kit quickly, please,' Jonathan instructed.

'How is Francesca?' she asked.

'Francesca will be all right — she's just had a little accident, that's all. To be on the safe side, call an ambulance anyway.' Guielletta nodded and picked up the phone, asking for the emergency services as Francesca looked around, her vision blurred.

'Jonathan, Massimo, Massimo,' she stammered and paused and then tried again, finding her own words extremely upsetting. 'Mass has been... killed, murdered!' she sobbed. Suddenly grabbing the man's wrists and shaking them tightly, she said, 'You must call the gendarmerie, right now!' raising her voice and seemed to have trouble focusing. Bewildered Jonathan stared as if she was suffering from a concussion.

'Calm down, calm down, Francesca, please. What do you mean? The gendarmerie, I really don't understand... are you sure, Francesca? Are you sure about this?' Jonathan asked her calmly in complete disbelief.

Guielletta then joined them. 'Are you hurt, Francesca? Oh, you are in an awful mess. Let us help you and tell us what has happened.' she spoke kindly to the bruised and battered systems administrator, although Francesca noted a hint of flippancy in her tone...

'*Grazie, Si, Si*, I am fine, sure, just call the damn gendarmerie — it's really important!' she shouted angrily. Francesca was becoming increasingly agitated, bordering on hysterical. As precious moments passed, Francesca tried not to lose her coherence and consciousness. So much had happened and so many questions were still unexplained, unanswered!

Jonathan placed his light trench coat carefully around the girl's shoulders and applied a dressing from an office first aid kit onto her skinned and tender knee. The man stared seriously at his colleague and shared a look of dismay with Guielletta. They needed to do something quick. He spoke to his assistant.

'Can you call the police, the gendarmerie, Guielletta? I think there has been a nasty accident downstairs.' Jonathan was now resolute in his decision and he directed his subordinate to make the call.

'No! No accident!' shaking her head frantically, 'Don't you understand — don't you get it? Massimo has been murdered! Shot! He is dead!' As usual, Francesca regretted being in their company. She demanded their full attention. 'Call the fucking gendarmerie, right NOW!' screaming a curse at them.

Jonathan's face straightened, 'Call it in, Guielletta,' Jonathan responded with a sombre nod to Francesca as Guielletta walked quickly back to her desk, opening her desk drawer and picking up her cell-phone. She called the gendarmerie, looking gravely over at her supervisor. This was as serious as it gets. Relieved Francesca at last had both their undivided attention....

****

Agata soon arrived on the scene unannounced; she had entered the office without being noticed by the man and woman, who were preoccupied by the unfolding events. She had carefully walked over to Francesca and watched her anxiously, a worried expression written all over the old woman's cracked face.

Jonathan stood up, rather surprised and annoyed at seeing the woman's silent appearance beside him. He was at first startled at being caught off guard, and in such occasions as this he had a peculiar habit of standing when facing someone. His leg would cross slowly and so it did, drawing his right knee across his left. Then, with a sudden movement, he would fully cross the leg over, to stand on both feet.

'Francesca my poor girl is there anything I can do to help you?' the kind old lady asked. Looking down at her sitting unevenly on her seat, cut and bruised, the cleaning lady gave her a comforting hug. 'Things will be just fine, dear. The doctor and the Fire Department are coming, I phoned from upstairs.'

Jonathan appeared to be shocked if not openly upset at the woman's initiative, not realising that as one of the few on-duty staff members of the night shift, Agata was used to taking action on her own volition.

'Oh, thank you, Agata. I'm sorry I ran away from you earlier—I was in a complete panic,' Francesca said quietly, trying to remember clearly what had happened.

'Francesca will be fine. She is a bit sore and *we* have already called for an ambulance,' Jonathan spoke condescendingly to the old woman. 'Why did you call the fire department as well?'

'Oh, *Si,* the fire alarm upstairs, it came on, it came on inside that room upstairs on "five" across from personnel offices,' she paused, taking off her expensive Omega watch, 'and there is a man lying inside — *he is dead.*' the woman sounded a bit upset, more at the man's insensitivity than anything else. 'I opened the door and there was Francesca! I helped her out, and then I called the authorities.'

'Thank you for rescuing me, Agata.' She swallowed, 'I would be dead now, if it hadn't been for you.' Francesca smiled. 'Had you not opened the door at that moment? Thank you so much, Agata. I will be in your debt, always.' Francesca felt that Jonathan was giving the woman too hard a time. The upstart!

Agata and Francesca kissed each other with warm affection before the cleaning woman looked with ill rebuke at the young man and headed for the door. Strangely enough, she still carried that pale green bucket in her hand, filled with dirty cloths and cleaning bottles. They were never parted....

Jonathan looked at Guielletta through the door and shouted at the old woman. '*Grazie*, you can go straight home, now, I am sure the gendarmerie will visit you later. Don't speak to anyone about this business, please. These circumstances are of Vatican importance and strictly confidential.'

The woman seemed most annoyed and unappreciated at being reminded of her duty, like a schoolchild, from that arrogant foreigner who just wanted to look self-important. The woman did not want any thanks, and the man's response was totally predictable.

Turning to Francesca, Jonathan said, 'Have you heard anything further about...' he hesitated, thinking again about being so direct, 'did you find anything else out about Michaelangelo's disappearance?'

She did not speak. 'Francesca, what were you looking for earlier to get yourself into so much trouble? Did you find where he might be hiding?'

'Michaelangelo is still missing,' she said quietly. 'I think he holds the secret to what is going on here.' The girl paused for a moment and continued, 'Do you not care about Massimo? I found him next to a computer, the computer was communicating when I found it in a hidden location. It is the machine which is being used by the mystery Apostol user! It stands to reason, that I am sure of — it is likely being used via remote access. Unfortunately for our mystery person, something went wrong. There was a fault and this disconnected him. Apostol was blind.

'I did not have a chance to look too closely at the computer. It is now connected fine on the network. I have to say that there was something strange about the back of the machine, though....' Francesca tried hard to remember. '*Si,* yes, that's it, I'll be able to find it in five minutes on the network right now, depending on the beaconing configuration settings.' The girl's mind was sharpening and already crystal clear! She seemed to be getting stronger with rest.

'What if we all go downstairs to the dungeons and have a look at it?' he tried to persuade Francesca with a reassuring voice. 'We are all quite qualified to check a computer

you know, and take care of Massimo.
Guielletta will come too, if you feel up to it — we
can go now. You could take us there...?'

*He is asking more questions than he is
administering first-aid! What a meddlesome turd. I
never even mentioned anything about Massimo
being downstairs...* Francesca was finding
Jonathan to be more than irritating than helpful,
as usual.

'Massimo is beyond help,' she was
infuriated. 'And, *when*... did I say that Massimo
was *down* in the dungeon?'

'Oh, I'm sorry — I meant upstairs, when
you spoke about escaping upstairs. I'm not
listening correctly,' he apologised.

'Surely you would be thinking that
Massimo was the man lying dead upstairs,
since I already told you that he was dead?
Agata already spoke of a man in the server
room upstairs.' There were two dead bodies in
the one building! What were the chances of
that? Francesca raged red with the project
leader's insensitivity. He never listened, the
bastard!

'Ha, ha, ha, my apologies,' laughing with
awkward embarrassment, although it was not

real. 'Francesca, you are quite correct. Pardon my stupidity.' The man looked shamed like a dishonest child caught out lying. 'Then who is the dead person upstairs, if not Massimo?' he questioned.

Francesca heard Guielletta's voice as she said, 'I would like to place a call to the gendarmerie, please.' Her voice was dull. Guielletta speaking into her cell-phone, which gave her a direct outside line rather than going through the automated switchboard.

'It's Zito.' Francesca answered.

'Zito?' Jonathan's face changed, he could not believe this! Zito was Vatican Audit Office!

'Hello? It's the *Istituto per le Opere di Religion in the Palazzo de Governmanato. Ah, Si,* we are having a critical problem in the administration building at this moment. There has been a serious accident, I think someone is... seriously hurt? I need urgent assistance. Can you send someone here please, as soon as possible?' The girl had an analytical tone of voice, almost like a computer program, without feeling. *Typical Guielletta – cold as ice.*

Then silence..., Guielletta appeared to be listening intently to someone on the other end of the line, and then answering one question after the next regarding what she thought had happened.

'We should not go downstairs, Jonathan, it is very dangerous!' Francesca responded belatedly and in all seriousness to his earlier question. Francesca suddenly had an idea! It popped into her head without warning, and she opened her drawer, picked up her personal cell-phone and called Michaelangelo's cell-phone number!

If it was active now she might be able to trace its location using some new free software she had installed earlier in the day on her own mobile phone.

The technician could accurately track Michaelangelo's location to the nearest twenty metres anywhere in the world, provided that his cell-phone was switched on! Francesca had noticed that the personnel section had downloaded a payable product like this earlier in the week.

Typical! *Those VIA Agents wanted to use it for employee surveillance!* She thought again of Massimo and that killer upstairs. She pressed Michaelangelo's number and waited....

```
Hopping... Hopping... Hopping...
Server has connected to client...
Transmitting data now...
```

"Connecting," the metallic voice chimed.

A map appeared like a trace on her cellphone and in about ten seconds, a satellite map and an image came on her little screen. Looking at the diagram, she saw that he was only about three hops away.

Francesca's call went transparently through the local firewalls and filtered routers to the nearest Satellite Internet service provider and replied back again, downloading data to...to ...where?

It was here... right here, inside this building! Michaelangelo was inside the Pallazzo? She thought of the empty pizza box upstairs. It started to make sense.

Next another message appeared on her display:

```
    ...feeding to ... Recipient
Voice Established.
```

A voice came instantly on the phone, sounding strangely familiar — it was speaking... to her....

'*Si,* the *Istituto per le Opere di Religion,* Administration Buildings, *Si* the Palace. Ciao ufficiale, I would like you to send some men here right away,' an anaesthetic female voice transmitted through Francesca's phone speaker...

Francesca looked up at Jonathan, who was shouting over to his assistant as she spoke into the other phone.

'I think this girl needs a complete rest, she has been through far too much. What do you think Guielletta, rescind?'

Jonathan nipped Francesca's cut face as he dabbed some more antiseptic ointment onto her wound. 'Call Internal Audit, Guielletta, they should know about any rescinding issues, as well as the Carabinieri.' He looked at Francesca, 'This won't take a moment. Keeps us all in their good Bible books...' the man laughed, though not with real jest, unaware of the woman's growing unease as she listened to each word on the voice on the cell-phone.

'Ouch!' the cut hurt! Clearly the woman's was not Michaelangelo's voice on the phone. She was trying to listen to the stupid man's rhetoric, but at the same time he was making it difficult to concentrate on the female voice in the phone....

There was some kind of interference, an echo on Francesca's phone. Looking up she set her cell-phone's visibility to *"on"* hoping that she would see the person at the other end. This required the other person to have the same vision technology. Michaelangelo's phone did!

Oh... just a picture of an ear, crap! She swore as the cell-phone seemed to pull away from the person's ear — she wondered if the person had suddenly heard a beep and became aware of her contact.... A red light indicator flashed, on indicating "live feed". Vision was set to on in BOTH directions!

A long instant passed in a split second reality, and then Francesca's unseen intuitive thought was justified as familiar eyes were displayed inside the tiny cell-phone screen. It was not Michaelangelo! The eyes were female and looked sideways... towards Francesca!

At that moment, Francesca turned her head to her right and tried to stretch around Jonathan's body. He was still standing above her and in the way! Staring past the stupid man and across the room, irritated by his immobility, Jonathan seemed unaware of these new developments around him and continued dabbing on more ointment onto her surprised face.

Francesca recognised that it was Guielletta! Horror! It was Guielletta's voice on the other end of the cell-phone. It was her eyes too!

Guielletta had realised the same a few seconds before, staring directly at Francesca's recognition.

Si, she knows too much and I will rescind her right now,' her clinical tone came through the phone, while Jonathan's eyes widened in perplexity.

Guielletta immediately opened her drawer and pulled out a double action Tanfoglio Force 99 carry semi-automatic, aiming it directly at Francesca!

Jonathan must be in on it, as well! I never mentioned where the mystery computer was located — he spoke about going downstairs first! He also got it wrong with the dead guy upstairs, why would it not be poor Mass? I knew there was something wrong! Shit! My God, she is going to kill me!

Francesca moved like quicksilver, tugging Jonathan with both hands. He stumbled off balance as she brought him in front of her and two bullets smacked into his shoulder blades! He fell towards Francesca and slumped to the floor.

'Out of the way, you fool!' Guielletta callously called as the man fell to the red stained carpet, blood shooting out from both open wounds like pressurised hoses!

Francesca was a natural and gifted survivor. Jonathan screamed in pain falling. This gave the administrator the valuable seconds she needed to jump off her chair and scramble around on the floor to the far end of the desk — out of immediate sight. The office desks were arranged in a star group of four. This would protect her for a valuable minute, at least. Another bullet passed over her head!

'Fuck me,' she instinctively dodged, 'not again! My luck is sure to run out this time!' Francesca hissed, knowing the female was walking over to finish her off. She desperately looked around on the floor for inspiration. Was there any way she could get out and stay alive? Searching below the tables, she could see the woman's ankles approaching slowly.

Guielletta stood above the bloody man screaming below her. Studying him, she spoke calmly at his torment, 'Poor bugger, Jon, it's turned out to be a real mess for you. Shouldn't have got in the way though…', 'I'll rescind this cow for you and think of something to say about all this later — it will not be too much of a problem. A cover up.' she said rationally. 'That, will be easy inside the Vatican with the help of VIA behind us. There is no one around just now. I'll kill the cleaner later.' She winked reassuringly at the anguishing man.

The man looked up in torture. 'I need help, Guielletta,' he groaned in a low, pained voice to his partner in crime, pleading for her help. After seeing into her blank eyes, he realised that she was a complete psycho! Guielletta cared nothing for him — her mind was transfixed on her kill. No compassion showed as she strode past the wounded man without a further thought. The 92mm shorter barrel Force 99 pistol pointed towards Francesca's hiding place....

Under the desk came a noise and Guieletta looked down. At that moment, Francesca appeared from behind the desk, swinging a long cable throwing at Guielletta!

Heavy and serrated, the cable was attached to an old style centronics metal plug. With great speed it struck Guielletta on her temple, causing the would-be killer to lose her balance and fall ungraciously over Jonathan collapsing unceremoniously onto her back, Guielletta instantly scrambled to regain her superiority. The dazed DBA attempted to get up, when suddenly another vicious blow landed squarely on her face! Francesca had run full pelt at Guielletta's vulnerable body, picking up a keyboard from her own desk on the way and swinging it around fast, smacking the woman flat onto her cheekbone!

Key pieces and bits of broken plastic and tooth flew off through the air! Guielletta reeled backwards in excruciating pain!

Half standing and half falling, the killer staggered back in agony and fell onto another set of star-arranged desks behind her! The woman's face instantly began to swell. Holding onto the edge of the desk behind her, she steadied herself for support on the star desk arrangement.

Guielletta's head spinning unbalanced was in severe pain. She could see that Francesca was closing fast the gap between them. *This was it!* The girl charged like a wild animal at Guielletta as the DBA readied herself for the final blow from Francesca's makeshift but effective weapon.

Francesca could judge the space between them — she saw that her own luck had finally run out, because the distance between them, although short, was still far too far away! She would not make it before Guielletta launched a counter-attack.

The systems administrator closed her eyes with a mixture of helpless rage and the awful realization of failure and her own imminent execution.

Guielleta's head was smashed and bloody, bruised, split-lipped and lost teeth. The

DBA aimed her pistol with outstretched arm straight at Francesca's head, pulled the trigger at Francesca.

'*Rescinded, you bitch!*' Guielletta slobbered bloodily.

Francesca opened her eyes, expecting to feel the impact and pain of a gunshot, but instead surprised.

Guielletta's body physically lifted and catapulted off the ground before her!

Francesca's eyes wide open watching the bedlam and hearing the short sounds of a repeated pop-pop-popping noises. Witnessing the horrors of Guielletta's organs burst in the air with soft sounds of hissing hot flesh as tissue burst from blood-spattered bullet holes, blood gushing out from her body.

A split second later, there came the sounds of the first short rattle of a mechanization — suppressed automatic machine gun fire!

It would only take a three second burst from an automatic submachine gun to empty a full magazine, as an accurate strafe of deadly bullets went whizzing past narrowly missing Francesca by a few accurate inches. The bullets impacted the airborne woman holding the lifeless gun.

Guielletta's body landed heavily on the other end of the office desk, tumbling through bullet-holed computer screens and torn sheets of paper, her arms and legs fell sprawling out widely over the tops until she finally rested perfectly atop the star-arranged desk cluster.

Although it appeared to Francesca that the scene had happened in slow, aching detail, in true reality it was over and finished in only a few seconds.

As Guielletta's body landed on the desk, her flesh shredded as it quivered like jelly, her head slowly turning to stare awkwardly at Francesca — she was dead.

Shouts and abrupt calls of male voices came from behind Francesca as she crumpled to the floor, stunned... Francesca was in a complete and bloody mess. Her mind numb, body exhausted barely recognising the sounds many of approaching feet, the moment overwhelmed her.

I-I'm still alive? I cannot believe it.... Francesca inspected herself with shock and disbelief, searching for a wound.

Traumatised, Francesca began stammering to herself quietly, beyond wrecked, slumping down on her chair to see the dead and mutilated body of her deadly and psychotic co-worker...

Then she heard commands from shouting voices all around in the room, although she felt too distant from it all, her senses began to close down. Her body implemented a force quit.

The noises becoming much louder when suddenly three or four Swiss guardsmen in camouflaged uniforms trained automatic submachine guns on the dead woman, checking her vitals while another crew attended to the critically-wounded man on the floor. Francesca seemed almost forgotten in the melee, although this could not have been farther from the truth once a gentle hand lifted her face upwards and through her blurred and misted vision she saw... *am I dreaming?*

It was the warm voice she'd longed for, penetrating her shattered mind, melting the ice — she felt the soft and kind touch of a man. Lifting her up and cradling the girl in his muscular arms, he held Francesca close to his chest, protecting her. She was safe at last!

'Francesca, I was so worried about you....' he said as the girl looked up carefully at the man.

She stared deeply into his starry green eyes. Francesca tightened her hold around his strong neck with pleasure. It was *Ciriaco!*

He had saved her life! Lost for words, Francesca could only sob softly onto his shoulder, whispering,

'Ciriaco...thank God it is you...' Completely fatigued she winced a little, her body hurt while she thought of her lost friend Michaelangelo's mysterious disappearance... *what has happened to Michaelangelo...*, her last thought was... *say nothing, not even to Ciriaco.*

Francesca somehow felt different... colder inside, clinical in mind it began closing in heartache and fear. What she had experienced below these floors seemed insane, horrific. It was no drug induced drink she ingested or hypothermic hallucination. Something awful lurked down there, deep inside the catacombs. The seven cursed Abaddon clerics, they wanted the *Links to God* for their dark master; *damn their rotten souls.* Supernatural things from another world. *The Clerics...* had let her go because of the prophecy. Truly, she was special.

Francesca felt safe for the moment, so her consciousness released its bounds to let her drift off into the mercy of sleep, a very deep sleep but someday soon he prophecy would soon come of age.

Colonnello Ciriaco Esposito, the Pope's personal bodyguard placing his stainless steel Beretta 92Fs Inox on the wrecked computer table beside him held Francesca safely.

Ciriaco waved some of the ambulance crew over to attend to her. His mind struggled with this new and crazy discovery. The pace of his investigation had just picked up and would continue. Shaking his head in disbelief surveying the bloody mayhem surrounding them, looked softly at Francesca, bruised and with blood stained cheek. Kissed her cut lips reaffirming his love and first assumption...

Si, this girl is going to be trouble.

CHAPTER X

THE VISITORS

>⊓□ ∧⌐∨⌐>·⌐∨

    The days passed by and the temperature had decisively dropped since the earth tremor in late October. Most of the roads and pavements were blanketed once more with hard frosts on top of the packed ice, disguising the roads' treacherous foundations. November moved on with more snow falls and bleak conditions that continued into a savage December.

    A once-thriving mining community last century was now just the simple village. Mauchline, a small tranquil place on west coast of Scotland where nothing much happened. The people inside the taverns laughed and spoke of things they had done years ago, and still found those same old stories fascinating year after year. A person might leave and seek his fortune elsewhere in the world and then come back twenty or thirty years later to find folks still talking about the same old things.

Unless you were born in the village and raised from an infant there, then you were always classed as an *"incomer"*. Such was rural life.

Coal mining had halted half a century before, as well as the digging for much-harder granite stone, which had fuelled the once-popular game of ice curling; these stones had then been cut, carved and polished in the local curling stone factory. This indigenous line of work too had ceased production a few decades ago, and the granite mine had long since closed. How extensive and how deep did these ancient granite mines go? One could only guess.

Ancient red sandstone quarries went further back in time, and were located not far away — just outside the west end of the village, next to the muir - moor. The quarry was started centuries ago by monks in order to build the village church and castle. Such buildings represented the beginning of village life proper. Some said that the village was as old as the sixth or seventh century.

The young girl Charity Fludd lived in a large the "Old Manse". It was a white-painted building with roughcast walls and a slated rooftop with several chimneys and extensive, mature gardens surrounding. Her house stood solid and sturdy behind a thick, twelve-foot high green hedgerow on front and sides, lowering to about six foot high at the rear of the house. The home had wooden front double doors painted dark-green like the windows frames, set to match. Everything was topped with thick snow.

To the rear of the house was Charity's bedroom window, which had a beautiful view of the bright open countryside and the smooth, sweeping, snow-sloped fields. The huge boulders that stood on top of the hill stood out clearly against the deep blue sky and the tree-lined ridges.

It was comfortable and cosy inside her large house, with its characteristic wooden beams. There was a large mantle-piece and a wide mirror above, and the furniture was old in character. The house had wooden floor with a rich Indian rug on top and a well-stocked bookshelf. On the walls hung peculiar artefacts from Egypt and other parts of the Middle East. The Fludds kept a lot of the original décor of the house, which they had inherited by their father's uncle, Captain Fludd, who'd passed away several years ago. Captain Fludd had no family other than his brother, Charity's father, Robert Fludd. Charity and her mother, Jessica, would forever be "incomers" to the village. Charity's father was hardly ever at home, which made life for Charity very lonely.

Her father had begun a niche medical company that was competitive and worth a fortune. His research team worked hard to develop the "$99 genome". It was a breakthrough then, a method that drastically cut the costs of the clinical testing of genes, set normally at $100,000. His patent would have been astronomical... but he did not have time to lodge the patent before the brutal takeover by another company.

Robert Fludd was a talented scientist whose science was not in question. The man had a poor head for business, however, and relied strongly on his associates and accountants for advice. They let him down and rewarded themselves with a massive pay-out, letting Doctor Fludd become nearly bankrupt. He had, without warning, lost a crucial, framed contract for the manufacture and supply of these specialised analytical tools — and that was only the beginning of his woes. After that, he became very unwell, suffering from a nervous breakdown after his business was acquired without prior notice. These days, Charity's father only a shell of a man who did not speak of his past work and stayed indoors like a hermit. He would go out seldom, and talked so little that it seemed to Charity that he was never really at home.

It seemed that the Fludds once had everything, and although they were still rich, they had a lovely home and both parents enjoyed great success until recently. Charity's school was second to none for providing a unique education for the gifted, and that was why they had come here to live. One thing that was missing, however, was a happy daughter.

Charity loved puzzles and crunching numbers of all kinds, although in contrast her mind was still that of little girl who liked to stir up a little mischief here and there.

At this moment, she sat playing with her long, wavy black hair, which was held back by an Alice-style hair band. Calculating coolly with her clear, crystal-blue eyes, a naughty immature smile spread over her freckled face as she studied her computer screen with bated breath. The girl almost teased her terminal into action.

She was searching to find out whoever was responsible for her father's illness. Remote access still appeared to be a bit lax, but there... there... *ah, in again!* The girl would leave a clue that she'd hacked the system, of course, because someone there needed to know that things were not right.

Outwardly, the girl had angelic features, although behind her cherub façade there was a cunning and clinical mind. The girl's project would require every ounce of her stealth and mischief, confidence in her ability to leave only a subtle electronic footprint, if they were up for the challenge. But not before she had found out the real truth!

Charity contemplated for a moment, looking out at the crisp, clear morning eastwards and admiring the sun shining across the countryside of white fields. Her fingers then continued to tap away like a mad pianist, pausing only for a moment here and there, although she did not understand the full legal implications of her actions. Computer hacking was a very serious business. Unknown to her, she had already started a chain reaction of inescapable events.... And, having a "sting" in her tail, she would use all her skilful dexterity in order to find out a little bit more typing again...

****

On the afternoon of the twenty fourth of December, the police had called in to see old farmer Kirkland. Apparently, more of his cattle had gone missing...

Sergeant Howie, the local "bobby" and the only constable stationed in this quiet neighbourhood. He was not an "incomer", being born and bred in the village, and had been waiting for this promotion after twenty years in public service. This was an opportunity for a quieter and much slower pace of life. His retirement from the police force was only a few years away. He reported only to himself, and to his wife, of course, although at times he worked overnight at the local police station. The farmer first reported a loss back in

October but Howie's gut instinct was that Kirkland was trying to squeeze his insurance.

Church service was later that evening and his wife needed him home as soon as possible to get ready. Kirkland's farm was not maintained very well, was quite dirty and run down. It had rusty old tractors and pieces of ancient-looking farm machinery scattered all over. The farmhouse and outbuildings were enclosed by dry stone walls known as dykes.

Another white topping of snow lay over the cold and reddish brown dry-stone dykes; although the farmer seemed too old to bother much about such things, the walls provided some sort of protection for his livestock in the wintry chill. It was muddy next to the farm entrance where a nasty and distinct odour always lingered.

The policeman drew up in his completely inadequate and stupid-looking, tiny white automobile — it was only fit only for the rubbish bin and was just another example of a cost-cutting exercise by the force. He had not expected such a poor vehicle when he had accepted this rural job, yet it still was better than where he had been previously stationed walking the beat in the streets of Glasgow.

Crazy hens suddenly appeared, running from behind the dilapidated farmhouse. He jumped, hearing the birds squawking loudly as their feathers flew about and their little legs scampered madly, their wings fluttering furiously in great protest! Like something out a funny film the farmer suddenly appeared quicker than his poultry, striding widely in his bigger than big wellington boots. The man was wearing the same old tweed jacket and frayed trousers, as always.

Drew Kirkland nodded his welcome as Constable Howie stood up and began walking towards him. Even minding his step, Howie slipped on the muddy quagmire of an entrance that marked Drew's home.

Taking a deep breath of cold air, he began to choke a bit, and wished he had filtered his inhalation a little first. Straining his face twisting it in automatic revolt of the sour farm smells, Howie could never get used to such unpleasant odours! Disguising this fact, his half grimace changed into a quiet and pleasing smile.

'Good afternoon to you, Andrew. A cold one it is and all this snow. How's the wife?' Howie looked around, trying to defuse the man's obvious anxiety.

'Afternoon, constable. Liz is fine.' he grunted and wiped his nose. 'Look, I'll come straight to the point. I cannot believe it! My whole herd is gone! Gone! Robbery! This is going to cost me dearly, man!' exclaimed the farmer.

'Now then, when did this all happen?'

'Yesterday night, sometime after milking.'

'What type of livestock is missing and where did you see them last?' the local bobby asked while taking out his notepad.

'There were about thirty in the herd, down at the lower fields near Sherrington Woods. Just outside the village. What do you think, sergeant?' he said, giving the policeman his proper ranking. The woods were at the far south side of the village, and the farmer pointed distantly in that general direction, over the hill.

'I'll take a run over there and see if there is any evidence, Mr Kirkland.'

'It's poachers for sure. There have been a few strange happenings and odd-looking strangers about. Have you seen them lately in the shire and around the village? Too many incomers, I say! There has been too many of them over the past few years and I don't like those Italian folk from overseas. I'd have a word with them if I was you.'

'Thank you Sir.' Howie nodded abstractly, not willing to commit to anything until he'd checked out the story.

'Ok then sergeant, off you go, lad!' Kirkland continued. 'You'll be going to the Kirk service tonight with the missus, I hope?'

'We'll try to be there! It's a busy night and I'll need to have a look for your missing stock, first.'

The farmer nodded in approval and headed back across the yard and out of sight. The policeman smiled a little at his summary dismissal. *What an eccentric old arse*, he thought and got in his automobile, scratching his head — still suspicious of the man's story. He drove off in the direction of Sherrington Wood, arriving there ten minutes later as the light waned slowly and redly, as it always did at this time of year. The woods looked lonely.

Sergeant Howie parked his inadequate vehicle on a single track road within walking distance of the small wood. The wood covered part of the south sloped approach towards Mauchline, and since he didn't want to drive completely off the road or fall into a concealed ditch, this was as far as he dared go.

Mauchline was cut off again — it often was in winter. This year was the worst weather that folks could remember in many a year! Snow had fallen the previous night, nine inches at least. The roads would take a few days to re-open, since the village was at the far end of Ayrshire.

Sherrington wood was classed as a "conservation area" and had stood for hundreds of years, thick and tightly packed with many varieties of deciduous trees. Its specific mistletoe white berries were found in clumps throughout this murky wood and were bigger than anywhere else in the country. This gave the area a protected status. It also included deep ponds and short swampland with a rich habitat for local wildlife and migratory creatures from other parts of the world.

Under the enclosed branches, the atmosphere clung low and heavy among the copious trees, and only the treetops could be seen from the distance on the high end of the village. The icy branches stuck up and out through the thickening fog, hovering purposefully over the lower meadows and moors. It was a frozen and most inhospitable place, fuelled by the greyish haze that swirled around madly, weaving through the trees, smothering and engulfing all bark and bush.

The only light left seemed to abandon the policeman as time passed and Christmas Eve was fast approaching, yet here he was, stuck on this forsaken path! The darkening mist felt intimidating and the woods became more menacing as night closed in.

This is a stupid search for cattle that never existed! Old shithead – he thinks I'm buttoned up backwards! Here I am, freezing my bullocks off and for what? Nothing! I should be back home getting ready for Church!

The man was irritated knowing that he had to investigate at least this far, or that otherwise the farmer would be back at the police station tomorrow. This annoyance focused his true and hidden feelings of fear as he walked on. It would be too easy to give up, so the constable persevered despite his better instincts, although somewhere in the recesses of his mind an alarm warned him not to go any further.

Walking cautiously along the featureless road as it narrowed, detail all but totally obliterated by the white downfall, he trudged onwards. The man was still warm inside his heavy coat and trousers, but was conscious that his heavy shoes were letting in water. His toes felt sub-zero as he tramped through more falling snow.

Constable Howie was a strong and able man, but walking through the snow made this wild goose chase hard work; he panted heavily in the deepening drifts. His breath condensed immediately in front of his mouth. *This place is frozen,* he thought, looking around. The old track was a lonely place, made much worse by the lack of daylight. It would be pitch black at any moment, and Howie checked his watch; it was 4 p.m. already.

No other tracks? The man could not see any sign of footprints, and even his own were fast filling up behind him. It was too dark to see properly, and he surmised that there would be nobody and nothing about in these parts today, in any case. Strangely enough, the place seemed... *too still and too dead,* he thought. There were no birds in late song, no sounds at all.

That's so odd, he mused. The unsettling atmosphere seemed to intensify in the lack of sound, almost as if nature was shouting a silent warning. All that he could hear was his own magnified breathing and the continual crunch, crunch, crunch of his footsteps in the snow and the odd creak or branch breaking off a tree somewhere deep in the woods.

His emotions were beginning to get the better of him. Howie had always thought that wearing his police uniform gave him a sort of protection, like armour, and now he wasn't so sure. A nice cup of tea back home was in order... he felt the looming disquiet sneaking up.

The woods grew taller on each side of the narrow track; the forest felt intimidating

and overbearing as the branches curved,
enclosing him in a roofed arc. Feeling trapped
by these overhanging branches, the man
tramped onwards underneath the cold white
umbrella, feeling like he was walking through a
darkened tunnel.

Trees bare and lifeless as the snow
encrusted laid branch to twig across the frozen
woods. Harsh cold bit his face—he knew it
would only get worse as the temperature
dropped and gripped the countryside again this
evening. Stumbling below the enclosing dark
canopy of trees he trudged onwards, following
the narrow track around a short right-curving
bend. The dimness came closer to him and then
suddenly the sky appeared above as the cold
grey mist cleared quickly, before his eyes. His
heart lifted at his escape from those chilly
woods!

Wonderful—he could see again! It was
still dark, of course, but the stars were
beginning to glow faintly. The constable
seemed easier when he emerged at the other
end of those depressing woods. He looked
straight ahead and not far away from him stood
a wooden gate with long icicles hanging

unevenly down. The gate was closed. Howie could see further to the lower fields and meadows — snow covered everything and lay thick over the long stone dykes. Even though it was dark and shady, eerie starlight reflected off the white snow, making a blue light that Howie's eyes quickly adjusted to. The snow blanket expanded as far as he could see, way beyond the moor.

No cows...well, I expected that. Regrettably the search for more clues has got to be done! I'll climb the fence and look around by those lower dykes, and that will be enough. A quick check down there and then I'm out of here — have a cup of tea and make a short report! It will be just a simple case of "poachers" — let's make life simple for us all. Sergeant Howie just wanted a warm drink, and for his quiet life to stay quiet. His numb feet felt like solid lumps of ice.

It took him another five minutes walking to reach the dykes, which were at the bottom of a large, white-crusted meadow. He clucked his tongue as he neared — the dykes appeared to be abandoned and badly maintained, neglected for years, crumbled in places here and there.

Howie thought that the cattle might have escaped and wandered off and onto the meadows and moor beyond, but then he remembered that no animal or bird ever ventured onto that uncanny place. As rumour would have it, the moor was meant to be haunted. And even the beasts uncannily knew it too! Looking over onto the nearby desolation of Mauchline Muir, the man could observe far off and away to the lowland hills miles beyond the village.

Much closer to him, here however were the old quarries that edged onto the moor. A mile away was the prophet monument, standing there stalwart like a castle. It dominated the hill approach on the northern side of the village. Standing alone and characteristically slim in its profile, the monument appeared silhouetted — silent and dark against the glinting skyline.

A few of the early stars were beginning to twinkle brightly. Only sparingly did bare trees grow on this white wilderness. What the policeman could not observe was the unnatural black mist hidden below eye level, concealed inside the depths of the open quarries close by — the cold, grey mist disguised the frozen blackness lurking underneath. It had been disturbed from a secret dwelling place and had been shifting around continually inside those deep quarries ever since the quake....

Sergeant Howie surveyed the bleak landscape for signs of animal tracks. Not even a hoof print could be seen! He looked up again as the rising moon shone through one of the moor's solitary trees, which stretched up with bare branches.

Even in the summer time when heather is in full bloom and the moor was at its most beautiful... there seemed to be always an uneasy tension around that place. A great battle had been fought here hundreds of years ago, between royalist troops and rebellious Covenanters. Their ghostly remains were thought to be the reason why animals would not graze on these lands.

Why did he put his cattle down here to graze, bloody idiot! Anyway, it's time to get going, the policeman decided, feeling small and insignificant here on the Muir; *I don't want to be here any longer.* The man had always stated to others that he did not believe in ghosts. *Still, I don't like this place, gives me the creeps.*

The man lifted his officer's hat to scratch his forehead as a deathly still silence pervaded from all around. His body shivered violently and his face changed as a feeling of great dread came over him; he could not comprehend quite why cold beads of sweat suddenly began running down his temples and forehead. The hair on his neck rose and his skin crawled when suddenly his spine stiffened, frozen.

The man's eyes stared straight ahead, fixed onto the distant monument. The constable then turned his head quickly to look fearfully at whatever was behind him... and opened his blue lips in utter dread; eyes bulging wide his mouth began to tremble uncontrollably.

Sergeant Howie tried to shriek in terror, but no sound was heard from him. The man's body dropped heavily into the soft snow, dead!

His mouth opened wide aghast to the sky, fixed in a soundless scream. The officer's skin was an icy, stone-grey in colour, as if he'd frozen. The big man lay petrified behind the stone wall, his lifeless profile stamped in the

deep, new snow. Darkness blotted out the light
of stars as a thick cloud blew in, and snow
began to fall, quickly transforming his body
from a black mass to a white lump to... nothing.
No living thing stirred on the virgin whiteness
of the Muir. Something unspeakably evil
moved silently away...

****

It didn't seem to matter that it was
Christmas Eve! Where the Prophet monument
stood was always a solitary place, and the
monument offered a most gloomy welcome to
anyone who entered Mauchline on the northern
approach road from the other village of
Crookedholm. The monument appeared as a
tall block-work of red sandstone with a grained
column and, for weeks now, the surfaces were
of the building were covered by ice and wind-
scored snow lines. Like the white swirling
countryside, this tall building was dulled by a
cold, opaque grey mist that seemed to linger
everywhere and appeared to thicken as one
progressed down towards the village cross.

Sitting quietly, the frozen gargoyles perched on their stone pillars on either side of the iron-gates entrance to the ancient monument, their glacial faces disguising any sign of idiom. Long icicles hung over their expressionless faces, growing downwards and off from their overhanging stone hoods, curving down and inwards to form sculptured and sharp-looking iced teeth. Grotesquely frosted tongues licked across frozen lips and managed to protrude out through sharp canines.

Snow was falling with little let-up, even though the meteorological office stated that it was going to be another mild winter. How wrong they were, it was going to be a white Christmas!

Older buildings of the village stood bold with solid character—they had been built to last. The church, constructed of thick red sandstone, had for its architecture many stone ledges and a slated roof and a gothic tower, which were all laden with snow and ice. Scotland was not alone in this extreme weather, of course—Europe was bracing itself for the hardest winter conditions on historical record!

The cold would seep quickly into anyone who was brave enough to battle the extreme bitterness, and the government was struggling to contain some bleak news.

It always took ages for the gritting trucks to reach the village, and today was no exception. A large Christmas tree was erected at the village cross with only a few coloured light bulbs flashing in the dimming evening. Some of the bulbs were removed — the bottom ones — "for a laugh" by the youngsters, which was disrespectful, to say the least. Villagers were furious about the missing ornaments, and although no one could prove his own suspicions, everyone knew who the culprits were. The local constabulary "was on the case" and, this year, like every other, the missing light bulbs were on their top list of complaints. The villagers did not see that this situation would ever change!

Many people were preparing for the festivities that were now only hours away. Tuneful choruses of Christmas carols could be heard from the choirs inside the old parish church; the choirs had been practicing faithfully together every evening for the past week with invited visitors from Germany and Wales. Over the past thirty years, the village had hosted a special service at Christmas time, inviting choir singers from other churches to share. Tonight was their penultimate evening

High above the altar, a large series of lighted, stained glass windows showed the story of "Christ and the Centurion".

The very Reverend Doctor Lintel Lewis Graham, Minister of the Parish, looked out from his vestry window. His collar was as white as the snow outside. Doctor Graham was a tall, cheery man, although a little rounded with badly-combed, sparse grey hair.

Through the vestry window, the old gravestones seemed to stare back at the Reverend, their frozen faces etched with many sad words. It had stopped snowing a little while ago and the mist lifted as grey clouds headed eastwards, opening up to reveal a clear and cold and clear night sky. The temperature outside was plummeting with the receding cloud cover, although it was a perfect winter's evening! Ten last chimes could be heard from the clock tower above before its mechanical hands stopped moving—ceased by ice.

Barren and lifeless trees stood in the graveyard grounds as they had for hundreds of years, stretching up high into this crisp clear night and almost reaching the heights of the clock faces on the Gothic Church Tower.

Long tree branches stretched up loftily into the air with iced, twig-like fingers trying to grasp at the stellar heavens as the minister looked through them and up to the full moonlight. The lunar light reflected off the white snow surface with dazzling luminosity and, like a photographic negative, this weird light cast a blend of black and white shadows off the dead stones and lifeless barks of these hallowed grounds.

Concealed underneath this gothic construction was a large private hall with high-arched ceilings held up by immovable pillars. An old green barometer hung high on the far wall, the gauge needle dropping well below freezing. Inside showed much evidence of past conflicts, and on one wall hung a battle-worn and ancient Covenanters flag, yellowing with age, once held solemnly and in strong hands with the pride of Reformation.

Reformation had been accepted in Mauchline and the rest of Scotland in the mid-sixteenth century and after the Scottish Parliament adopted the "Confession of the Faith". Disguised behind this once proud "Standard", a secret message was chiselled into the stone long ago—an enigmatic Masonic scripture and a code-work of strange symbols with some unknown significance....

Above this closed hall, up in the vestry, two men of the cloth stood. This was going to be an *extra special celebration,* because this evening he would join together to praise the Lord with Father Poletti and his most welcome catholic congregation.

'If you could lead the service please, Father', he smiled with genuine friendship and a passionate tone. Contented, they both walked slowly together with clasped hands towards the lecture-hall as their flocks gathered and waited with murmuring anticipation, listening eagerly to their approaching footsteps.

The Papal Father was wearing a silk white Mitre Simplex on top of his head and in keeping with the rest of his attire, a holy crucifix hanging on his robes. The Father had gathered here with his Catholic Community this evening for a joint service. Both religious men had discussed the procedures and protocols earlier and agreed to keep their sermons light and open, with lots of carol singing and few prayers. It would be up to individual, family and religious beliefs to outline what the parishioners would accept.

The community turnout was excellent, bringing together both catholic and protestants alike… at long last, both churches could worship together inside the parish Church! Who could have thought this to be possible? It was seen as a blessing of God.

The village, like most small places up until about forty years ago in the West of Scotland, exposed a raw, bigoted and racist attitude from both the majority protestant and also minority catholic orders; now, however, much of that dreadful behaviour had all but disappeared through education, religious tolerance and the understanding of good-minded folk. Some peoples' stubborn attitudes would never change, however, and some would always harbour a disturbing resentment.

So how could religions hope to live together until they at least respected each other? Could this small village show the way and find the true path to the Creator? The Minister revered this change of attitude—village life had so moved forward since he had been a boy—savouring this precious moment as he entered the Nave of the Church.

The <u>rushshshhh</u> sound of everyone standing up simultaneously echoed the start of the service as the parishioners' heavy clothes rubbed together, reverberating sounds all around the Church in unison. The air felt charged with spiritual electricity. It was, after all, Christmas Eve!

'Please, Father Polletti. Our flock awaits us.' The Minister gestured towards the Church Lectern. The members of the congregation were all standing and looking at the dignified papal figure. The man was thin and tall and of regal stature. Father Polletti then made the sign of the cross and stood forward, while the jovial doctor Graham stood no less elevated and in equal importance beside the catholic father and seen by all.

The altar was large enough for both men as they overlooked the communal congregation, and it was Dr. Graham, being the host, who first opened the Holy Bible. Bowing slightly towards the good father and turning to meet the many eyes of the congregation, he began his sermon.

'Welcome everyone to God's holy place. We have all come together on this very special evening to celebrate together the birth of our Lord Jesus Christ! I believe that through our own eyes, which are the windows to our souls, we see many good souls here tonight. Thanks to God and his son Jesus Christ who looks through our eyes.

'It is a cold night, a winter's night and a holy night!' the Reverend paused slightly, 'We are joined together through misfortune and yet it has given us this special opportunity to pray together with our catholic neighbours, friends and families in this parish church—to pray and sing together and worship the great Almighty. We are all his children.'

Doctor Graham spoke with a strong Scottish, his voice lilting up and down melodically. Then he looked at the Father. 'I swooping flight with its strong, elevated wings curving like cupped hands, enclosing a smaller shield with a blue background. Inside this shield was an upturned and red enflamed dagger with an open parachute on top.

The bird fiercely gripped its claws in immortal combat these words: "*Silendo Libertatem Servo Mobil*", a motto translated "Serving Liberty Silently in Motion", and indeed it was a most eminent award of posthumous distinction in recognition of an elite fighting unit and individual's ultimate self-sacrifice! Inset into his fur headgear above this unique military ensign was a much smaller object. It was more like a crescent-moon — a waning shaped silver symbol of intricate design with an origin much, much older and of a very different nature... and as his head turned it glinted a little in the light.

So cold it had suddenly turned that nothing and nobody walked outside in the village streets this evening with the exception of a fleeting shadow. At some point after those mysterious visitors arrived, a dark shape progressed unseen and silent along the graveyard outside, concealed by the moonlight shadows.   Stealthily it moved uninvited into the church. There was another way in!

Finishing the service, the minister stepped back from the altar as Father Polletti raised his hand high in blessing.

'Praise is to our Lord Jesus Christ,' he exclaimed, his hand making the sign of the holy cross. 'We all leave as children unto God almighty, who looks upon us all this Christmas Eve. Under God and under one roof all friends together, we are saddened that our own church of St Mary's was destroyed by fire on October this year, when our village witnessed a freak of nature; some would say it was the work of the devil. However, time has moved on and I have news, which arrived today.' The Father paused and some of the congregation murmured together and then listened as he spoke,

'Unfortunately, the holy pontiff's office could not release any extra monies at this moment. The Vatican treasury is tasked with the relocation of essential finances for other important missions, although assurance they give to me that our church will be rebuilt at some point in the future. Come, let us pray.'

found outside the village on the hilltop. All badges displayed a golden motto underneath: "Flexible of Intellect, Conceptual of Idea and Strong of Spirit." On their front breast pockets and sleeves were gold braid, with cuffs and collars to match.

Headmaster Collins sat proudly near the front, unsuspecting as the solitary shadow stood static and unmoving above the congregation. It was a vague image and partially hidden behind a solid stone pillar that supported the high-arched ceiling. The shadow moved and shimmered in the darkness, and for a short moment it was silhouetted against the candlelight, projecting its wavering dark grey form against the deep reds and rich blues of the stained glass windows, and then it was gone. Did it ever exist?

Underneath, the quiet visitor sat and all his senses agreed. It was time to leave.

The hymn finished and Reverend Graham began a final prayer. Before he closed his eyes, the man narrowed his gaze to the back of the narthex, seeing a glint of light and a figure? *Who is that?* It was a silent movement that he saw, at the back of his church, recognising it to be a man's profile. Could he identify him? The Minister thought hard for a moment and then closed his eyes and bowed his head in prayer. *I am sure I know that person....*

Not able to recollect the memory, the minister had no sooner finished praying then the bells rang out loud and audibly from the tower belfry! Loud and far the chimes could be heard across the whole parish. His attention was completely distracted.

'Blessed are all his children, go forth and enjoy this happy Christmas!' he shouted. The people cheered in excitement, happiness coming over their faces.

'Happy Christmas!' they shouted with much laugher and hand shaking as many other people hugged each other warmly. All the choirs chorused together "Silent Night" as everyone began to slowly leave the church.

Out they went into the cold night, pulling up collars and hoods, buttoning up their warm duffel coats, shoving their gloves on quickly, throwing bright and colourful scarves around their necks as they braved the Scottish elements. Their eyes watered as a bitter wind began to suddenly blow. They tramped along

'Merry Christmas, Scott, I love you so much!' his mother came across from the window and hugged her son.

'Mum. Merry Christmas! Cool!' Even though he was sixteen, the boy still got a "Santa sack". After all, it had always been the tradition inside the Hrycuik family — no matter what age!

Later on, at about two o'clock in the afternoon, Mrs Hrycuik was preoccupied with making the Christmas dinner. Scott thought that his mother had made a bit too much food, considering it was only for two.

At the front of their house was a garden with a short hedge about three-feet high that surrounded their sizable home; their driveway opened onto the street and the village cross was about half a mile away. Other houses on Scott's street were built in "Miners' rows".

Gradually, Scott could hear the sound of an approaching automobile or something heavier — like a Jeep engine, which turned into the street and came up fast. By the sounds it was a large four by four, and it skidded to a halt right outside his home. Preoccupied, the boy did not bother to check who it was until the door-bell rang.

'Mum, mum!' Scott shouted in a deep voice. 'Mum, that's the front door!' his voice had broken earlier that year.

'You get it then, son; it might be your friend, Cammy!' The kitchen was hot, but Mrs Hrycuik moved around like a professional, too busy to answer the door. Juggling numerous pots, pans and hotplates, she shouted back, 'Hurry up, Scott! Get that *door!* Scott — *right now!*' She knew that Scott was quite spoiled and shouted again at her assuming son as she heard the door ring more urgently.

At last, Scott jumped up and ran through to the hallway, quickly unlocking the front door.

'Skoosh! Skooshy... Happy Christmas! Happy Christmas, little brother!'

A young man stood on the doorstep for a moment and then stepped inside; a cold draught surrounded him as they stood in the small hallway. The man hugged tightly his younger brother, still feeling that same strong bond between them.

many long hours; hand in hand they sat on the sofa and soon fell asleep. Her son was completely exhausted. What a trip it had been to get here...

Christopher was twenty-three years old with short black hair. A tall young man and very athletic, fitter than fit, he had always been very religious, just like his father. He was well-educated, displaying a keen aptitude towards Biology in his early years. His eyes were piercing-green with a fine, black-speckled quality about their appearance. He had always displayed attention to detail.

His mother looked at his sweetness and had to remind herself that her son hunted all sorts of horrible looking insects and brought them back for dissection, to her horror! At a very young age, he had left university with a doctorate in cell biology and biochemistry. What a proud day it had been with all the family at his graduation! Christopher was now a distinguished bio-technologist and was offered a research fellowship with his current employers, Oncol Scientific Corporation, specialising in the biosynthesis of new cancer inhibiting enzymes and precursors.

Proud of what he wanted to do also as a Priest, Christopher a catholic like his father and although the young man did not like the commercial aspects of the organisation he worked for, his dedicated life took him into the heart of the South American rainforest. Not before he made a quick trip to Italy to see the Vatican City, however!

Two days later the village roads were cleared again of snow and Mrs Hrycuik had a long bus journey to make, to the city of Glasgow. It was the annual "Christmas Sales!" day. She never missed the sales and so, kissing her boys goodbye, she headed off bargain hunting for the day with her friends.

Partway through the trip, the snow started to fall again, heavier than ever before and soon they were turning the forecast to blizzard conditions! Mrs Hrycuik didn't return home as scheduled that afternoon.

Her sons were extremely afraid for their mother's welfare and safety waited anxiously because the village was again cut off, all roads impassable, and there was nothing any of them could do. Everything possible was already being done to find all the missing people!

'Listen Skoosh, we are all in a bit of a pickle,' a concerned Christopher began. 'I don't really expect you to understand any of what I am about to say, but...' He paused, studying his younger brother's uneasy face. 'First, I have a confession to make...'

CHAPTER XI

OPERATION AEQUINOXIUM
ᒷᓵᑎᖴ⏌ᐳᖴᒷᑎ ᒑᑎᘉᐸᖴ ᑎᒷᐳᖴᐸᒑ

John Paul's eyes appeared patient, his ears listened closely and his holy stature seemed, as always, thoughtful. The late Pope's figure silently gazed downwards as if in prayer as he stood inside his own magnanimous, gold-framed mirror with its fine symbolic details. His reflection was fixed thirty feet higher and onto the wall, erected on top of a polished marble mantelpiece with a solid silver crucifix anchored at either end.

Across the way his real portrait hung, sanctified and secure and most elevated above the great entranceway. A large silver cross was embedded into the wall above the pontiff's dominant portrait. Magnified by the wizardry of skilled craftsmen, Pope John now stood large as life on the walls of his old office. His presence lived on forever after his untimely death, his soul appearing always on the distant mirror. The cardinal sat reading a secret dossier with studious deliberation. A sacred silver cross shone above Pope John Paul's theological prominence as if his spirit was still influencing the dark walls, even after his death.

'*Grazie,* I understand.' Sitting inside the great St Peter's Basilica within the Secretariat Office, Cardinal Giovanni Dalla Gassa placed the receiver back onto his large marble table. It had been the chaplain. The cardinal was deeply disturbed by the shootings in the Palazzo del Governmantorato. It was an unfortunate and unexpected turn of events that had almost uncovered the secret... Inevitably there would be an inquest, but behind golden Vatican seals. nothing would emerge. There would be no loose ends. He knew this. Nothing would detract from his Godly quest. The funding he had secured over the years was easily in excess of a billion dollars; he could afford to take care of this matter.

Seeking for the Reliquae had been his first real test, and its conclusion was now indeed very close and within his grasp! It was the first fruit of a lifetime's searching and covert pursuit. The Illuminati remained an ever-useful and vigilant part of his intricate plans, but he did not work for their sake. Sooner or later, the man Michaelangelo would turn up and seek help from the girl. The Illuminati insisted that Michaelangelo's execution was mandatory and, against the cardinal's better judgment, he had no other option.

He read the interim report with immense interest. "Operation Aequinoxium" had reached the green continent in order to secure the holy Reliquiae and save the remnants of an archaeological as he had pre-planned with detail. The last communication from Amazonia was that a combat force of Suisse guards had arrived and was by now in position, ready to move. For security reasons there would be complete silence from that classified location until this Reliquiae was secured. There were others, of course, other godly powers still to be found. He would find them all.

Giovanni had seen one much closer to him in his dreams. 'Si another…' he hissed quietly, 'I have seen it in my dreams…' knowing that the time of the Reliquiae had not yet arrived. *It will be here soon, very soon*, he thought and finished reading the highly classified and top-secret report which had been sealed with Papal Sphragistics and crossed with the golden bull. The Secretary of State sighed a little apprehensively, feeling the urge for sleep overcome him. His great mission, his private holy grail, was taking its toll on his health. Dalla Gassa found it difficult to sleep, he was afraid to sleep—he did not want to sleep because of the dreams. He hoped against all hope that sleep would only last a few moments.

His dreams of late were becoming more distressful than ever. At first, they had been infrequent, bright and wonderful when God's angels had spoken to him. Now, the dreams were of hooded things, dark and frightening – *the unliving* eating away at his mortal soul. The man's face began to twist and twitch as tiny beads of sweat began to appear, exuding out from his pores and then rippling down his temples like the rivulets and tributaries that flowed through the great Amazon jungle.

His head rested uncomfortably on the hard table dreaming of his magical links to God, his arms wearily outstretched drifting into darkness. The patient Pope looked down sympathetically at him from the mirror above...

GOD'S CHAIN compelling sequel continues inside

DEVIL'S TEMPLE.

The mystery of GOD'S CHAIN unravels in this desperate search to find the fabled Reliquae.

Universal laws are breaking in the cosmos threatening the very existence of god. One link is flawed allowing the arrival of a dark Lord to exist on Earth, who's intension is to take this link, complete GOD'S CHAIN and become a destroyer of worlds.

Only a few know of the existence of the Temple of MalisIblis. It holds one of the links to God. Each link being a magical object of ultimate power. Whoever harnesses them will be able to shake the very fabric of the universe.

Cardinal Dalla Gassa endeavours to complete his holy mission by sending a military mission to the lost temple and secure this link. It is here, inside Amazonia where the greatest war mankind has ever fought begins…

These are the dark days.
The time of the prophecy.

CPSIA information can be obtained
at www.ICGtesting.com
Printed in the USA
LVHW081619100420
652974LV00013B/49/J